HERE STILL

DYING INTO LIFE ANEW

*to my trench buddy
Art
with blessings,
Yaz*

Praise for *HERE STILL: Dying Into Life Anew*

We invite you to join this journey and feel, think and learn. Read and find within you the inspiration as Dr. Yaz did. Showing up for life, noticing what occurred a year before a cancer diagnosis, listening to one's dreams, welcoming intuition, living to 100…

All these concepts I teach she is living (well, still working on "100"); and has expressed in her writing with the rawness of a first-person account.

–Bernie Siegel, MD
Author of *A Book of Miracles and The Art of Healing*

Reading Dr. Yaz Bolkan's book is a wonderful adventure. She is a dynamic author – a storyteller with an ability to see situations in Technicolor and to put the right words in the right order.

There are moments when the reader is touched by tenderness and others when it's a knock on the head. It is a beautifully presented, complex but colourful fabric of relationships that surrounds this challenging journey.

This is a very well-written book and it is also an important book. I am thankful for the opportunity to read it.

–Dr. Blair Little, Harvard Business School
President, Society for the Enhancement of Quality of Life
Author of *Freeing the Light of Soul*

Dr. Bolkan writes beautifully, in a very direct, somewhat urgent and unsettled voice, an engineer who only in the course of time discovered that she is also a poet. This is an unusual, gripping work; a story told on many levels and in a highly original voice.

If survival from terminal illness is one part of the story, and a fitting together of different cultures another, then a cancer survivor's leaving her marriage, an admission she had never allowed herself before, is a third.

Three stories interwoven in complex and seamless ways, all of which will appeal to large numbers of readers, related in a compellingly fresh and subtle voice, by a person who experienced the alienation and the horror of cancer as few people have.

I learned a great deal about the survivor spirit in the course of reading this book. I learned something about myself as well, enlarging the horizons of my understanding. You will too.

> –Dr. Gordon Brittan, Regents Professor of Philosophy
> Montana State University
> Author of *An Introduction to the Philosophy of Science*

I invited Dr. Bolkan for a talk about her book in my class. This was an incredible opportunity. As an individual, it encouraged me to consider my values and what is important for me in life.

As a professional, it encouraged me to challenge my ideas about patient centred care and our responsibilities for our patients.

> –Erdem Yazganoglu, MD
> Health Information Science, University of Victoria

HERE STILL is a page-turner. A brave story, well told.

–Ellie Stein, MD, FRCP (C)
Psychiatrist in Private Practice
Assistant Clinical Professor, University of Calgary
Author of *Let Your Light Shine Through*

I highly recommend this book as an invaluable tool for self-discovery for cancer survivors, professional care givers, and those individuals open to seeking greater self-awareness.

This is a deep and reflective case study depicting the process of losing oneself and finding a new self in the context of an on-going life crisis.

It is easy to read, and in addition I find it accurate from a psychological and social perspective.

An honestly lived human life is a work of art and this journey reflects it with distinct clarity. The raw details of family life, addictions, and human relationships dissolving and re-configuring all play a stark backdrop to Ada's cancer treatment and subsequent healing.

Hope emerges as she surrenders to the life-transforming experience of illness. Her psychological wellness and eventual freedom arise from a life shattered.

On a very practical level, I believe this work will add value to the body of knowledge being developed in the interdisciplinary field of psychosocial oncology. It could well be a useful adjunct to medical or social work curriculum.

–Michael Boyle, MSW RSW, Professional Counsellor
Former Professional Practice Leader, Patient and Family
Counselling Department, BC Cancer Agency Victoria

I couldn't put it down. Brilliant. Insightful.
—Francine Khan

This is such an impressive story. I was up all night reading, lost in time. Thank you.
—Iryna Spica, Bookdesigner

An astonishing saga! Told entirely in the first person, Dr. Yaz's style truly allows us to be part of the experience. I hear a universal message in her words: "Life is worth it; live it well while you have it."
—Ann Frost, Counsellor, MEd, MA

It brought tears to my eyes. So tender, so bold and yet so raw... A must read to understand the survivor spirit. And beneficial to relationships.
—Sandy, Cancer Survivor

Loved the book. Got goosebumps, it's amazing...
—Jessica Kaman, MBA, Lifesciences

A clear, fresh and very personal story of a deep and raw struggle. Refreshing and cause for reflection whichever path your own quest for life takes.
—Myra Reinheimer

A tribute to the human spirit's ability to endure, recover and fly again. Incisive, thought-provoking, yet also full of tenderness and love.
—Margaret Ardan, Teacher

I LOVED it! Couldn't put it down. What a compelling story!
—Lynette Edison

HERE
STILL

DYING INTO LIFE ANEW

DR YAZ BOLKAN

Virtus Ventures

Copyright © 2014 by Dr. Yaz Bolkan

All rights reserved. No part of this publication may be used or reproduced in any form by any means, electronic, mechanical, graphic or otherwise, without the prior written permission of the author. Contact information is available in the "About the Author" section. Please avoid piracy and purchase only authorized editions.

The author thankfully acknowledges the support of the Canada Council for the Arts. The author is also pleased to acknowledge the support of the Province of Alberta through Alberta Foundation for the Arts.

This is a work of fiction. Any resemblance of characters to persons either living or deceased is purely coincidental.

This book is not intended as a substitute for the medical advice of physicians. Readers are advised to consult healthcare practitioners regarding their health and wellness.

Printed in the United States of America
Virtus Ventures

Library and Archives Canada Cataloguing in Publication:

Bolkan, Yaz, author
    Here still : dying into life anew / Dr Yaz Bolkan.

Issued in print and electronic formats.

ISBN 978-0-9938469-0-8 (pbk.).--ISBN 978-0-9938469-1-5 (epub)

    I. Title.

PS8603.O4624H47 2014   C813'.6   C2014-904897-1
                                                                         C2014-904898-X

tear my heart open to infinite love

INSPIRED BY MEVLANA CELALEDDIN RUMI

Invitation

I was about to bear my first baby at the fertile age of twenty-five. Now, in lieu of embracing an adult child, I am holding this book in my hands, marking the eighteenth anniversary of a rude – but every bit worthwhile – awakening to life.

As with all precious things, losing it made me aware of how much I love it – life that is. Terminal illness overtook my life, I died and returned, and picked up my pieces, more than once. Amidst the turmoil, certainties vanished and the unknown became familiar instead. My perceived strengths proved useless while seeming weaknesses transformed into allies. Vulnerability revealed unforeseen gifts.

Making sense of dizzying turns of events is an undertaking I had not imagined in my wildest dreams. Living this improbable life opened my eyes and heart in marvelous ways. In honor of being here still, I find myself drawn to guide others by example.

This journey became an initiation into being truly alive. It taught me that living full-heartedly invites a certain kind of presence and attentiveness. I witnessed mysterious healings in this very body once I surrendered to being here and being still.

Discovering life anew has been the greatest adventure of my life. Join me in this fateful year. I came out far richer and I trust so will you.

1

Thirst

I'm so thirsty... All I want is to gulp down the water in the glass by my bedside. *Grant me this one wish and afterward kill me if you like... God? Have mercy please.*

Hours pass... I know this solely because the sun has moved long ago out of the window's frame, and my thirst has only intensified. Nevertheless, I still cannot move.

Nothing is tying me down; no needles, no tubes. I am home, *a reason to celebrate!* After months of back and forth from the hospital, I am lying in my own bed now. *Firm yet comfy, just the way I like it.*

Why don't I leap for joy? For being alive, being free – or so my mind likes to believe. My body tells of another truth, of an imprisonment in depletion. I am so fatigued I cannot move a finger, let alone stretch my arm out to reach the glass of water next to me. *Let it be a bad dream. Please let it all be a nightmare!*

At each blink, infected eyelids rub on my eyeballs with the abrasion of rusty hinges. Radiation across my body and several rounds of chemotherapy have shriveled me up, turned my mucus membranes first into open wounds and then closed them up altogether.

Wasn't it just a few weeks ago that my tongue peeled off leaving the underlying raw skin exposed? Time has warped lately, but the sensation remains clear: *It hurt like hell!* Then a thick fog set in; *courtesy of continual morphine I'm told.*

Grateful I am to be alive. *Really?* I question myself. *I am, I am,* I try to convince myself, especially in view of my cancer-ward roommate's swiftly declining health. The other day I caught words foreign to me come out of my mouth: "Dear God, please help Cecilia. She's a good person, ease her pain." *Whom have I begun praying to? Me, the perfect agnostic.*

"Celia," I whisper, "I miss you." We bonded deeply in the short time we spent together. While sharing a hospital room, we felt safe to voice our innermost struggles, even laughed sometimes. *Something I didn't tell you is how scared I was of you when we first met; scared of your strong-built frame, your thick blond hair and big blue eyes.* As I think of her, a favorite Simon and Garfunkel song plays in my mind once again. *Ceeelia, ratatatata... How I wish I could sing.*

Wait a minute! When these non-urgent thoughts can zoom through my mind, how come my desperate wish to move my hand doesn't compute? Angry, yes, I'm really angry that my body doesn't obey such a simple order – just like when I used to be in the habit of getting upset with my thighs. *So chubby,* in my opinion, not that they had a say in it. My egoic insecurities were calmed ever so briefly by dismissing a body part as though it were my subordinate.

Oddly, my thighs have slimmed down from fountain-like vomiting and violent diarrhea. Along with the weight though, all my vitality is also gone. *Watch what you wish for!*

Cancer treatments nearly killed me while the doctors struggled to save me. What remains is a shadow of my prior existence... and a lingering question: *How many more pills does it take to finish off the job?*

Fang

"Got your supper, Ada." I wake up to my husband speaking softly as he steps into our bedroom with a food tray. Sleepily, I reply "Whaaat...?" while covering up a cry deep inside. An unheard voice screams: *Honestly? Roast chicken and fries? Have you looked at your wife for more than a fleeting moment lately? That type of food is a thing of the past! When I could chew, when I could swallow!* Instead, I utter through dried-up sticky lips, "Thanks for the ginger ale."

I am embarrassed for my unthankfulness as Ross places the can of pop on my chest and wraps my hand around it. After the relief of the first sip, I awkwardly add, "Thank you for dinner, Sweetie, but I think a cup of instant soup will do tonight. My mouth is a bit sore." He nods quietly and leaves the room. *Serving is not his strong side – and asking for help is not mine.* I am at a complete loss as to how to walk this tightrope of showing appreciation for his effort while learning to assert my mounting needs.

That conundrum aside, *whom am I kidding with my cool stance?* I find myself acting as if my life depends on it, when in actuality what is left of it depends on facing the ugly truth. *When have I turned into a liar? How did I end up in this mess?*

Why the heck am I still here? I want to escape! I do the arithmetic on the number of pills I last saw in the medicine cabinet; *eight spare sleeping pills, another five codeine painkillers, a few leftover anti-nausea meds – do they count at all? Bummer, is that enough? Or does that get me no more than a few numbed hours? And, if Ross finds me unconscious, a pumped out stomach?*

I'm robbed of the choice to sign off! Disappointed – yet deep down relieved, I divert my mind from suicidal urges. *What a fluke my whole life really is. It might be worth hanging in,* I reconsider. *Who knows, maybe it'll take another sharp turn for the better, like five years ago...*

Back then, while still living in Turkey, I recall opening the official letter confirming my scholarship: "We are looking forward to having you join our research team." *What a nice bunch these Canadians are*, I had thought to myself. Truthfully, I only had the faintest idea about this country and its people. And that stemmed of all things mainly from Jack London's novel *White Fang*.

As a child, the story of this part-wolf, part-dog creature had gripped my imagination – *probably because I was a hybrid myself.* Just like the wolf-dog struggled between its wild nature and domesticated life – *often disowned by the pack*, I, too, grew up between two worlds.

In my innocent perception, I referred to this snowed-in cold place up north where my hero roamed as "igloo-country" which, however mistakenly, stuck as an image for Canada in my mind for years to come. Later, when I was told that downtown buildings were linked by structures named "sky walk", and that an electrical cord hung from the front bumper of most vehicles, I was convinced that these tales were more outlandish than my concocted depiction.

Shell

Unable to get out of bed, or read, *or kill myself*, while waiting for Ross to bring me soup, I resign to continue pondering the twists and turns of life... *that led me to regularly shovel piles of snow off our driveway, plug in my car's block-heater at night so that it starts in brutally cold mornings, and often walk the +15 Skywalk system as though I have done these things for all of my life.* Except, nowadays I do none of these activities – *nothing, but lie in bed day and night.*

To avoid this feeling of helplessness, I refocus on my memories. *The possibility of going abroad was bitter-sweet.* I was torn between loyalty to my family and the call of adventure. I grew up in Turkish culture at a time when young women usually left their parents' home only to move in with their newlywed husbands.

Thanks to my mother of Dutch and German descent, I was raised to be more independent than most girls, playing sports, even riding a bicycle as a kid. She was born in Amsterdam and, as best she could, instilled her liberal heritage in me. This was empowering, yet it left me struggling for a coherent identity in a conservative culture. I came to believe that a woman was as able as a man in theory, though in practice I was continually confronted by the seeming "fact" that anyone without the male organ was not a complete human being.

"Be polite, appear strong academically if you like, but in the real world bow your head to your elders and especially to all men regardless of their age. And, oh yes, above all, keep your virginity." These were the basic rules my aunt spelled out for me.

My timidly rebellious response was to choose the male-dominated field of engineering and to excel in it. I worked so diligently throughout the first three years of my studies that I was set not only to graduate the youngest of my class, but also surpass the highest grade point average of any student in recent memory.

"What are you trying to prove?" my older cousin Murat asked me point-blank when he learned of this. "It's not normal." "What is really?" I tried brushing his comment aside. I was not expecting jubilation, but his dismal comment startled me. *What was driving me to such lengths?* It had become my "normal" to supersede all academic standards.

In my mind, I wanted to be taken seriously, to be recognized as a whole person – without any qualifiers such as "She's doing well for a woman." However, my hopes for a genuine sense of empowerment conversely diminished with each achievement, which instead fueled ever-increasing expectations from my surroundings and eventually from myself. *If only I could outrun it all!*

Fool

A hard knot in my gut pains as I am reminded of how my idealism was further crushed shortly afterward. During the summer leading to the final year of my bachelor's, while working as a trainee engineer at an international company, I was given the task to organize applications for an upcoming engineering position. *This was beneath me, but I wasn't about to complain.* While sorting the resumes in order of the best candidates, and separating them by gender as had been requested, I was glad to see that a number of women were well-qualified. When the personnel manager called me in, I excitedly reported on my findings. He cut me off coldly, "Hand me the male candidates' documents and trash the females'." I froze in my tracks in disbelief as he ripped the "unworthy" pile out of my hands and threw them in the garbage bin. Rendered speechless, deep inside something rebelled, rumbling in my core like hot lava, achingly searching, but unable, to find an outlet.

The next day, I requested my transfer to work at the factory. *I prefer to dirty my hands with machine oil,* I determined. Over the following days, I glanced at my own application packages for post-graduate schools with dampened enthusiasm. My grades at the particular college I was studying at guaranteed a fully funded admission to some of the best schools in the U.S. – presuming I took care of the paperwork.

It was an exceptionally warm evening when I decided to put the tedious job of filling out forms on hold and phoned my cousin. Murat and I had begun spending more time together since his move to Istanbul from Bursa, a nearby town my father's family was from. Being new to the city, he wanted me to show him around. In return, he proved to be a convenient chaperone for me.

A curfew as such was not imposed on me – *except that when I rarely arrived home minutes past nine o'clock, Moeder would throw me a look to say "You know better", while Baba wouldn't speak to me for days.*

For the sake of retaining peace with my parents, and appreciative of the overall level of freedom I enjoyed compared to my girlfriends, I did not protest – even at the age of twenty. Instead, I included my cousin in my outings, his male companionship extending the unspoken rule for my return home to eleven o'clock.

Murat answered my call, "Zamanlaman harika," commenting on my timing being right on. "I was on my way to the Joan Baez concert." "She's here? Right, it's Istanbul Festival. You're learning your way around town quickly! Hadi gidelim," I replied, *let's go*. While locating our seats in the open-air amphitheater, the moon was rising over the darkening city-skyline. We went onto listening to well-loved songs amidst countless cigarette lighters being waved in rhythm.

"Büyüleyici," my cousin remarked how captivating it all was. The exuberant spirit and body-heat of the crowd made up for the cooling air as night set in over this roofless structure. Everything was indeed so harmonious that the roar of a steady traffic in the background along with the sea breeze carrying in horn-sounds from ships passing through the Bosporus did not take away from, but added to the ambiance.

The audience remained in unison even after the show ended as we all walked up the crowded aisles that were dimly lit by moonlight. I sensed a push on the back of my shoe. "Pardon," a voice behind me said, "I think I stepped on your foot." I turned around, about to say "Önemli değil", *that it was no big deal*, yet went silent instead.

I did not believe in love-at-first-sight. *Romance was a dreamer's pitfall in my books.* At that moment however, my cautiously sensible persona was nowhere to be found... *It was blowin' in the wind...* On the spot, I fell head-over-heels for this handsome stranger.

Ozan embodied everything I was not; a free-spirited painter, ignorant of anything but himself and his art. *And his magnetic melancholy...* The rest of the summer passed by rapidly as our physically platonic yet emotionally passionate relationship blossomed. Entrenched in the conservative cultural values we lived in, "There is no other option," I said and he conceded. A future without him became unthinkable and my graduate school application forms turned into scrap paper.

At a New Year's party five months later, I met an American journalist who in conversation mentioned living with Ressam Ozan, the painter. All the while I believed him when he never invited me home, claiming to be hosting his sickly mother. *And there, I gave him credit for being a gentleman, when in reality he had a cow, free milk and a fool!* My world collapsed as dramatically as it had taken flight. I could only confide my sorrow in Murat since he had been witness to our initial chemistry at the Joan Baez concert.

Canada

Preoccupied by my heartache, I recall going through the final term on autopilot. I had no motivation left to follow up on applying for overseas studies. I also had no interest in international companies when their representatives came to our campus. Nonetheless, once my department head sent me a memo that he put my name on the interview list, I knew I could not let him down altogether by not even showing up. The recruiters mistook my disinterest for cool bargaining; the more I said no, the more they pursued me with promises of increased remuneration and other benefits. *I couldn't get away soon enough from this zoo!*

Professor Erkan Etken approached me at the end of a class. He was on a yearlong sabbatical from a Canadian university and was more personable than the rest of our professors. "How are you doing?" he asked. "You seem absentminded in class lately. Is the pressure of the final year getting to you?" "No." "You have a bright future ahead of you. Must be nice being wanted by so many." *Except by Ozan,* I sulked inside. "I know your answer from our earlier conversation when I invited you to join me at the U of C. I respect your decision, but if you change your mind, let me know."

Between the painful separation from Ozan and the disillusionment I experienced as a trainee engineer, going away into the complete unknown became surprisingly appealing. As it turned out, Western Canada was so far away that going much farther would have meant coming back from the other side of the planet.

What about my family and friends? I feared, as the possibility of leaving became increasingly real. I was born and raised in Istanbul. *Where else could I take a sleepy commuter ship to cross over the picturesque Bosporus from one continent to another? And walk out of an ultra-chic shiny skyscraper to enter an age-old building with its marble steps worn down to a curvy wave? Or stand on the cobble-stone path between the basilica of Hagia Sophia and Sultan Ahmet Mosque, tapping into the conversation between these historic giants?*

This was the center of the universe for me. I could not conceive leaving behind my loved ones or living anywhere other than this vibrant city. Nevertheless, after further contemplation, along with my mother's encouragement to see the world, I agreed to accompany my professor upon graduation to a city named Calgary. *I'll be back in no time,* I consoled myself.

Dive

I didn't bargain for this! I desperately want to return to dealing with worldly worries of calculating career moves and fretting over romantic entanglements. Instead, my health – rather, the lack of it – demands my undivided attention. *My gut hurts!* Besides the skin of my tongue peeling off the other day – *or month, it's all gone foggy,* my intestines are rotting from recent treatments.

It's as if a family of skunks resides in my gut. I cannot blame Ross for moving to the guest room, slipping away with a mundane excuse, "So you can rest better." *I can barely endure* the stink myself. *But did we have to fall into a sickening silence, too?*

Where is my hubby? I wish he would put his much-used idioms into action, especially: *When the going gets tough, the tough get going! Why is he not walking his talk?* "Got to speak eloquently as well as colloquially," he taught me. "The trick is to fine tune your tone of speech just right for the present company." That sounded similar to when I grew up, having to adjust my speech accordingly – *for sheer survival,* it had felt.

Ross, however, uses his abilities to his advantage, capturing everyone's attention around him at will. His reticent appearance lights up when he is in the mood. *At school it's skillful debates, and at home he lets loose and throws great parties.* "We can sleep when we're dead!" he proclaims while dancing into the night. This dramatic shift catches me by surprise each time. He then grins at me, "Grand-Papa comes through I guess." Though he rarely speaks of his mother's francophone father, it is always with a sparkle in his eyes. "He was loved – and hated – by the family for his flamboyance!" *When all is said and done, mon amour,* as he likes to be called intimately, *also knows how to snuggle up. I so wish he lay beside me right now.*

My eyes drift over to the wall alongside our bed. *That was a nice idea, Moeder,* I thank her in my mind. During a visit two months ago, my mother had asked me to pick my favorite pictures out of photo albums and then rearranged most of them into a poster-size collage. Noticing that she omitted photos of her son-in-law – *on purpose or not?* – I had placed a framed wedding photo on my night table to include him. *Now all of my family and friends keep me company in my solitary hours.*

What a pleasant focal point, I glimpse at the poster and then close my aching eyes. This is my version of reaching for a breath of air before diving once again into the cold dark place of immobility. Whichever image on the poster draws me in at a given moment entertains me for the next while.

Gin-ger

This time it is the picture of my mother and me, holding each other in a tight embrace only hours before I left my parents' home in Turkey. *Moeder dreaded losing me altogether, but she gave me the necessary boost to stretch my wings.* I was equally stirred. I had no experience living on my own and suddenly I was to live all by myself in a country – *continent!* – I had never set foot in. I remained indecisive about staying or going throughout the time leading from receiving the U of C acceptance letter to my planned departure date. "Don't believe it until I'm on the plane," I claimed repetitively. I was still muttering these same words at the airport to my parents and my cousin who came to bid me farewell, whilst fighting back tears in a vain effort to appear casual.

After walking through airport security, sitting quietly – *and alone* – in the departure lounge, I found myself overwhelmed by ambivalence. Once the plane took off, I knew the point of no return had arrived. As my much-loved Marmara Sea faded in the background of the small oval window, the last bit of anticipation I felt was overridden by apprehension. *I'll return for a visit in the summer,* I calmed myself.

When the flight attendant came by to serve supper and drinks, Canada Dry Ginger Ale caught my attention. "I'll have one of those please." Once she handed me the pop can and a cup, I studied the label; English print on one side, French on the other. *Neat, this is just like home,* I thought, reminiscing on my bilingual upbringing.

My pedagogy-trained mother had chosen German over Dutch for practical reasons and taught my elder sister and me to speak nothing but German with her, and Turkish with my father – no exceptions – ever. In hindsight, I appreciate her intent; this firm training led her children to speaking these two languages accent-free. *It was no small feat for Moeder to succeed in her endeavor single-handedly.* However, people were often offended because they could only partially follow our conversations as we strictly switched from Turkish to German when our mother was present, and then back to Turkish when addressing them again. *It was like a United Nations summit without earphones.* As a result, my sister and I were alienated by most of our friends, who retaliated by excluding us from their inner circles.

Being born to two unyieldingly unique cultures, *and parents*, led us into a split existence. Aylin, my elder by three years, grew into a recluse with an attitude. She later spelled her name "Eileen", stating in her teenage rebelliousness: "It's pronounced exactly the same way!" Her bold statement of preferring a globally accepted language over the rather rich mixture of Turkish, German and Dutch, was an added injury to my parents who had named her after a deceased fraternal aunt.

The name my parents picked for me was more versatile: Ada was a Turkish first-name as well as a short version of Adelheid, *after my great-grandmother whom Moeder admired as a forerunner of feminism.* I subconsciously picked the opposite response to my sister and attempted to please everybody as best I could. Only now do I see that in the process I became a wind-up doll, embodying one or the other nationality and language, depending on whomever I was with – *always fitting in, never at ease.*

Flight

Maybe Canada was the answer to the tiresome duality? As I take another sip from the ginger ale Ross brought me, I find myself back at the first instance I tasted this fizzy beverage: *It's gazoz with a twist,* I determined on the overseas flight, noting its similarity to a Turkish drink. I threw another look at the dual label; *it'll please Moeder that I brush up on my French.* Then I overheard the stewardess speaking to another passenger: "funny, eh?" I was appalled. *Is that how my English will sound soon? That's funny indeed – more "odd" than "ha-ha",* I worried what I had gotten myself into.

"Mix it up with gin," I remember the traveler in the next seat suggesting. *Did she notice my trepidation?* "I'm Natalie," she smiled. "Ada," I replied skeptically while assessing this woman at least twice my age. She asked the flight attendant who was still serving our aisle to pour a generous amount of gin in my half-empty cup. "This'll help you sleep. It's going to be a long, and bright, nine hours; we're traveling with the sun." *As if resting was an option in the tight seat.*

"Tasty," I acknowledged Natalie's cocktail recipe. Not being much of a drinker, the gin went straight to my head. *Is the plane spinning or is it my head?* My shyness was instantly overruled and my nervousness turned into chattiness. "See, Berna forewarned me," I blurted out. "I beg your pardon, who's Ber..., Berna? Is that short for Bernadette?" my friendly companion inquired. "No, it's Berna without the 'dette," I replied, my inhibition washed away by the strong drink. "It means youthful in Turkish," I lectured in my tipsiness. "Berna and Fulya are my closest friends," *more like my only friends, besides my cousin and my sister,* I admitted to myself.

"Nope, it's not 'fool-ya' either," I added defensively before she could open her mouth. "It's simply Fulya, named after a fragrant flower. We met at high school. It took a year longer than others, but granted us a Turkish diploma and Abitur – admission to universities in Germany. After the stress about my sister going to the Netherlands for college though, I didn't follow up on it." "Interesting," Natalie managed to squeeze in, probably out of pure politeness. "Aylin and I were inseparable. Playing and fighting, always together, until she was sent to boarding school. That's my sister. 'That'll cure the wild streak in her,' I had overheard my father. She became the black sheep of the family instead. I kept quiet after that, petrified that Baba may disown me altogether."

"Do tell more," I heard my flight companion, not that I required any reinforcement to go on. *Does all this sound like a bedtime story to her?* I noted in a sobering moment, which I smoothed away by taking another swig. Either way, I was happy to talk about my friends and family; it released my unease about stepping into the unknown. "Our pajama parties were something else," I giggled under the influence, I recall disgruntled. "Berna had the toughest dad. She was forbidden to leave for sleep-overs. But her aunt let her stay in her apartment the few times she was out of town and her dad went along with it since it was right above their home. She'd get permission from her parents to call Fulya and me over, pretending we had to study.

I brought candles which we lit at night and Fulya snuck in a bottle of wine. At ten o'clock we turned off all lights so that Berna's dad thought we went to bed." A smile spreads on my face as I see in my mind's eye the three of us tiptoeing across the living room and whispering to each other over candlelight. "Berna's big secret was sleeping with her socks on, silly girl. That's how strict everything was at her place." *Why did I indulge in such details?*

Fulya had a real secret, *and I'll take it to my grave.* One time when Berna went to the washroom, "Ölümü gör," she had threatened me, daring me to see her corpse if I told on her. Fulya then blurted out that she had terminated a pregnancy. I nearly fell off the sofa. *Sex was taboo. Abortion?*

After this confession, I became her faithful alibi. I shake my head remembering how tense I used to get on school-day evenings when Fulya told at home she visited me while in reality she met up with her boyfriend. Knowing I would mess up if her mother called, I unplugged the phones, only to face my annoyed parents, requesting an explanation from me while plugging the cords back in the wall jacks. I kept silent. *I was pathetic at lying, but my lips were sealed for my friend's sake.*

"I continued living with my parents after high-school," I recall my conversely chatty disposition on the intercontinental flight. "Fulya went on to study medicine." It occurs to me only now that helplessly watching her father die from lung cancer may have been her motivation. *We all knew about his illness, but had no language for it, so we ignored it altogether.* "Berna and I entered Bosporus University – the first-ever American college outside the U.S." I boastfully informed Natalie in the same tone our rector had stated during a speech. "Berna enrolled in management and I in mechanical engineering." I further added, "This was the first foreign-language university in Turkey. We studied the same textbooks as in the States."

I feel like burying my head under a pillow recalling this – *where did such an urge to sell myself come from, and that to a complete stranger when I hadn't even done so to recruiters?* We were indeed the educational elite, a tight-knit circle that I found smothering while in it. *No more than a few hours into fleeing it, I was already nostalgic about it.*

Homesick, I went on: "'Honey, you just won the top student prize,' Berna exclaimed at graduation – she talks like that," I remember my words too well. "'Here we're the crème de la crème, and you're a shiny cherry atop! Your next obvious step is an ivy-league school in America. What's up with Canada? What's the name again, Calgary? How far is that from Toronto?' She wasn't impressed when I told her, 'It is in America'." "Good one," Natalie grinned, half asleep.

Effects of my drink fading, I became self-conscious about having revealed my life-story to a random traveler. I am relieved to recall I kept my busy thoughts to myself from then on: *Berna figured out life well.* She was about to marry a Princeton graduate and move with him to New York State – not just to be a housewife, but to enroll in the MBA program at her fiancé's school. Fulya had also aligned herself successfully. She and her new husband were moving to Palo Alto; he was recruited to work in Silicon Valley while she enrolled in her master's in biotech at Stanford. *And I?*

Serpent

I open my eyes and look at my graduation picture that my mother pinned in the center of the collage she hung on the bedroom wall. *The cape, the gown – symbols of status.* I recognize that at twenty-one I had begun having some clout in Turkish society. Academic achievement came easily and being part-European gave me an added edge in the growing international market. But, I felt disconnected inside, *no more than a racehorse with blinders on.*

I had no female role model to guide me in a workforce steeped in gender bias. The lure of a successful engineering career felt crushing at the same time; *nothing but ever-building expectations.* The anonymity of a faraway place became more and more appealing. *I don't want fame, I want freedom,* I knew in my heart.

On graduation day, holding the award with a juvenile clumsiness, I defended my decision: "Isn't it serendipitous that this prof came here on sabbatical and ended up supervising me?" "More like serpent-ipitous," Berna remarked at his well-planned timing to teach fourth-year students right before he returned to Canada. "He was in recruiting mode."

"At grad-level it doesn't matter what school you pick," I continued justifying myself to Berna in my professor's words. "I don't buy it. Are you in love with him?" she cut in. "No way, absolutely not. Wha-what are you talking about?" I stuttered. Not because of any feelings I had for Etken. My heart still ached for Ozan, but I was too shy to divulge my failed romance. Rather, I blushed like a teenager because I had no chance yet to mature emotionally in my performance-driven young life. "He arranged a scholarship and promised me my own lab," I steered away from her tease.

"'Why go the beaten path when you can be a pioneer,' my prof said. That's when he won me over." *That's a sensible decision,* I convinced myself. I did not, could not, admit that leaving home all by myself, without a fiancé or a husband, was too daunting. I had no interest in a relationship so soon after Ozan; therefore going away under the wing of a male professor offered a much-needed break.

None of us could have unveiled, but all of us knew deep down that, beneath the emancipated surface, we lived by the rule that a woman could not exist without a man. This was so engrained in our psyche that it was not a mere belief – it was an unspoken law.

"What will it be; tea or coffee?" the flight attendant startled me hours later on that life-changing flight. "Tea, please." *It'll be all right*, I reassured myself. After the lengthy trip, I was relieved to stretch my limbs. The courteous Customs Officer at the Calgary airport helped me feel welcomed in this new country. I was further relieved when my two suitcases showed up on the conveyer belt. I put them on the baggage cart with the care of embracing long-lost friends. They were all I had to my name in this foreign place.

I romanticized about the pioneer spirit of the European side of my ancestors for a moment, some of whom had arrived on this vast continent with nothing but the clothes on their backs, plunging into the unknown in anticipation of the new and leaving behind their life in the "old country". Disturbed, I snapped out of daydreaming, reminding myself I would be no more than a guest, destined to return home after the two years allotted for my master's.

Rockies

My arm aches. When has it become too much to hold up a pop can? It is also too much to reach over to the night table. Choiceless, I let a few drops drizzle out of the near-empty can of ginger ale onto the bed cover while having to relax my arm. *My once-athletic body, how I've taken you for granted.*

"Mountain goat", Berna and Fulya nicknamed me for my love of climbing hills, unlike their passion for roaming shopping centers. Later, when my girlfriends heard I might be going to live near the Rocky Mountains, they laughed at how fitting this was. "Ada will go to the mountain," they played on a religious quote. Indeed, within the week of my arrival in Calgary, I got a ride with fellow graduate students driving out to a National

Park. Our destination was apparently a hiking trail near the lake on the twenty dollar bill at the time. *It didn't matter, it all looked alike to me.* I simply wanted to see "the Rockies".

I could hardly contain my excitement as the mountain range grew closer in the windshield. Once I stepped out of the car in the Moraine Lake parking lot, I felt the reverence of having entered a majestic temple. *The peaks surrounding us were colossal, and the lake at their center glistened like a turquoise gemstone.* I was awestruck. *I was in love.* From then on, my weekend routine became first hiking, and then learning scrambling, rock climbing, and later downhill and cross-country skiing, in Kananaskis, Banff, Lake Louise, Sunshine, Jasper...

As my eyes became more acquainted with the incredible scenery during my frequent visits, I began to make out figures out of the initially faceless wall of mountains. A relationship of sorts grew in me with individual peaks, each with its unique character; initially the most distinctive ones such as Mount Rundle along the skyline of Banff with its form of a massive wave about to crash, Castle Mountain with its shapely fortress-like cliffs, Mount Assiniboine overlooking us all from afar... and then, in time, many more.

What had been simply a range of rock formations became so familiar and personable that spending time on them became a home-coming; tranquil and invigorating at the same time – *a wonderland to lose as well as find myself in.*

Home

Home... how is it that I find myself not feeling at home in my own four walls? *And how about in my own skin?* What has happened to my body that used to work so well? *Ouch, my bones ache! Where are those painkillers? Wait. First I need food in me to dampen the stomach-pinching side effects.* I expect my sweet should be back any minute.

Somewhere in the back of my mind, I recognize what an insurmountable challenge my husband and I are facing. A little while ago we were an ambitious professional couple with somewhat ordinary marital issues. When we met two years ago, attending the same course in graduate school, I had completed my master's and moved on to doctoral studies. "Ross McMillan," he stretched his hand out confidently. *So European,* I enjoyed his gesture, and replied "Ada Akanay," while shaking hands.

"Isn't that an English first name? But your accent?" he inquired. "Français, peut-être? My grandpa was French. Wishing I had learned the language properly." "Non, turque et allemande." It was fun mixing it up. "Intéressant," he smiled. "How about telling me more over coffee sometime? During term I'm real busy, but let's meet after the finals."

Following a brief hesitation, "Sure," I replied, though I was anything but that at the thought of meeting a man I did not know outside the safety of the classroom. My rigid upbringing kept its firm grip over me even after living in Canada for three years. While conservative and liberal voices went on arguing in my head, I concluded; *I don't expect we'll ever meet up. And he's old, probably married. So, if we did, it'd be nothing but a friendly chat.*

My respect grew quickly for this stern-looking classmate who was highly focused on his studies. Through brief conversations during breaks he revealed emigrating to Canada twenty years prior – *at about the same age as myself.* "Jobs were tight for a young geologist in Scotland. Canada sounded like a good choice. For Grand-Papa's sake I went to Montréal first – fun place. Better pay was in Alberta though." He was a self-made business man holding a daytime job while completing his master's degree in the evenings. Conducting research for my Ph.D. and teaching at the university sounded easy in comparison. *His family must be proud of him,* I presumed, *so studious at forty-some. He surely has a couple of kids and a loving wife waiting for him at home after class.*

As we got to know each other over the duration of the course, I became intrigued by a defiant twist in this man's disciplined manners. When he got into an intense debate with our professor, I had to hide my grin as a saying I had recently learned came to mind; "swimming against the stream". His willpower reminded me of salmon swimming upstream in a mountain creek I had seen during a hiking trip on the west side of the Rockies.

Don't be silly, I told myself, aware that the long hours of teaching before the late evening course were the reason for my mind wandering. Having been trained to courteously fulfill societal norms, I was fascinated by him going his own way without compromise. I became his biggest fan, so much that when he won an argument, I had the same satisfaction I had while cheering on salmon when they managed to jump up little waterfalls.

Ross, on the other hand, my elder by almost a generation, told me later, "After my first marriage I quit that whole business, but then you came along. You think like a man but move like a woman. And that cute accent of yours; I had to have you." Sensing beneath his coolness an admiration for me was intoxicating. I felt seen for the first time.

We were both hard workers and right after our wedding I found myself immersed in building our business, completing my studies, teaching extra hours at school to prepare for my next career move and assessing the most opportune time for our first offspring, until...

2

Happy

"Aaah, thanks Sweets," I whisper while Ross holds up my head to sip the warm soup he has brought. *We're on good terms today.*

"Here you are," he slips a handful of pills through my chapped lips one by one, each one causing a sensation of sharp rocks scraping down my dry throat.

Finally, pushing through the most-awaited painkiller, he adds, "That should help. You rest up now." I wish I had the strength to hold him tight when he gives my barren head a little peck. *No such luck.* He leaves the bedroom as swiftly as he had entered.

The codeine in the medication settles throughout my body with the softness of fresh snow. Soon after, the gnawing pain is smoothed over – *life isn't as horrific as it was a moment ago.* In the temporary relief that the drugs enable, my mind returns to the last pleasant memory it has from before the recent madness:

It's a blissful summer day half a year ago – July 29th, to be exact. My body pressed against the railing of a tour-boat, I stretch out my face toward the bright blue sky, merging the sun's radiance with my inner vibrancy. The mild lake breeze dances on my hot cheeks. I am a beam of happiness on this day that marks my first wedding anniversary. I glance over to my beloved husband and my favorite cousin sitting together on the bench behind me – *I have it all.*

Murat is with us for a month-long English course. Apart from my parents who have come once, my cousin is my first visitor in the five years I have been in Canada. Ross and I have taken off the day for our special occasion. My sister-in-law will only be able to join us in the evening. Being a community health nurse, she is out of town for the day as usual. *Lennie has become a true sister; I know how much this means to my hubby.* "She's all I have for family. None of the others took me up on helping them move over here," he had said, referring to his parents and remaining four siblings in Glasgow. We are both pleased to observe Lennie and Mick, as he is nicknamed here, taking a liking to each other in the short time he has been with us. *Who knows what may come of this by the end of his stay in another couple of weeks?*

Lightheaded, *from the heat I guess*, I sit down beside Ross. "How broad your shoulders are," I sigh while leaning onto his manly chest. Selfishly, I wish he did not work so much and that we could have more days like this. *Come to think of it, since our wedding we haven't had a single uninterrupted day of such peace, not even on weekends.* This makes me tease him: "Have you married me or our newly budding business?" "Let's not spoil the moment," is his usual reply. Apart from the loneliness, I appreciate his work ethic.

All of a sudden, I realize how tired I am. Ever since developing some sort of a thyroid problem several weeks ago, frustratingly I find myself in need of rest. Both of them go along with my request to cut our outing short, and Ross drops off Mick and me home before driving on to work; "I'll squeeze in a few extra hours."

Mirror

I feel energized and cheery after resting. "Wear something sexy," my cousin calls over from the guest room when he hears that I am up. "No baggy stuff, tatlım, you hear me?" Mick, *my Murat*, adds endearingly calling me his sweetie. "It's your anniversary!" *He sounds almost like a native speaker,* I am impressed. *How quickly his English is improving.*

His voice from across the hallway evokes childhood memories of hearing him run around in our grandparents' seaside home, which we visited during summer holidays. Once my sister was enrolled in boarding school, she had turned from an amusing playmate into a temperamental bookworm. *Aylin hated it when I called her boredom-schooler.* Unaware how much she was wounded by this educational transfer that made her live away from home, I went onto seeking new companions.

None of the girls wanted to join me in my adventures, which was incomprehensible to me. *Who wouldn't want to hunt treasures – be it climbing tall mulberry trees for the sweetest fruit at the tip of a branch or digging through garbage piles for scraps to build a dollhouse?*

My cousin became the only alternative. He was the one boy our grandfather permitted me to play with, both our fathers being his sons. At first, Murat did not want to be seen with a girl and insisted on telling everyone that he was older than me by two-and-a-half years, to make it look like he were babysitting me. *Any of this aside, we all knew not to mess with Dede's orders.* He was the head of the family. Even my mother did not object to this restriction on my playmates, understanding that some lines in the sand cannot be crossed.

"Alright," I call back to Mick, content about our friendship having grown strong. I try sounding pouty, attempting not to let on how glad I am for his boosting suggestion. *I ought to wear something nice for the occasion, even a touch of make-up.* While putting on lipstick, the lump on my neck catches my attention in the vanity mirror. I shudder, remembering the first time I saw it – *nearly fainted at the sight.* The prior night to that morning, I had not been able to sleep, tossing and turning in excruciating pain. My bones felt on fire all night, so much so, that I was afraid that I could not ever walk again. *What a relief it was stepping off the bed.* My feet were able to carry me to the bathroom, however, I had to hold on to the sink when I saw myself in the mirror. *It looked as if a golf ball was stuck in my throat.*

Isn't it looking bigger? I lean in for a closer look. *Looks more like a tennis ball now. What is this?* When I tense up, I refocus on the specialist's words to calm myself: "Your thyroid is enlarged from a viral inflammation. The gland will deflate back to its normal size within a month's time. It'll have to run its course like a cold virus. There is no need for any intervention."

Hearing Ross and Lennie enter the front door, I hurry getting dressed. While my husband comes up the stairs, I walk toward him wearing a sleek long dress. The subtle lift of his eyebrow tells me how amazed he is by this sight. "Oh là là," he responds to this drastic contrast to my habitual attire of jeans and sweaters. Partly it is Mick's comment, and partly my happiness, that has helped me tonight to overcome my usual inhibition to dress feminine. When we enter the restaurant, I am content that my appearance suits the ambiance.

My hubby picked the fanciest spot in town. Dinner turns into an incredible party thanks to his extravagant orders, filling the table with appetizers, side dishes and entrées, and plenty of the most costly wine to wash it all down. "Happy first, Babe," he grins at me. Tonight, I indulge in this feast, *I won't get wound up about the spending,* I promise myself. Too reluctant to exclaim it, I quietly go on thinking: *I'm as happy as on our wedding day – and more in love than ever.* I knew in my heart that I would eventually grow to love this man who shows such adoration for me. *But I couldn't have guessed how deeply I would truly bond with him.*

Vie

All our eyes open wide when Lennie pulls out a small velvet box and presents it to Mick. Apparently, the joyous occasion of our wedding anniversary, *along with her liquor consumption,* I suspect, encouraged her to propose. This past year, she teased me that she wanted a handsome Turk. So, when my cousin came to visit, I told her, "Your order has arrived."

The joke becomes reality when he accepts her proposal and engagement ring. *Isn't it the man who should propose?* I feel old somehow, even though I am the youngest of the four of us. Ross and I exchange a brief look; it relieves me that I am not the only one caught by traditional thinking.

He then winks at me, "C'est la vie, let it be." *I'm glad in a way that Lennie is the one who initiated things. She's a decade older than Mick, so all in all it kind of makes sense,* I justify with a disjointed logic. Most importantly, I am relieved that this negates any doubt someone could have about my cousin possibly having an ulterior motive to stay in the country. *What a wonderful family we're becoming.*

In the late hours of the night, we run out of celebratory toasts drinking up the last drop of wine and end up closing the restaurant with the owners. Being the designated driver by default, I cram everyone into my tiny two-door hatchback which soon overflows with my companions' ecstatic chatter. Once home, while washing off my make-up, I hear my husband's snoring already, which loudens in proportion to the extent of preceding partying.

Upon entering our bedroom, I notice him curled up halfway inside the closet. Witnessing how he could not make his way to bed once again causes something in my gut to twitch. *He's lying on the floor much like a drunken homeless man crumpled in a street corner.* Confused by why it bothers me so much seeing him "crashed out wherever" in his words, I lie down in the empty bed and let exhaustion draw me into sleep.

By morning, I am at home alone. Ross has left for work, and from the note on the kitchen table I gather Lennie has managed to take the day off and is out for breakfast with her new fiancé. I imagine them moaning and groaning over their post-party headaches while sipping on a virgin bloody mary – "best remedy for a hangover," according to her. *Great, I got the house to myself. I'll work on my PC today,* I decide. *My computer code needs some tweaking anyway.*

Gland

I study my neck in the bathroom mirror while brushing my teeth. I remember a month-and-a-half ago calling my family doctor's office to consult her the day this lump appeared out of nowhere. It was disappointing to hear that Dr. Jackson had left for her annual summer vacation. There was no way I could delay this matter. Besides the worrisome lump, my pulse was rushing – *I trembled as if on a constant coffee buzz.* I knew I could not handle this for long and decided to visit the neighborhood clinic.

During signing in at the front desk, the administrator informed me, "You'll be seen by Dr. Eliot. He's the general practitioner seeing walk-in patients today." *Doesn't that name rhyme with... What if he's an id...?* I found myself agitatedly thinking while waiting. *Oh get serious,* I ordered myself, *this is a doctor's office. Besides, just anyone will do to stop this racing heart.*

While examining my neck, the doctor commented, "You've developed an unusual thyroid condition and your heartbeat is 120. I'll refer you to an endocrinologist and request that you're seen within a week." *Relief must be around the corner,* I reassured myself while awaiting the appointment.

When I met Dr. Dubois, the comfort of receiving expert medical care diminished. His response to my restless tone of voice, especially shaken by a fast heartbeat, had been: "Let's not be a hypochondriac." *I felt as small as a mouse and from then on kept my mouth shut unless I was asked a question.*

Upon a brief examination, he concluded: "The abrupt onset points to a viral infection." Squeezing the lump on my neck once more, he continued, "It aches when I press on it, right?" "No." "The swelling is an inflammation. It's a type of thyroiditis. You've also developed hyperthyroidism from your over-functioning gland," he remarked while writing a prescription. "Take these pills every morning and your heartbeat will normalize. You'll feel much better."

"Thanks doctor," I replied trying to gather my thoughts. "Isn't an inflammation usually sore?" "Of course," he responded. "Why does this not hurt?" "You say you have flu-like symptoms lately," he diverted from my question. "That's a result of this. It's simply an atypical presentation if there is no tenderness." His mind was made up. "It'll take a month for your thyroid to decrease to its original size by itself. Nothing to worry about."

Alright, this was reassuring. As I began trusting him, his mannerism softened. "When I asked you about your history you said you're from Europe. I'm too; from France. And you said you are doing your Ph.D. in engineering? That's ambitious." "Not unlike specializing in medicine," I added, feeling less tense. "You could've been one of my students," he smiled. Our interaction shifted from an expert preaching to a layperson to a friendly conversation.

By the end of the appointment, I felt more like a favored student than an annoyingly tense patient. Not wanting to risk this pleasant status, I did not raise any more questions regarding his authoritarian diagnosis – *even when I felt it didn't match my symptoms*. Trusting this amiable professor/doctor was far more tempting than doubting the state of my health.

The month, that Dr. Dubois promised on that day would cure me, has passed by now. The only improvement is that my heart is calmer since taking the prescription drugs. *But the swelling hasn't gone down at all,* I analyze. *Wouldn't that be the true indicator of progress?*

Until today, I have resisted contacting him in an attempt to keep my faith in him – *also afraid of being labeled again.* I cannot restrain myself anymore and call his office. It takes persistence to convince his administrator to eventually put me through to him. "It keeps growing and is changing its shape," I report frightened. "Nonsense. Patients with similar conditions often claim that, but it doesn't," he annihilates my experience. Defeated, I hang up.

Pub

I try to forget about it and concentrate on my project. At 5 p.m. the phone rings. "Pick me up at the office," Ross requests. "We're meeting Lennie and Mick at the pub tonight." "I'm on a roll at the computer," I reply, wanting to stay home. "Your cousin <u>and</u> sister are getting married. How often does that happen?" "You're right, but I just don't feel like it." "It'll be good for you. Shake it off with some fun. We'll shoot pool and throw darts. Don't spoil it now." *There is no arguing with my strong-willed hubby,* I note, *he's probably right.*

Half-heartedly, I drive downtown as told. An hour later, I announce: "Sorry guys, don't mean to be a party-pooper, but I have to go home." "Good, you're catching on with the pub lingo finally," Ross replies, referencing the many prior visits when I used to talk in what he refers to as "Book-English".

"Remember how you'd sound like a snob and I'd even gotten in trouble when my buddy Harry called you an uptight you-know-what? C'mon now, don't act like a curmudgeon, stay a little longer. Have another drink," he sways me. "Feelin' no pain Babe." "You know one drink is my limit when I drive," I respond, wishing I did not sound so rigid. In a gentler tone I add, "I really got to go. The three of you can come with me or take a cab later."

"One for the road for my buddies," Ross exclaims to Lennie and Mick as well as a few other guys at the bar whom I do not recognize. Once the drinks are consumed, he states agreeably, "OK, let's pay the bill and get going," looking at me and then pointing at the bartender. "Not again," my voice tightens. "Are you gonna rub in that they took away my credit card?" he pouts with a tipsy voice. I do my best to answer with a teasing tone, "Remember how you say 'cash is king' Sweets? Bring some with you next time." But the tension in my voice seeps through, revealing my fading patience. *Oh, he's trying me, but I'm not going to make a scene,* I promise myself. Struggling not to snap completely, I pay the hefty bill in order to get going.

On the way home, with my three companions packed in my little car, Ross says, "Turn in at the mall, I got to pick up something." *Why do I follow his orders?* I begin getting mad at myself. Even then, I do as he wishes. He directs me to the liquor store parking lot. "What now?" I ask rhetorically, wanting to stay calm with Lennie and Mick in the back seat. "Scotch for the Scotsman," he justifies. "Got some change?" "No. I can't keep up with you," I sound shriller with each word. "At this rate, we'll lose my credit, too."

I hate myself when I lose control over my emotions. *However provoked I may be, I ought to hold it in*, I order myself while clenching my teeth. "You know how to hurt a man," he replies sheepishly, still under the influence. "Fine," I hand him my card, "put it on." "But your signature?" Lennie instinctively jumps in to suggest no one but me should sign for the transaction. I involuntarily throw a dismissing look at her to say, *don't you know your own bro?*

While the party continues late into the night at the house, I cannot stop shaking in distress. I take a shot of the scotch before the bottle is emptied. *This better knock me out for the night.*

Angst

In the morning, my mind is flooded before my eyes open: *Why am I so lethargic these days? I've to get my experiments running and iron out the bugs in my computer program. When am I going to prepare my teaching notes? The house is a mess.* Demanding thoughts press on, stirring further concerns.

The confidence of strong earning power was instilled in me throughout my privileged education. Even so, influenced by my frugal parents, I saved with great discipline, aiming for a bright future, for the family I was going to co-create one day with my partner-to-be.

Reality turned out differently. Ross admitted his finances were not in equally good shape once debt collectors locked his accounts. While asking me to pay off his loans, he assured me, "The business I dreamt of for so long is our baby now." At this point, I have no choice but to trust in his success to recover my savings: *I'm all in, as he'd say playing poker.*

I'm too edgy lately, can't even let go of worrying about this weird lump in my throat, I realize disturbed. Before the week is over, I gather the courage to call Dr. Dubois's office a second time. The administrator books a consultation, possibly in the hope of ridding herself of me.

"It's getting bigger, it feels like something is growing inside me that doesn't belong there," is the only way I can convey my perception at the appointment. "Have you been watching Alien movies?" is a response I did not anticipate. "You need to wait it out. Your thyroid will shrink soon. It's simply an unusual case of thyroiditis, taking longer than expected."

Upset, I revisit Dr. Eliot who referred me to this specialist in the first place. With the exception of speaking more patiently, he repeats the same message: "Relax and wait. You'll be well soon."

3

Date

The thought that Dr. Jackson must have returned from her summer vacation crosses my mind. I am drawn to seek her advice; however a respectful obligation toward the other two doctors holds me back from contacting her so far into this health condition.

I am also scared this may look like actions of a hopeless neurotic. *Two doctors concur. Seeking a third opinion, for what? To be further scolded? Besides, I'm too tired as is. And I've so much on my plate.*

In this insecure state, I am left to believe that taking the time to book an appointment with her and tell the whole story over would be frivolous.

It's time I quit indulging in my concerns and pay some attention to my cousin, I add, not having been able to tend to Mick since the exciting news of his engagement to Lennie.

I decide to put my seemingly excessive worries aside and trust Dr. Dubois, who after all has the proud composure of a well-respected expert. *Maybe the belittling attitude stems from many years of success in his career.*

Having convinced myself that I am basically healthy, I go shopping with my cousin to choose his wedding tux. During our outing, Mick fills me in on the news I have missed in the past week and tells me why everything is happening at a head-spinning speed. "We'll get married on the day I'd have flown back to Turkey. That'll make things easier, paperwork and all."

"Murat'cım, I'm thrilled that you're staying," I tell my cousin. Yet, I also have an urge to suggest taking things slower, especially having detected some hesitation in his voice. "What about flying back home at the previously planned date and mulling it over? Romantik olur," I emphasize how romantic it would be staying in touch across the continents.

"Picture receiving handwritten letters on perfumed paper or hearing your lover's voice on the phone from afar. This little break could offer you some quiet time to come to terms with the next big step you're about to take. This is for the rest of your life, you know." I persuade him, "Lennie flies over to visit her parents at Christmas. It's just a hop from Scotland to Turkey. Surely she'd visit you in Istanbul. That's only a few months away."

I sense that my caution stems from having rushed into marriage only seven months into dating. *That was confusing enough.* Doing it within one month, as Mick and Lennie are about to, is inconceivable. I feel guilty for having been misleadingly encouraging my cousin toward marriage in an earlier conversation. Ten days prior, while enjoying a summer evening together on a park bench, my cousin had asked, "How's married life anyway?" *Was it the happiness of having him here? Or was it the softness of this summer day?* I heard myself, my voice a pitch higher than usual, go on about how great it all was.

"Dating was fun." *Mostly, that is,* I qualified in my mind. *My usually oh-so-serious man willingly made a fool of himself announcing to the world his love for me, be it serenading on the streets after midnight or getting into a fist fight over me.* He knocked at my door one night in a torn dress-shirt stained with dribbles of blood. While I dabbed his bleeding nose clean, he told me proudly how he defended me against his friend at the pub who called me uptight. "My hero," I had whispered and found myself ripping his shirt further as I kissed what he called his "voluptuous love-handles". *Was it my strict upbringing or his pub-breath that kept me from showing the same affection to his lips?*

This I did not reveal to my cousin, or that Ross often got drunk on our dates – disappearing right in front of me, his eyes glazing over with each additional drink. *Then comes the low-point of the night, predictable profanities and sometimes getting pushed around. But afterward he turns into a teddy-bear, warm and cuddly. I feel safe again in his strong arms.* "Yes, rough moments happen once in a while, but they only make our bond stronger," was how I summed it up for my cousin.

Then one day, Ross had asked me to meet for lunch, and on the spot said, "Marry me. Now or never!" *A dare devil's declaration of love – charming in a spooky way.* He looked dead serious. Faced by such a swift ultimatum, my mind had devised an implausible logic: *If I'm going to trust this man for life, might as well begin now.* After all, he was seventeen years older than me. *If he's so adamant about it, he must be right,* I justified in my youthfulness. Shortly afterward, we promised our lives to each other.

I also did not share with Mick how my husband's focus shifted right after the wedding to breaking loose from the firm he was working at to establish his own consulting business. "It's our baby now," he would say anytime I asked for closeness. "A geologist and an engineer – the perfect combo."

The man who could not get enough of me suddenly turned into a ghost, snoring on the couch by early evening, "spent" as he would call it, from a long workday and numbed by a few too many drinks. *It'll all get better when we have real babies,* I assured myself. Aside from such issues, I was concerned about our love-life. *How are we to get pregnant without getting intimate much?* I cried myself into sleep at times.

Mick remains obsessed about getting married regardless of whatever I could bring myself to share, I realize. As he puts it, "Most of my friends are settled by now and the thought of being a loner in my thirties is horrible." That he has two good years before leaving his twenties happens to be no consolation. While telling me how satisfied his parents will be that he is marrying a Canadian *(really? Is that how my uncle thinks?),* he mentions his involvement with another woman back home. "She's British – typical UK accent and dry sense of humor. You'd like her. Bummer is she hasn't got a steady job."

"What?" I am drawn from my side-thought back into the moment. *Is he dreading to face this woman upon his return to Turkey? Afraid of losing both women in his indecisiveness? Or is he clinging onto Lennie out of convenience?* Lost for words, I drop the topic. *My comments are misplaced amidst handsome tuxes anyway.*

Is he looking up to his father's elder brother, my father, having chosen a Dutch wife? I consider. *Is that what drives him to court a foreigner – or two? Or have both Baba and my cousin been inspired by Ottoman sultans who picked western women to mother their heirs? If that's the case, I sure hope they haven't picked up the harem idea along the way.*

Mick has fortunately narrowed the choice of suits down to two – *in accordance with his present state of mind*. "They all look black to me," I add helplessly. *The shop-athon wore me out.* Seeing how jaded I am, he replies, "I'll come back tomorrow to finish shopping."

Lead

Following a long night's sleep, I wake up refreshed, yet feel badly for not having been to my lab in days. After trusting the doctors with my health, and spending some time with my cousin, I am keen to get back to work.

Am so excited about my new job. Receiving the instructor position offered to select doctoral students gives me a boost. Attending this department for the past five years has undoubtedly worked in my favor. *I'm also right on schedule to defend my dissertation in half a year.* Anticipating the new teaching duty in the upcoming term – *yikes, that's in a week's time,* I recognize the pressure to complete the finishing touches on the research equipment I have been constructing.

As I am about to move a piece of my apparatus at the lab, I have to admit my recent weakness. *It's made out of plexiglass – when did it turn into lead? What's wrong with me?* Having no other option, I give in to asking fellow students for help with carrying. This does not sit well with my tomboyish personality. Yet, it is clear that without assistance I would not be able to get any work done at all.

I must enroll in yoga this term, I conclude. *Maybe building core-strength will help. At the start of summer I was scrambling up peaks on our camping trip to Waterton Park just fine, so why on Earth am I so weak?* I am confused. *I heard it's good for stress, too. Yup, yoga it is.*

Welcome

With my days spent at the university and evenings filled with the final preparations for Mick and Lennie's wedding, the special day arrives even sooner than anticipated. It is a small yet cozy ceremony at home – a justice of peace, and Ross and myself performing the roles of best man and matron of honor. "Meet Lennie McMillan-Akanay and Mick Akanay-McMillan. Doesn't that sound neat?" my cousin states satisfied, kissing his new wife. "What's with your name?" I catch myself asking. "You ladies hyphenate. Why shouldn't I? This is my contribution to feminism!" Though not completely convinced, I go along, "Good point." *He's becoming a whole new man,* I observe with mixed emotions.

We invite the bride and groom out to a fine restaurant of the same caliber as last month's pick. *Another festive event celebrated in style.* After the many hours it takes to conclude that we are partied out, it is time to head home. Stepping out into the cool late-summer night sobers up Mick enough to hurry. The brisk wind has no such effect on either of our hardy partners. He makes a dash for my car, parked at the other end of the block. *Should've chosen valet parking,* I think to myself, noticing that the temperature has dropped markedly since the early hours of the evening. As Lennie follows him, I start walking faster, too. Ross catches up to me and hooks his arm in my elbow. He then pulls the keys from my hand. In a childishly drunken state, he shouts at them, "Run as fast as you like, but nobody is getting in without these babies!" He triumphantly shakes the keys in the air to demonstrate his point. Rendered powerless by his strong grip, I resign to his foolish joke and laugh with him along the slow steps that bring us to them.

"Kanada'ya hoşgeldin," I teasingly welcome my cousin in this country. "It takes a while to get used to," I refer to the drastic changes in the Alberta weather. Once all of us are in the car, the cheerful chatter I recall from the outing on our wedding anniversary is replaced by a suggestive silence.

The deceptive quiet is interrupted moments later by Mick's sharp voice, irate for having been left waiting in the cold. In a rage, *far deeper rooted than simply being drunk,* he goes on to threaten his brother-in-law: "Don't you ever do that again!" My husband's tolerance to being told what to do being nil, he responds with an equally aggressive tone of voice, "Go to hell!"

Troubled by the unsuspected turn of events, I am relieved when we arrive at home and retire into our respective bedrooms. In a desire to resolve the quarrel, I ask Ross, "You're the host Sweetie, and Mick's senior by more than ten years. Could you please apologize tomorrow for having been unintentionally insensitive to his needs?" "No bloody way!" is enough of an answer to know the conversation is over.

He has no problem falling asleep whilst I remain wide awake, bothered by the explosive confrontation between the two men I love; my spouse and my cousin. *My hubby's behavior doesn't surprise me much.* In the short time we have been married I have had ample opportunity to experience his temper first hand. Initially, this used to disturb me so much that after such a bout I was convinced that our relationship had ended. In time, I adjusted myself to the cycle of volatile fits followed by sweet make-ups. *Nowadays I find myself sucked into the vortex with him, only noticing my own loudness well into the shouting match.*

No-go

During sleepless hours in the night, having thought back to my arrival in this country earlier in the evening, I am reminded of my first ever encounter with Canadians. It was in Cyprus, on the Turkish side of this hotly contested island. In our college years. Berna was given permission to travel on the premise of being accompanied by her studious girl-friends, myself and Fulya –

good thing, no one ever found out about her secret. Even though both were set on spending yet another day shopping, for once, on this beautiful spring day, I was able to persuade them to join me on the open fields at the outskirts of town.

As we strolled along the rocky hills, enjoying water views from the gentle peaks, Fulya thought she heard a noise, but we went on. Then, all of a sudden, we heard a harsh man's voice loud and clear: "Stop! Don't move!" Seeing the fully armed soldier waving from afar, we knew to follow his orders promptly. Childhood memories of gunmen terrorizing the streets of Istanbul had taught us an obedient respect for weapons. And when the civil war had ended with a coup d'état in 1980, rough-looking rebels had been replaced by soldiers with clean-shaven faces and bigger guns – *leaving the rest of us in terror as before*.

To our surprise, this mean-looking soldier quickly changed his demeanour and proceeded to wave in a friendly gesture as he walked closer. He began speaking in a softened tone. Apparently, he assessed these three girls in light summer outfits to be of no threat. Shortly afterward, his partners joined in; tall muscular men, handsome in their uniforms. Even then, we remained cautious as we had learned to be wary of soldiers and their heavy weaponry.

Then again, these guys were different, smiling at us while pointing their machine guns away. They introduced themselves as Canadian Peacekeepers and looked glad to chat with a group of young women in this otherwise barren United Nations no-go zone. This pleasant afternoon set the tone for our amicability toward the people of this far-away country.

Turkey

I think back; *what if I had stayed in Istanbul? How would've my life turned out then?* I smile, noticing that my nostalgia has intensified how personally I take protecting the image of the country I grew up in – *as if I were its ambassador*. A fellow student, a born-and-raised Calgarian, invited me to join his family for Thanksgiving dinner when I was new to Canada. This was my first opportunity to socialize outside the university environment.

I appreciated Sam's thoughtful gesture and felt welcomed in his parents' home. At dinnertime however, his uncle unstoppably made jokes playing on the word used in English both for the food we were eating and the country I came from. It did not help explaining: "It's 'Türkiye' actually. 'Turkey' is simply an unfortunate English translation." Sam's apology afterward helped lessen the hurt I felt – which was rooted more in my dinner companions' resistance to absorb new information than the joke itself. *Ignorance and prejudice is human nature across the world,* I gathered.

I had developed a passion to defend Turkey when I came to realize how it was misrepresented at times by the western world. Attending Turkish as well as German classes in school had led to a unique perspective: I found out that history was "in the eye of the beholder" while witnessing how the hero of one culture was a villain in another. The same applied when I traveled from Turkey to my relatives in Germany and the Netherlands. A news item I had just watched and read about in Istanbul was often enough delivered with opposite commentary in Europe.

Recognizing the irreconcilable differences in underlying cultural values, I learned to distance myself mentally from immersion in any one culture. While this had its emotional price, it also facilitated a clearer insight. *It's rather paradoxical that offspring of multicultural families, like myself, carry the solution to world peace in our blood, while world leaders continue waging war on countries that appear to threaten their differing values.*

A protective loyalty grew in me toward this side of my heritage, not as much out of a sense of belonging to modern day Turkey, but as a passionate supporter of an often misunderstood and beaten down culture. My nomadic Turkish ancestry was something I did identify with, honoring the land and nature not as exploitable property but as a gift. This later led me to an affinity for First Nations. When I saw the life-size photograph of an elder in the Museum of Anthropology in Vancouver, I uttered "Dede," upon the uncanny resemblance in facial features and posture with my Turkish grandfather.

On my European side, my namesake great-grandmother's pioneer spirit seemed to guide me. Upon my arrival in Canada, in the freedom of anonymity, I loosened up on overachieving. Even then, the habit of "being first" took another form by default; I happened to be the sole female graduate student in my department. Seeing my reflection sometimes in a glass display along the corridors of our building startled me – *what are curves of a woman doing here?*

Discrimination was palpable in engineering even in Canada. Even so, compared to the intensity of my upbringing, this setting overall was a dream come true. *My landlord let me sign a rental lease as a single young woman. No one at the car rental office asked me who the main driver of the vehicle was going to be and instead let drive away all by myself.*

Canada began feeling more like home over time, leading me to assimilate not by force but by choice – *even embracing "eh" in my speech as a symbol of my love for this country.*

Rank

My relationship with my favorite cousin was not shaken when I left for Canada straight after graduation. On the contrary, our bond strengthened through frequent letters and occasional calls. Murat, now Mick, was closest to me in age of all my cousins. We had started out as involuntary playmates, but when he later was my confidant while breaking up from Ozan, he also became my best-friend.

For the people-shy person I was back then, it had been a relief to build a deeper friendship on our familiarity. *Some thought we looked like a couple, but we were first-cousins, what were they thinking?* That aside, *he is here now, starting a new life.* At this pleasant thought, I get to sleep.

Mick and I share a cup of tea in the morning. Still disturbed by the intensity of last night's argument, this time I explore the possibility of reconciliation with him. "Have you lost your mind? Your husband should treat me better, I'm his sister's husband now!" I am astounded by his infuriated tone, which is in stark contrast to the easygoing image I have of him. *Is this contagious or what?* I wonder. *Just because my hubby has a temper, what's going on with my cousin? And why am I acting up sometimes, too?*

My contemplations come to a halt when Mick questions: "Alkolik mi?" implying that Ross is an alcoholic. "Hayır, he's not." *Why am I so defensive?* "He likes his booze alright, just in the evenings though. By morning his mind is sharp as a knife."

At the office, in between preparing class notes, my thoughts fall back to the unresolved issues at home. *Maybe it's the stress of living in close-proximity lately,* I justify. *Our townhouse isn't big enough for four adults.* So far, the three of us have been managing well; my sister-in-law, being often away on overnight trips, usually spends only weekends at home. My husband works seven days a week, which leaves me with household chores. When in town, Lennie gives me a hand getting the groceries and willingly cooks meals, while I throw in her wash with ours and clean the house. We enjoy spending weekend evenings together, which is the only time Ross isn't at work. *Also, the house being in Lennie's name and us paying the mortgage works out fine.*

However, shortly into Mick's visit, Lennie managed to arrange her work-schedule temporarily to be back in the city every evening. This has doubled the occupancy in our small home for the last month. *It's inevitable that some dissonance occurs,* I console myself. *We'll have to put up with it for a little longer until she sorts out her job.* "I may be getting a promotion," she had announced the other day, "it's a better position at a medical center in Squamish." "Where is that?" "In British Columbia, halfway between Vancouver and Whistler." "Oh good," I replied, "just an hour's flight, and we'd get to see you, the ocean, and take in great skiing, too." We all cheered her on, aware that Lennie and Mick's move would bring about a needed change. "You'll be close enough for a weekend visit," I added wanting to keep our growing family together.

Monkey

With this matter settled in my mind, I can finally attend to the demands of the new academic term. *Once term starts, things get busy in a hurry at the uni.* Classroom teaching fits me well. I get an exciting rush from conveying scientific ideas to young minds, *and get them to understand concepts – and even enjoy them sometimes.* I am content to have my hands full with teaching and research. Though, I have to accept that speaking to a class of sixty students with a lump in my throat is wearing. *I may have to give in to using a microphone until it goes away,* I note to myself.

Attempting to smooth over the recent rough patch at home, I take time to chit chat with Mick at breakfast. "Yoga is fun, give it a try," I share, recognizing what a good decision it was to enroll. "I don't know about those poses," he smirks, "could break a limb." "It's kind of intriguing, the stuff Tamasi, this yogini from India, talks about while we stand like a tree or a downward stretching dog," I try enthusing him.

"The best part is it gets me away from work for an hour. Instead of munching on a sandwich leaned over my computer at lunchtime, now twice a week I gulp down my lunch while running to the gym for yoga." I add, "You're right, the poses are a bit of a stretch – pun intended, but they take my mind off the many thoughts that usually ring through nonstop. 'Monkey mind' the teacher calls it. I laughed out loud in class when she said it – I really feel like a monkey sometimes. Just as my mind bounces from one thought to another, I, too, zoom from one spot to another. On that note, I got to go."

I have become so busy lately that I have no time left to walk anywhere, be it rushing across hallways at school or jogging across the parking lot to get to meetings. No time to chew before I swallow either – *except these days,* I note, *nothing goes down that swollen throat of mine unless it's turned into mush. Porridge and soup every day is starting to get boring – have to find ways to spruce it up until this swelling is gone.*

Tamasi approaches me at the end of a yoga class, "Are you alright? You can have a rain-check for the course if you want." "Thanks, I'm fine," I defend my self-image of being agile, but then soften. "Am surprised how some of the postures are so hard. My belly feels heavy, and this thing in my neck is awkward." "I see. Take your time, do what feels good," she replies. I catch myself near tears at these words. *Why?* Hastily I roll up my mat to get back to my hectic life.

Complete my doctorate; build my career and our business; keep the house in order and the fridge full; tie up loose ends at school, at home, at our office; shop for my hubby to make him look good downtown – I do treat him like my boy sometimes. It's about time I have a real child. I also want our children to relate to him as a dad not a granddad, so better hurry up.

If I get pregnant six months before handing in my dissertation then I'd defend at seven months, good. I'd have a big belly, but not about to burst, then I'd take care of the committee's final requests in time to deliver my doctorate and right afterward my first baby – perfect timing. I could take off a month with my newborn before starting my next job.

Oh my, this math takes us to about now. Better tell my sweetie I have to quit the pill. It's really overkill, popping so many pills. But after Fulya's secret abortion, I promised myself to never have to face such a decision. I focus on my newly changed plans. *Baby-making-time is ticking! Is this "life on the fast lane" or what?* I attach myself to this speedy state of mind.

Call

The disharmony at home continues haunting me in spite of the busyness of my life. *It was ignited by a silly incident on Lennie and Mick's wedding night, but why is it dragging on?* Things are worsened when Ross examines the latest phone bill listing hours-long calls to Turkey. "Is it you?" he asks. "No, Sweets, I haven't got the time even if I wanted to chat that much with my parents," I respond.

Mick, what are you up to? I question in my mind not wanting to know why so often I hear his muffled voice from across the hallway when I return home in the evenings. Ross then shows the phone bill to his sister. "No? I'll pay for it," she replies, trying to trivialize the matter. *I can tell she knows about the Brit.*

The next day, upon coming home, I notice that Mick has locked himself in the guest bedroom again while Lennie is away. *I want to believe that they had no time to talk things out yet.* This does not make matters any better, but at least it would justify why he is on the phone once again. *Surely, he must be aware.* If not the phone bill, the extension cord sticking out from under the door as well as the compact housing we share reveal his lengthy conversations. "Why don't you get cordless phones?" he had complained the other day. "Exposing our heads to a headset emitting such electromagnetic radiation isn't healthy," did not seem to be the answer he wanted to hear.

Mick's tone of voice, audible through the thin walls, gives away that the recipient at the other end of the line is the girlfriend he left behind. I am flabbergasted when he keeps chatting one evening after Ross arrives from work, who clues in right away. Outraged by my cousin's audaciousness, he shouts over, "I'll drive you to the airport to unite you two lovers for once and for all." Mick screams back mockingly, "What's it to you?" to which he responds, "My sister's well-being is very much my business!"

It is as if the name change has transformed my cousin's character. Besides being confrontational, he is unapologetic about leading a double life. *Dare I think that his new boldness may in any way be related to a sense of entitlement – a change of status from guest to landlord in our home, and from guest to rightful resident within this country?*

Once Lennie is back, I hear Ross corner her in the kitchen, "What's going on Len?" *It's rare that I hear him call her this,* my mind diverts, *but this makes sense for "Helen". Why would anyone get to have a nickname with more letters than their real name?* I am back to things that do not make sense when I see the intensity in her eyes, begging him to drop the matter. "He said he's sorry and won't do it again." "He's a liar!" he confronts her. "Please Bro," she walks away to the washroom.

Next, I sense my husband's drilling eyes on me. "Yes, I knew, but what was I to do? I was sure Mick had sorted things out. Sweetie, I was stuck between a rock and a hard place, as you'd say."

Over the following days, it becomes evident that Lennie has chosen to stand by her weeklong husband instead of her brother, rejecting his warning for the sake of saving her young marriage. Consequently, their lifelong bond suffers deeply, and so does mine with my cousin-turned-brother. He blocks any attempt to talk. Whether his behavior is caused by paranoia that I could be a spy rather than an ally, or by a desire not to face the mess he has created for himself, I am left witnessing how my cousin, my best friend, slips away from me.

My attention is forcefully drawn to my health in the midst of this frenzy. By now, observing my thyroid grow has become part of my morning routine. I have resigned myself to the prognosis that in due course it will normalize by itself. What alarms me right now is that my period, which never lasts more than seven days, has completed its second week without any sign of subsiding. Concerned, I call Dr. Dubois again. In the three weeks since our last conversation, his position has not budged. "Ignore it," is his quick response, discrediting the seriousness I feel about my condition. "Your present symptoms are from the hormonal imbalance caused by the recent changes in your thyroid."

A few days later, while rolling onto my side in bed, my hand brushes against unusual lumps in my breasts – *they stick out like hard knuckles*. Once again I contact Dr. Dubois. "Are you sure you didn't have this a few months ago already? Then it must be hormonal, as well. They've grown too fast to be anything serious." Not finding his explanations convincing, I visit the general practitioner: "Please give me a complete check-up," I plead wanting to put my qualms at rest about something more extensive than a localized infection. He chooses to back up the specialist and decides, "We'll wait with the physical exam until after your current condition is resolved."

Blood

Ross, Lennie, Mick and I are eating together at dinnertime for a change. There is little talk but no apparent hostility – *the closest thing to a cease-fire*. I try thinking pleasant thoughts, but "creepy" is what comes to mind. *Is all the tension in the air going to disappear like "poof"?* Before I can think or say anything else, out of the blue, my heart begins racing – again. *It's not supposed to do that, I take my meds right on time,* I assess distressed.

"I'm going to stretch out," I excuse myself and walk away to rest on the living room couch. A few minutes into it, I realize that this is not helping. I reach for the phone directory under the coffee table. *What if I've to call for an ambulance?* I am ashamed of feeling unwell, especially on this peaceful evening.

Why am I frightful of sharing my worries with my dear ones? I question myself while my husband, cousin and sister-in-law are merely a few steps away. *Where could the number for the ambulance be?* I go back and forth through the phonebook. *I'm the strong one, that's who I am.* It has never occurred to me that I could ever be needing help. I did not spend any time in the five years I have lived here, nor ever before, to learn about the health care system. I am competent in the engineering world, but a step beyond it is all a foreign land to me.

"What are you doing?" Ross calls over, seeing me turn through the pages from across the room. "Looking up the number for an ambulance," I timidly reply, "just in case." All three break out in giddy laughter. *Now I know why I didn't want to mention this in the first place.* Their reaction is more about releasing the unbearable edginess at home, but I inevitably take it on.

They may be right to ridicule me as the hypochondriac that I must be, just like the doctor said. I close the phonebook and return to the dinner table. I still feel sick, but pull myself together long enough to appear normal.

I prepare for bed soon after. While in the bathroom I become aware of my clenched teeth and tightly hunched shoulders in the mirror; *that's how hard I was forcing my body to hold together to get through a supposedly friendly supper.*

The peace pact still holds on the following evening. The four of us play pool in our basement, temporarily smoothing over the intense tension with booze. I enjoy this game of playful physics. *But why is it so hard to keep my eye on the ball? It's so annoying to miss my shots.* It is upsetting not to be fully in charge of my body. *I should get some rest,* I go to bed early. *Maybe it has something to do with my period being heavier than usual.*

I am awakened in the night to a strange sensation. My clothes are wet to the touch. Upon turning on the nightlight, I see a bright red puddle on the sheets. Quietly I check on the mattress underneath; it is soaked through. *No wonder I feel so drained,* I comfort myself. I cover it up, change my nightgown, double up the feminine pads and try to sleep – *I'll sort out the rest once Ross gets up.*

I find myself faced with yet another shocking reality when I wake up in the morning: I cannot focus my eyes on anything. I developed double vision overnight. *That for sure is not hormonal.*

My patience has run out with the specialist's invalidation and the referring doctor's repetition. *I've paid due respect by staying committed to them for so long.* Suddenly, I realize three full months have passed since the initial onset of symptoms, *and none of them is resolved yet.* I have been lost in a trance all this time, confused by the doctors' mystifying behavior and overwhelmed by the commotion at home. As I come out of this daze, I do not care anymore about being judged neurotic.

Empowered by what feels like the dispelling of a curse, I call my family physician. *I'm sure she's back by now.* I am told that Dr. Jackson is booked up, but willing to see me after office hours. Her eyes fixated on my grossly swollen neck, she assures me in a firm yet caring voice, "I'll make appropriate arrangements. You go home and rest."

Next morning, Dr. Dubois phones me in person. *To what do I owe this honor?* He refers me to a needle biopsy the same day. "Afterward we'll meet at the hospital," he ends the call. *Does Dr. Jackson have something to do with this?* At the biopsy, I am instructed not to meet him at his office in the hospital, but to go to a room that is booked for me. *Now he's really gone overboard.* Nevertheless, I go along with his plan.

4

Granny

Here I am, sitting on a bed at the General Hospital, expecting to meet Dr. Dubois as per his instructions. Half an hour into the wait, I am bored and ready to leave. *I've had enough of gloomy rooms, first the biopsy, then this. Besides, why am I assigned a bed that I have no reason – nor inclination – to sleep in?*

Keen to go home and start my weekend, I get up to look for him. I spot him at the end of the corridor; he is on the phone. I walk toward him to remind him of our appointment. In order not to be invasive, I stop at a courteous distance.

Even so, I overhear a few sentences – something or other about a woman that is terribly ill. From the little I capture, the image of an old lady comes to mind, *a granny whose time is up*. I feel sorry for her and walk back to the room so that he has the necessary time and privacy to tend to her case.

Shortly afterward, Dr. Dubois walks in. He sits down beside me on the bed. He is out of sorts, contradicting his customary confident appearance. Although I am not particularly sympathetic toward him anymore, I assume that his uneasiness is related to the phone conversation I overheard, and offer him a smile and my full attention.

When he finally starts speaking, I detect an exaggerated tone in his voice that sounds like a misplaced attempt at displaying compassion. He says: "We received tentative results for your biopsy. It's a malignant tumor, a type of lymphoma." While he goes on using technical jargon, the only comprehensible phrase to me is, "This was unpredicted."

My mind splits off struggling to process his words. *What's he trying to say?* I remain stuck at the word "tumor", which is the only term I am familiar with. *Alright, that means some sort of an abnormal growth. What about "malignant"? That goes with "benign", right?* I know one of them is safe and the other dangerous.

Ross would know this, I admire my husband for the way he speaks this language so well. *Then again, when he throws the dictionary at me in heated arguments, it hurts,* nervous chatter overtakes my mind, *not as much physically, good thing it's the concise version usually.* In truth, I do not understand why he gets so angry at me for not knowing some of the terms he uses. Sometimes I reply equally angrily, "Next time we'll fight in Turkish, or German, your pick!" Even then I feel inadequate, just like now.

Where is my sweet? He who yelled at me for not speaking up to the doctors. I so wished he would have held my hand and defended me against them. *But then again, I was too proud to ask for his help.* I also was concerned to be thrown out of medical offices due to his confrontational attitude. *It's bad enough getting banned from pubs around town after rowdy nights.*

I feel lonesome in the hospital room. *It's so cold and white everywhere. And this doctor is freaking me out. Anyway, whatever big words he throws at me, things can't be too serious.* I hang on to what I have been told over and over; not to worry so much – nothing is wrong with me.

A shiver runs down my spine when Dr. Dubois mentions, "I'm off the phone discussing your biopsy results." *The "granny in despair" is me? No, no, no. This guy doesn't know what he's talking about. He treated me like an overanxious mental case, and today he changes his mind, telling me I'm sick with some ugly sounding disease? I cannot trust this man anymore. I wish I could visit Dr. Jackson, but I know she leaves early on Fridays.*

Word

My only other choice is to consult with the general practitioner. I receive permission to leave the hospital upon agreeing to report back first thing on Monday morning. *Silly really, nobody could've forced me to stay in that sterile setting.*

When the nurse at the walk-in clinic takes me in, I blurt out what I remember from the prior appointment. "Needle biopsy to your thyroid gland?" Dr. Eliot restates. "That's not a very reliable procedure. I'm sure it's a mistake. You don't have thyroid cancer. Trust me, my wife had it. Go home and enjoy your weekend."

To my relief, this time his comments differ from the other doctor, *and best of all his conviction is based on personal experience.* I also appreciate the simple language he uses, allowing me to decipher the specialist's technical terms, *while he was skipping around the touchy "C" word in spite of my clearly confused look.*

Following the reassuring chat with Dr. Eliot, I hang onto his hopeful prediction and make an effort to disregard Dr. Dubois's dire verdict. At night, however, dark thoughts surface. *What if the biopsy results are right? What if it is cancer? The few people I know who had it all died.* I look at my husband sleeping beside me. *Just one word ago, I was in the same reality as him – sleeping and waking, rolling through the cycles of everyday life, filled with hopes and desires for the future.*

I cry silently as I see our unborn children in his face. "CANCER" rings loudly in my ears. *The world is drifting away from me. My future is no more. I'm dead!*

Fluff

I become more optimistic with the rising sun. *Ross's attention helps, too.* Lennie and Mick busy themselves with outdoor errands during the day, offering us privacy at home. The weekend passes quickly as I am booked up with blood tests and CT-scans – *had no idea such tests are possible on weekends.*

Reluctantly, I return to the hospital bed on Monday morning that had been assigned to me on Friday. *Haven't seen so many doctors and nurses in my life.* Their names and faces are all but a blur. I am escorted from one place to the next: an MRI, a second CT-scan, numerous blood tests, and a surgical biopsy. I catch a glimpse of the tissue the surgeon removes from my breast, a white fluffy substance. It reminds me of a bundle of fat cells hanging together like tiny grapes that I had seen on a surgery show on TV. *Looks harmless enough to me.*

At the end of the day, I have had enough. *I'm beat.* I ask the nurse to call my husband so he can pick me up. She evidently calls someone else, because shortly afterward a doctor walks in and bends over the bed, his face awfully close to mine: "This is no joking matter. You're not leaving the hospital. There is no time to waste. In fact, unless the chemotherapy works wonders, you have no more than a few days to live!" The anonymous doctor leaves as abruptly as he entered the room.

It is not panic that pours over me; strangely, it is relief. *Finally, someone acknowledges how ill I am.* I so wish I had been wrong all along as the previous doctors told me. *I'd rather be a hypochondriac than right.* But the ugly truth is sinking in. Receiving confirmation that it was not all in my head is a surreal liberation, and, combined with the exhaustion from rushing around all day, carries me into sleep.

Blue

In the morning, I awake to wearing a pale blue gown. While attempting to grasp all that has happened, a doctor I have not seen before storms into the room. "The initial test results are confirmed. Your body is full of malignant tumors." *By now, unfortunately I know what this means.* "Plainly put, besides the grapefruit size tumor in your neck and orange-size lumps in your breasts, there are multiple melon-size growths in your abdomen."

Her words are so overpowering that, even though I appreciate the simple layperson descriptions she gives, I cannot grasp the significance at first. *If it weren't for the grim look on her face, I'd think she's describing a colorful marketplace.*

It's absurd, is all I can think. Over the recent past it was an uphill battle to be taken seriously – *the more alarmed I felt, the more I was ridiculed.* It took me some time to get convinced that I was well enough to simply sleep off my ailment. However, shortly into trusting medical experts over my suspicions, I find myself confronted with a deadly diagnosis. "Furthermore, the double vision probably stems from tumor development in your head," she concludes. The relief I felt with yesterday's doctor is gone. I close my eyes, wishing this strange dream would end.

Nonetheless, this doctor goes on talking. "I'm Dr. Olsen – the oncologist assigned to your case. The diagnosis is Stage IV Lymphoma with multiple masses in vital organs. This particular type scores nine on a scale of ten regarding its rate of growth. The tumors double in size every forty-eight hours and squish your organs one by one. There is no time left to consider any other option. Once you sign these forms, we'll start preparing you for your first chemo session." Before I can think of anything to ask, she adds: "If all goes well, you may have a fifty-fifty chance of one-year survival."

The numbers shake me up like a sharp slap in my face. *If my chance is one-in-two, I might as well be the "one" that makes it. Let's get on with it then.* Hearing this vigorous statement in my mind, I am left wondering where it comes from – such energy is not to be found in my body or spirit anymore.

Some place deep in my consciousness has been shaken awake, recognizing *this is it*. An emergency compartment of sorts is unlocked in me, which I did not know existed; *a "final-aid kit"*.

Before signing the forms, I tape up my right eye; although this limits my vision, at least I can focus again. Upon completing the paper work, a nurse calls me to the front desk to take a call. "Dr. Jackson?" *How did she know where to find me?*

"How are you doing?" She does not wait for my answer, knowing too well what state I am in. "I wanted to make sure you got admitted alright." "Was it you?" I grasp the events behind the remarkable change in Dr. Dubois's mannerism.

"We had a chat," she tactfully clues me in. "How did you know?" "It was blatant," she refers to the cancer diagnosis. "Thank you so much. I owe my life to you." "I simply did my job," she humbly remarks and reassures me before hanging up, "I'll follow your case."

While standing by the phone, I decide to ask the nurse behind the counter for permission to call my department head. I apologize to him that I will step down from teaching for the rest of the term.

"It bothers me to have to bail on you, but fixing this health trouble may take a little while. We can't just keep substituting my classes with teaching assistants. I thought you'd like to know so you can line up another instructor. I'm very sorry." "Thanks, that's good to know," he replies. "I mean, sorry to hear about your bad news. And thanks for letting me know. Get well soon."

Heaven

I return to the hospital bed and try to gather myself. *Is this it? What if I don't make the cut for one-in-two? I haven't begun living yet!*

Think hard, I prompt myself, *when have I felt truly alive?* Disappointedly, not even a handful of memories come up, one being the day I had gone hiking with two colleagues, about two years ago. We had done a good day's hike to Lake Bourgeau near Banff and were enjoying our lunches on a big boulder beside the lake.

"Let's go up Mount Bourgeau, too," I suggested while munching on dried fruit for dessert. "No time today, we had a late start and the hike back will take nearly two hours as it is," one argued. The other added, "This has been a full day for me; I don't want to drive back in the dark."

Something overcame me at that instant, over-shadowing my team player attitude. "Alright then, forget the hike up the trail, I'll climb this peak right beside us. The view will be the same." "That's six hundred meters straight up," the cautious one observed. "I'll be quick," I grinned as I began running toward the cliff before anyone could talk me out of it. *This climb was so exciting.* It was not as much the physical aspect as it was the impromptu instinct that had moved me. It was as if I was driven beyond myself.

Wish I had worn my boots, I thought when loose gravel started filling in my lightweight summertime hiking shoes. The sharp pieces hurt at first, but then the pain disappeared the further I scrambled. I came to a sudden stop at the steep ridge – one more step would have led me tumbling down the other side.

"Heaven!" I exclaimed standing tall, overlooking mountain peaks in every direction as far as the eye could see. I lost myself for a moment in the exhilarating view and the howling wind. "I am alive!" I yelled at the sky above. Utterly satisfied, I speedily slid down to join my buddies. "Your legs are bleeding," one remarked looking below my shorts.

"Right," I responded. "The old snow I stomped through up there is abrasive like ice. Ha ha, now I know why my feet quit hurting. It wasn't just gravel but ice that got in my shoes and froze my feet." Once the freezing effect faded, I wailed feeling the cut wounds at the bottom of my feet. I emptied out my shoes and walked back the seven and a half kilometers to the car, each step's pain reminding me of the godly scenery I had just soaked up all by myself. *That was worth it,* I confirm contently.

Settle

A nurse comes in the room with a blood-testing kit. "Bloodsuckers," I mumble. "This is the third time already. Please take enough this time so I don't get poked again." Apologetically she proceeds to wipe the needle site clean. She starts crying, "It's not fair." "I'm sorry," I reply. "Didn't mean to be harsh to you. Just been a rough day." Now breaking down in sobs, she repeats: "Not fair. You're so young." *What's this about?* "I saw your CT-scan. It's packed in there, six tumors in your liver alone. That's not good." She pulls herself together, "I'm sorry, I shouldn't be saying anything." *I get it, she thinks I'm about to die.*

While my mind comments internally, *unprofessional but touching*, something else blurts out of my mouth: "Don't you worry, I'll live." How these words pass my lips, I may never understand, but the deep-rooted calmness it is accompanied by is soothing. *Probably a sign that I've gone mad.*

The nurse pulls herself together and, after having filled the little tubes with my rich red blood, she adds, "I'll give you a hand moving to a room to yourself." *Hadn't noticed that I got company in this place with all that's been happening.* "Let's make it as comfortable as possible for you." Dr. Olsen drops in later, "Expect to stay a month, at least." *No way*, I think to myself, *I'll be out in a week.*

Ross comes in later. "They called me at work and said to bring your personal belongings. Here are your slippers and pillow. And a letter. I can bring more tomorrow." Both of us know that even if he moved the whole bedroom over, it is impossible to create "comfort" here. Over the past two days, the tumors have multiplied in size once more. My belly has expanded so much that I look pregnant enough to go into labor.

Why isn't it a baby growing in my tummy? When I manage to stand up with help, the extent of tumors becomes further evident; I can only walk slowly and bent forward like an old crone. Swallowing becomes alarmingly tight due to the growth in my throat pressing on my esophagus, while its suffocating pressure on my vocal cords results in an unrecognizable voice.

Double vision is the easiest of them to deal with. *The patched up eye gives me a sense of being a tough pirate.* And it enables me to read the letter Ross brought along. Specially-picked stamps exhibiting Australia's natural beauty cover half of the envelope. The rest of it is decorated with a stylish handwriting on the address lines. Sender: Gülin Tekin. *Bad news travel fast.*

I feel her hand on my hair. That was the only time I didn't protest staying indoors in the summers of my childhood. "It's too hot outside," nor "you're badly sunburnt," held me back on scalding days, except for my Abla's invitation to brush my hair. I called her an elder sister in accordance with Turkish custom even though she was not a relative, but a neighbor's guest at my grandparents' seaside home. *She was "twice my age",* probably fourteen years old.

I see both of us on the divan, with a gentle sea breeze dancing in the curtains. I did not tire of her caressing and softly playing with my hair on these lazy afternoons, trying to put me to sleep – *so much so that I'd wake her to continue when she dozed off.*

We rarely met after that year, but she remained a distant friend. I had heard she moved away from Turkey, *and converted her religion?* Here she is soothing me once again: "*I hold you and stroke your hair, Kardeşim,*" she calls me her younger sister. "*Geçmiş olsun, may your sorrows be a thing of the past soon.*" She ends her letter, "*Let Mother Teresa's words guide you: Life is a dream, realize it.*"

Gülin Abla feels far yet near in this moment. I silence emotions rising up in my chest by deciding that I have no time for dreaming in my pragmatic life.

Choice

Once the diagnosis is confirmed, Lennie and Mick visit me at the hospital. Everyone is in disbelief. My sister-in-law leaves in a hurry. *I'm sure she's a good nurse, but this is hitting too close to home,* I guess. My cousin, whose behavior toward me is showing signs of softening, remains with me through most of the day.

"You were always one for extremes." The accuracy of his statement surprises me. *Beneath the recent estrangement, we go back a while,* I acknowledge, pained by the loss of our close connection.

The next day Mick comes again, thoughtfully supplying me with a salad and some fresh fruit for good nutrition. After he leaves, the nurse inquires about our relationship, and remarks, "How blessed you are, to have close family by your side." An awkward smile is all I can respond with while my insides crumble. The promising shift in my cousin's attitude fades quickly.

Rather than dwelling on this hurtful topic, I focus my attention on the upcoming medical procedures. I am told that the final step before chemotherapy can be started is testing my bone marrow for cancer cells. An intern comes in; she has a fresh-out-of-school look. Nevertheless, I warm up to her when she smiles at me nicely, which I don't recall from the other oncologists. She tells me, "Lie on your side and curl up. It's crucial that you don't move during this procedure."

"A simple process." She goes on, "I'll use a device that looks like a corkscrew to reach into the hipbone through your lower back and extract a small amount of bone marrow." What is not so straight forward is that the assisting nurse notices halfway into the drilling that I am not connected to the intravenous tranquilizer. "Too late, can't disrupt anymore," says the intern brusquely, who, I suspect by now, is applying this procedure for the first time to a living person. I am relieved when she is literally "off my back".

The nurse apologies while tidying up after the doctor has left: "I'm so sorry, I didn't see it in time. But how could you possibly remain so still while she was digging into you?" "She told me so." *Did I have a choice?*

The nurse's animated mannerism lets me understand what a painful procedure this was. Evidently, a protective mechanism inside me spared me registering a sharp tool being pushed through my flesh and bone. *Did my overloaded nervous system know to shut down somehow?*

Charm

Ross has become protective of me since the hospitalization. Evenings are the only time he can spare to visit me. "I want to be by your side, but during daytime I got to be at work." *Now that my income is in jeopardy, the onus is on him to pay the bills.* He comes straight from the office – *rather, via a detour at the pub,* I notice from his breath.

We spend a rushed hour catching up on the news, and he disappears quickly in order to get something to eat and get ready for the next workday that he starts at the crisp hour of 5 a.m.

When he hears about the bone marrow testing incident, he is outraged. "I'm moving in on the weekend!" This is against regulations in this hospital, but thankfully the nurses close an eye for us as we are gaining their sympathy. "Want to know how I heard them refer to us?" I smile. "The charming couple of the ward." "Of course we are," he confirms. "Let me hunt down something half-decent to sleep on."

Once he leaves, I drag myself to the washroom. I had thought that things had gotten as bad as they possibly could the day before, forgetting that tumors don't stop growing because a diagnosis is confirmed. Yesterday I was hunched over, but today the growths in my gut have continued expanding, making walking near-impossible.

In my technical world, when a virtual bug is found, the computer program would be stopped and the code corrected; that simple. *Reality is so messy*, I acknowledge while my husband rolls a heavy recliner chair alongside my hospital bed. The washroom door is wide open. I feel uncomfortable at first. *It isn't that he has never seen me "on the throne", as he'd put it.*

However, the thin hospital gown is inadequate at concealing my by-now disfigured body. He walks over and gives me a kiss on the cheek. "Let me know when you're done." "Help yourself to my dinner," I add as he closes the door behind him. "The tray is on the bed."

"Great. I'm famished," I hear him. "Don't know how you can swallow that stuff," I add. I find it difficult enough to attempt eating anything at lunchtime. *If I hadn't lost my appetite from stress, I'd get an ulcer from these greasy meals,* I am convinced.

Sometime later, he knocks at the washroom door. "You alright?" "Not really," I reply hesitantly. "Want me to come in?" "Hm hm," I nod in tears. "Here, let me have that," he takes the sheets of toilet paper I helplessly hold in my hand and proceeds to cleaning my bottom.

The tumors are so bulged out that I cannot twist or bend at all anymore. *Is he dreaming of his wife right now,* I wonder in despair, *the one he calls his "Hot Babe" when naked like this?*

I cannot recognize who or what my body is anymore. *What sick plan is this that my hubby is left wiping my bum instead of our baby's?*

Trick

The following morning, a group of medical staff enters my room. One takes blood from a new spot on my arm, the other one inserts a sizable needle onto the top of my left hand; the end sticking out of my skin is connected through a tube to an intravenous stand. Yet another one scrubs me clean and places a catheter in my bladder, its extension collecting my urine in a bag beside me. These lines only amplify the debilitation I already feel from the ever growing tumors.

I'm nailed to bed. Did Gulliver feel this powerless when the Lilliputians tied him down? Unfortunately, I realize further that this involuntary surrender extends beyond the physical realm –

any control I had over my life is now in the hands of hospital staff.

A chemotherapy bag is placed on the IV stand after hours-long preparations. I drift off while watching this transparent liquid, looking as inert as water, trickle into my veins drop by drop. I awake to the ceiling moving fast – I am being rolled through the hospital corridor. Once in an elevator, the nurse standing by my head explains, "We're taking you to Emergency. You're bleeding." *Oh right, I had that lengthy period.*

I experience an unusual sensation in between my thighs while being lifted onto the surgery room bed under blindingly bright lights. *The warmth feels nice.* When the nurse proceeds to cleaning me, I notice something spongy between my legs that looks like a chunk of a liver in a pool of blood. "What's that?" I screech. "Your endometrium is too enlarged, it's peeling off in big pieces," I hear a calm woman's voice. "I'm a gyne-oncologist." *Why do I know all these terms that were wonderfully foreign to me just a few days ago?*

"We have to stop the bleeding." *Duh,* I say internally, *the puddle under my bum is growing faster than the nurse can mop it up.* "I'll inject you with high-dose estrogen now." "How high?" I find myself asking. I wish to be a participant and not only a piece of meat. *Seriously? Who's talking?* I mock myself in the same breath.

I'm dying here and some brain cell of mine is left having a conversation with the doc. "Basically three months' worth of birth control pills," she replies. "It's a lot, I know." "How about clotting?" *There I go again.* "We've no other choice," she says while shooting the drug into my artery. "Hopefully this'll do the trick."

I wake up in my hospital bed to hearing that same voice again. "Wanted to check on you. You fainted from the blood loss. We got the bleeding under control and gave you a transfusion. "Sorry," I say, "for the many questions." "It's quite alright," she smiles. "It's your body we're dealing with." She adds, "We'll put you on the pill continuously from now on to avoid any such surprises." "Thanks for your help, doctor..." "Knowlton," she completes my sentence. She touches my shoulder lightly as she prepares to leave. "Keep up the tenaciousness, you'll need it."

Dawn

It must be the weekend, I gather, seeing Ross enter the room. He is holding a bag under each arm: "This one is for Monday morning," he demonstratively lifts the white one first, a customary package of fresh shirts from the dry-cleaner. "And this one..." he mischievously grins while lifting the brown paper bag – another familiar sight.

"Had to bring my daily medicine, Babe," he adds triumphantly, having smuggled in a six-pack. He hides it behind the shower curtain until the last nurse has left and the footsteps in the corridor subside for the night. He retrieves the beer and settles into the recliner chair. Within moments after his last sip, he is out like a light. His snoring becomes a lullaby for my troubled mind.

Days and nights start blurring into each other while the chemotherapy treatment takes effect. Nurses and doctors come and go... Sometimes I manage to get out of bed for a short while, presumably to have lunch sitting upright in a chair, leaning on my weakened forearms to prop me up. Soon after, I stay put in bed altogether; *I have no will to move, even if I were freed from the many tubes dangling on and off me.* I am drained of each and every drop of life energy I have ever had.

A hazy cloud overcomes me. From an otherworldly distance, I witness my being slip in and out of life... *in and out... in... and... out...*

Hypnotized by this ebb and flow, I begin floating away, *far far away...* farther with each swing, drawn into an ever deeper slumber from the sleep I have already fallen into. I have no want. I have no need. *All there is, is absolute serenity...*

While my being eases more and more into this enticing trance, somewhere in my subconscious a subtle tug registers, a gentle occult force of sorts. *A last thread of life pulling at my departed being? An invitation to return perhaps?* Uninspired by the effort it takes, yet seemingly void of any choice on my behalf, bodily sensations begin returning. I vaguely become aware of a warm glow embracing my hand. In the darkness of the night, I make out the shadow of my husband sleeping in the recliner chair, his arm stretched over to me. *His hand feels so good on mine.* I go back to sleep.

I awake to hearing Ross getting ready to go to work. He is a morning person and I am not in the best of times. But this dawn, I am more alert than I have been in days. *I'm not even grumpy at this ungodly hour.* "This chair is killing me," he complains. "It's been five nights on this piece of shite." "Glad to have you by my side even in a foul mood," I smile at him.

He remains distracted, disengaged rather. "Got to focus on work, Ada," he says walking toward the door. "I'll tell the nurse they can take the recliner back. You're in good hands here," he blows me a kiss before disappearing out of sight. I remain gazing at the empty door with the numbness of a child being left behind at an orphanage.

After sleeping another while, I wake up when breakfast is served. *Good, jello. I can't bear to put anything in my mouth, but at least it's fun to mess around with.* I sense a hue of a dream; *where was I floating?* Even though I cannot make a clear connection, I recognize the significance of the prior night.

A hand... Ross's hand... But now he's gone. Has he fulfilled his job and hence left this morning? Could the lifeline I felt have been the warm blood flowing through just anyone's hand? My mind is too tired to process any of this, though recollecting the pleasant sensation from last night I fall asleep again.

Intrathecal

I awake this time to hearing footsteps; Dr. Olsen is approaching my bed. She holds a needle of respectable size. *Is there any spot left on me to poke?* She explains that this one goes right into the spine. Her coldness sounds reassuring to some degree.

If I'm to judge from her detached voice and impersonal gestures, she's surely not referring to the spine of anybody I know.

Momentary denial leaves me when her assisting nurse comes over and moves me onto my side. She places me into position after considerable adjustments, trying to avoid pulling the many lines or squishing organs under the weight of the tumors.

"I'm here to administer intrathecal chemotherapy. It'll require a lumbar puncture." *There go a bunch of new words I haven't heard of before.* My antenna goes up, *should I be worried?* "I'll insert the needle into the lower portion of your spine in-between two vertebrae in your back," Dr. Olsen explains, "I can't give you tranquilizers for this procedure. It shouldn't hurt much."

"Been there, done that," I refer to the mishap at my bone marrow testing. The subsequent lengthy pause lets me know that my feeble attempt at joking is not appreciated. "It's crucial that you don't move at all. Watch for any changes in your legs. The slightest shift off target can cause irreversible nerve damage." *Alright then,* I quietly try to kid in my mind to release tension, *I've good practice in "remaining still" from last time.*

Fortunately I had been clued in by a nurse before, "What Dr. Olsen lacks in bedside manners, she more than makes up for with her impeccable expertise." This strikes a chord with me. *Is this the sort of professional I'm turning into? Does it have to be this way?* The more sensitive one is the more toughened up one has to get – *calloused by the relentless abrasion of climbing the metaphorical ladder in a male-dominated career.*

True to her fame, Dr. Olsen proceeds with utmost precision, and absent of any empathy in her voice, describes the procedure as a scientist would while handling a corpse.

"Once the needle reaches into the spinal canal, an amount of spinal fluid is extracted exactly equal to the amount of chemotherapy to be injected. This is followed by a steady and slow injection of the drug. The spinal fluid envelops the brain, and is extremely sensitive to any alteration. Even the smallest pressure change can cause substantial pain – often headaches." When done, she adds, "I'll be back to repeat this as part of your treatment protocol." *Oh joy.*

I come to experience Dr. Olsen's impersonal sounding lecture in the form of a skull-splitting migraine. After being tormented for hours, I beg the nurse. "We can't give you any more meds to alleviate your pain," she replies apologetically. I lose the last bit of control I had left. This turns out to be not just another insult to my body, but the last injury that breaks me.

My will succumbs to maddening pain. *Time, space, life... dissolves.*

5

Light

My eyes open up. Shapes form out of a blurred grayness. *I can focus!* I become aware of my body; the level of pain is more tolerable. *Obviously someone eventually had mercy on me and knocked me out of my misery.*

It's great to stretch. "Ouch!" I am sharply reminded of the IV needle. *How did it get up higher on my arm?* I notice a trail of puffy dark bruises indicative of prior puncture sites.

Never mind. I'm moving. I palpate with my free hand my neck, breasts and belly. *The lumps are gone!* So much so that wrinkled skin hangs off me as if my body were an overstretched bag. *Nonetheless a bag that has rid itself of weighty rocks. Sweet lightness of being...*

"Good. You're awake." A nurse is standing beside me. I am sure I recognize her. "I'm sorry, but may I ask your name again?" "That's alright. It's Hannah. It's been quite a while since we last talked."

Of course, the one who told me she's from South Africa. I had enjoyed her slightly Dutch-sounding English. It was a treat to hear a familiar accent spoken by this striking African woman from the opposite end of the planet. I wonder for a moment, *what may have brought her here? What views does she have on the world?* Yet, I must solve an immediate puzzle first. "How's that?" I count. "I was hospitalized no more than a few days ago." "A few weeks," she explains. "You've been unconscious for a good part of it."

"Shall we get you up?" she asks. "Gladly," I reply and attempt to curl over to the edge of the bed, but my knees do not bend. "Easy does it," she intervenes and pulls off the blanket. "Look, your legs have fluid retention from lengthy immobility." "Those big fat logs can't be mine," I stare in disbelief at my shapelessly swollen limbs. She consoles me, "Once we get you moving, they should normalize soon."

I gradually manage to stand up on my wobbly legs. As I start taking a step with the nurse supporting me and keeping me untangled from the IV stand, Ross steps in. "Let me tuck under your other arm." "You're here?" I am surprised. "Yes, I checked on you several days ago, too, but you were out of it. We thought we lost you there for a while." *He hasn't completely forgotten about me.*

The three of us walk a few steps together. *Their touch feels so good.* I soak up the first physical contact I have had outside medical procedures. After settling me in the chair by the window, Hannah excuses herself. "I'll leave you two be."

"I'm dying for fresh air," I am besieged by a sense of suffocation. "Let me open the window," Ross replies. "Damn it, where is the handle?" He calls in a nurse walking along the corridor for assistance. I hear her mutter something about the delicate balance of air conditioning in the building. "For a minute, please," I cry out. Then comes the underlying truth: "Windows are kept locked for patient safety. We're on the top floor, you know," she says facing him while avoiding eye contact with me. *I'm furious.*

"If I wanted to kill myself, do you think I'd be putting up with this hellish cancer treatment?" I apologize right away, "Sorry, all I want is real air to remind me of life beyond the hospital." The nurse, about to leave, says, "hospital policy." Ross steps in with all his fierceness, "Fuck this shit. Give me the handle now!" A short while later a lovely breeze fills my lungs.

I know my husband to be usually courteous in public, never swearing outside the privacy of our home or the accepting ambiance of a pub. *My sweetie's nerves are frayed,* I conclude. This volatile discourse spreads quickly through the ward and puts an end to our popularity.

Use

"Take it easy," Hannah reminds me when I am being discharged from hospital a week later. "You've had a rough time. Rest up." *Should've asked how exactly I was supposed to do so,* I contemplate once back at the house.

Now that my fight to stay alive is done with, the drama at home hits me full blast. Ross is in a bad mood for the short time I see him in the evenings. Lennie is often on out-of-town assignments, supposedly to enhance her upcoming position, *but I have a hunch that avoidance motivates her as much or more.*

And my cousin is nowhere in sight, especially when it comes to running an errand for me. The medications I have to take, the stairs I have to climb back up after getting a snack in the kitchen, rotating bath-towels in bed to avoid soaking the sheets altogether with heavy sweating, standing upright for the duration of a shower... all are insurmountable tasks.

To make time pass while having to stay home, and also to feel useful, I set myself a new goal each day. *Sit upright at the table throughout a whole meal; clean out the bathroom garbage – don't forget to wear a mask and gloves; tidy the coffee table in the living room...* I also sort through piled up mail. Two pieces are addressed to me: a package from my friend Berna and an envelope bearing the university seal.

First work, then fun, I decide. It is a typed letter signed by my supervisor: "I regret to inform you that you are removed from the university payroll. For your convenience, attached is the sick-leave form for employment insurance. Get well soon." *Is this it, Ricardo? I'm away for a month and you discard me already?*

Gone are the days I was pursued. Three-and-a-half years prior, toward the end of my master's degree, several professors in my department competed to gain me as their doctoral student. However flattering this was, my determination to return to Europe upon completion of the initially assigned two years superseded all else. With my heart healed from my first romance and my self-confidence boosted, I returned home, carrying the same two suitcases I had left with. I communicated right away with universities in Turkey, Germany and the Netherlands for my doctorate. My solid technical background evidently proved enough credibility to receive invitations from prominent engineering faculties. In order to ensure the most suitable next step, I visited the top three campuses on my list.

At the end of my expedition, to everyone's surprise, mine included, I found myself on a transatlantic flight once again. This was a decision more from the heart than the mind. Unlike any other place I had been to before, I felt most at ease in Canada. Ever since the day I arrived, I felt accepted – *with my accent and all.*

I took a liking to a people who truly welcomed multiculturalism. This embodied most realistically my personal vision of cohabiting peacefully with our differences. In contrast to other countries that emphasize assimilation into a predefined mold, I found Canada's identity flourished on individuality, creating an enriched space for co-existence. Before I knew it, I had developed a caring loyalty toward this land – *and a beautiful one at that with its rugged nature,* I reflect while missing hiking and skiing in the Rockies.

When I made myself at home once again in Calgary, I chose Ricardo Rivera as my Ph.D. supervisor since he gave me the most freedom in defining my research project, but also out of nostalgia.

This warm-blooded Venezuelan felt so "mediterranean". Being my parents' age, he also fulfilled a need in me for a father figure. However now, in my weakest moment, I feel betrayed by him – *or by life, or by my body?* I cannot discern. *Couldn't he have at least picked up the phone and told me in person?*

What happens to my research and lab experiments, so close to defending? My classes are already assigned to other instructors. Noticing that the world is turning just fine without me overwhelms me. *Why then have I bothered to work so hard, always feeling obliged to pitch in more than my share?* I feel utterly disposable... and useless.

The package from Berna takes my mind off oppressive thoughts. *It's a teddy-bear. Never been into plush toys,* is my first reaction. *But this one is cute,* I reconsider. I hug it, *yup, snuggly,* it passes the test. Beneath the packing noodles, I find a second item; a diary. *Never been into keeping a journal either, but could give that a try, too,* I assess.

Moved by my friend's considerate gesture, I call her in the evening. When she hears my voice, she replies "Canım," an ardent Turkish expression of closeness, telling me I am as dear to her as her own life. "What I wanted to give you is a warm embrace and to listen to your sorrows." "I see; what a neat idea sending me a teddy and a journal to symbolize your wishes. Sağolasın," I thank her with good wishes for her life. "Your gifts mean the world to me." She says, "Let's visit soon," as we hang up. A tear trickles down my cheek.

Moeder

Barely starting to envision a remote resemblance of normalcy sometime soon, I receive a call from the hospital; I will have to go back for a second round of chemotherapy. *I'm summoned back. Did I not know this or did I suppress it?* I cannot recall. Upon admission, this little mystery is solved when a nurse greets me for the "intensification phase" which she explains follows the "induction phase" I recently received.

"I'm coming to visit you," my mother phones. "Murat called us." With the cheeriest voice I can muster up, "It's alright Moeder," I reply. "No big deal, I'll manage. You can't just take vacation during the school term to fly across half the planet." "It's done, I got my ticket. I'll see you on Saturday. I managed to get a sub for three weeks."

"Tschüss,"I hang up in order not to burst into tears. Recalling incidents my mother had shared with me over the years, I am aware that by taking time off she is risking her job security as an art therapist for the German Consulate's school in Istanbul.

Unlike last time, I am conscious of all the days I spend at the hospital, including the most unpleasant details about chemotherapy. The stomach-turning nausea is accompanied by troubling dizzy spells and I sweat so profusely that often I am left dripping wet as if having freshly stepped out of the shower. None of the side effects lessen even when treatments are stopped at regular intervals. A bucket and a hairdryer become my steady companions for when I cannot make it fast enough to throw up in the washroom or when I don't find the strength to change my clothes repeatedly.

Awaiting my mother helps me get through the renewed hospital stay. Upon her arrival, she rushes into nursing me – *just like she used to whenever I fell very ill as a kid.* At all the other times, our relationship was far less tactile and more intellectual. *Moeder treated Aylin and me as little adults.* This allowed us to grow up more independently in a culture that did not encourage this, especially for girls. Her reserved attitude would soften only at times that she deemed to be an emergency. *My current state evidently qualifies as such.*

My mother rescues me from hospital meals during the day by feeding me little-by-little homemade stews made palatable for my queasy stomach. She also tailors two brightly colored nighties so that they fit over the tubes attached to my body, breaking the monotony of the hospital gowns. She massages me daily, first with rubbing alcohol to reactivate my blood circulation and then with a mix of oils to soften my skin that has hardened from the toxins in the chemotherapy.

The stubborn bruise from repeated IV needles on my hand, along with other blue and purple spots on my arms, gradually subside under her touch. She also takes me on small walks along the hospital corridor. And at night, she goes home to cook fresh broths and wash my sweat-soaked nighties, to return early the next morning.

Fifty

"How's Murat doing?" I ask my mother. *I miss him.* His visits having stopped since my first hospitalization and Ross refusing to talk about him, I have had no contact with my cousin except for the brief interval at home, *when he mostly played hide-and-seek.* In her typical pragmatism, she says: "The house was filthy dirty when I arrived. Murat acts bored when Lennie is not around, and spends most of his time in the bedroom. Oh, and there is a telephone cord hanging out his door, I nearly tripped over it." *Is he still ringing his lover?* I am concerned.

"We call him Mick now." "Yes, I heard, but he'll remain Murat to me. I couldn't get my head around his hasty marriage business. But I'm not here to debate that," Moeder is quick to let me know her position. "I'm trapped in a Thomas Mann line!" She goes onto quoting, "Viewed from the summit of reason," halfway talking to herself, "all life looks like a malignant disease and the world like a madhouse." *There goes one of her typical literature lessons.*

"It really feels like that," she emphasizes. I go on to suggest, "Could you talk to him? I think he's in a bad crisis," I make the mistake of tuning out her underlying message. She is quick to clarify, "I haven't come all this way to entertain Murat!"

"I wish you hadn't invited him to stay with you in the first place," the deeper truth comes out. "Let's not get into that now", she regains control. "One right thing Murat did was getting in touch with your father. Why didn't you tell us how sick you really were? And why didn't your husband call us when it got so bad?" Her voice wavers.

"What do you mean?" I am perplexed. "I'm sick, but things aren't that grim." She replies sternly, "Murat didn't call just about anything. He called us to say Ross had told Lennie that it was time to say their farewells. And apparently when he went with her to see you, the nurse told them that you were dying and that they were keeping you as comfortable as possible."

"Really? That sounds like the longest chain of whispering in a telephone-game," I reply, trying to be silly. Too frail to accept the weight of reality, my mind focuses on an irrelevant tangent: *What luck, the one day my cousin came to visit, I was unconscious.*

"We were worried sick," my mother continues. "Your father broke down weeping. I went onto planning to be by your side the soonest I could. To double-check what Murat told us, I asked at the front desk and was referred to a nurse – Hannah, I think. She said they didn't expect you to live, especially once your vital signs faded."

Hmm, no one told me that. Matter-of-factly, she adds: "I'm glad you came back and my priority is to help you get well." Her comment straightens my thinking, making me realize that I need to soak up all caring she has to offer to survive this nasty illness.

My mother and I settle into as much of a routine as possible amidst ongoing activities at the hospital. Then, Dr. Olsen announces that I can go home early – *two weeks before schedule*. My excitement is clouded by doubt. I have come to dislike abrupt changes in doctors' decisions.

Something is obviously not going according to plan! I am additionally troubled hearing Dr. Olsen repeat her initial prognosis: "There is a fifty percent chance of one-year survival."

"But didn't you say that before?"

"Listen carefully," Dr. Olsen slows down her speech, "one... year... survival... Be glad you made it through the first part. You still have half a chance of making it to next year." *After all I have gone through? Isn't it time for a bonus, a raise, not even a cookie? Something, anything, to show for the hardest work I've ever done in my whole life!*

It is disheartening that the great news of the day is simply that I am alive still – *so far*. I get an eerie sense of how significant this is, but my mind cannot bend that far at this time.

Letting go of a basic reference point I have counted on for so long feels impossible – *being alive and fully functional is the absolute norm, isn't it?*

Miracle

Once Dr. Olsen leaves, my mother is determined to find out more. "I'll see what this early discharge is about." She returns to my room with the head nurse by her side. "It's indeed good news. Ada responded to this second set of treatments exceptionally well. She was spared complications she had during the first set. Therefore, the doctor was able to adjust the treatment schedule to continue at the outpatient clinic."

"That's lucky," Moeder cheers. "I'd say your daughter was indeed lucky to get medical care in the nick of time; she's our miracle girl. But she's also a real trouper and persevered through it all. She takes her meds without a fuss, zealously follows everything we tell her to help her get better, and also keeps us on our toes by asking pertinent questions. Polite and assertive; you raised her well." She looks at my mother and then waves at me on her way out, "Take good care now."

I'm a grown woman! I react to being referred to as a "girl". It had also taken me quite some time to get used to Ross calling me "babe", feeling uncomfortable with such infantile connotation as a term of endearment – *truth be told sweet talk was not part of my upbringing.* At this moment, however, it is actually the reference to a miracle that causes my scientific mind the most discomfort; *isn't it too convenient to label matters that we cannot comprehend as such? How on Earth did I pull through?*

It is disconcerting not to have a logical answer either to why I fell so violently ill or to why I survived thus far. At the same time, an uncanny expansion of sorts is taking place in my awareness, forcing me to acknowledge that life is far too complex to be contained within my rational worldview.

I am reminded of a dream from a previous night. It had started out like a nightmare: *I was free falling through the air, certain to burst into pieces as I saw solid ground get closer and closer. Upon contact, however, concrete turned into an ocean and I found myself immersed in gentle waters.*

I had awoken sweating in mental disorientation. This was accompanied by an unfamiliar yet oddly calming sensation. Three words came up: *falling through illusions...* This sounded so insensible that I had forgotten about it until the nurse's comment triggered me.

Exit

My mother proceeds to pack my belongings. "Ross said he's waiting in the car at the entrance." While she carries my bag toward the elevator, I sluggishly make my way over, too.

I cannot believe my eyes: *Dr. Dubois?* As tense as I am, he is excited. Before I can get into the elevator, he grabs my neck as if to assure himself that the big lump is really gone. *Don't touch me*, I want to say, feeling strangled by his grip. He victoriously announces, "I'm writing a scientific paper on this case!"

The initial illusionary student-teacher bond lost its appeal long ago. All I can think about is what makes a person become so desensitized to another human life. *Will this man ever realize that there is a living being behind the screen of an academically interesting "case study"?*

To my dismay, I have no strength to voice myself at this time. I slowly maneuver away and slide through the elevator doors as soon as he lets go of me.

Best

It's great to be back home and have Moeder with me. I am freed of needles, nauseating drugs, terrifying doctors... *well, for most of it.* I continue receiving chemotherapy twice a week at the outpatient clinic, *but compared to the roller coaster of my recent hospital adventures, this is child's play.*

Another change since we arrived back home is that I don't see much of Ross. From the minute we arrived at home he has buried himself even deeper in work. *Distancing himself from the stress of my illness may do him some good.* While he is away for long hours every day, I get spoiled by my mother's uninterrupted attention during the tail end of her visit. I relax into her energetic care. She cooks for me, massages me and, whenever I am able, takes me out on short walks around the block to get my limbs moving.

Moeder offers me a wig for our outings. "Thanks, but I can't stand this itchy thing on my head," I point to my hairless tender scalp. A few minutes later she returns, laying a variety of the most elegant silk scarves onto my bed. "I picked them up at the Grand Bazaar just before flying over. I had a hunch you might not like the wig." "Super," I grin, excited by her choices. "I love their feel against my skin." They keep my head warm and their colorful designs cheer up my pale face.

Our walks are the highlight of my day, allowing me to leave the sickness behind – *if only for ten minutes at a time.* My mother keeps my spirits up by entertaining me with bigger goals to aim for every few days. First, "Let's walk for half a block," then, "Let me drive you to a nearby park for a change of scenery," and later, "How about visiting the park by the lake to watch the ducks"... Little by little, life and color start coming back into my life.

With the exception of these brief strolls, I spend most of my time in bed. *My mind is foggy from chemo;* it only now occurs to me how hard it must be for Moeder to sleep on a foamy on the living room floor without any privacy. *Why haven't I thought of this before?* The senior would be given priority back home. So my cousin, being the sole user of the guest room during most of the weekdays, would have normally offered the comfort of a private room to an elder, especially to his "Yenge", his aunt. But this thought does not seem to enter his mind.

Neither has it occurred to Ross to switch places with his mother-in-law, offering her our bed while I was hospitalized. *Startling that Moeder hasn't complained at all; she's obviously aware of the already enormous tension at home.*

One afternoon, I awake from a snooze to the door bell ringing. When I look down the stairs, I see two handymen unpacking a fashionable sofa-bed, replacing the ragged couch from my husband's bachelor days. "Danke Moeder," I grin, appreciating her fine taste as well as generosity and resourcefulness in solving the matter. *Now we have a nicer living room and she has a decent bed to sleep on.* "Keine Angst," she calls up that there is nothing to worry. "I cleared it with him; the old one is going to Goodwill."

Murat is the only one who is unenthusiastic about the new piece of furniture. *In actuality his opinion matters least,* I finally look at him from a realistic perspective. For the first month of his visit, during the English course he took, he was naturally welcomed in our home. *Lately though, the air at the house could be cut with a knife.* Since marrying my sister-in-law, he has technically become even closer to me, but ironically, emotionally has turned more distant.

In an attempt to make my cousin feel comfortable while Lennie arranges their move, I had remarked, "Now you aren't merely visiting, but virtually own this place," referring to his wife holding the title of our home. This comment eventually backfires on me: Having taken over the house chores from where I had left before hospitalization, I hear Moeder turn off the vacuum cleaner and tell Murat, "Pick up your coat and shoes from the floor and store them in the entrance closet like the rest of us. I can't clean the living room otherwise." "I do whatever pleases me in my own house!" is his scornful response.

Lieb

Even though I am discouraged by witnessing this discourse, later I find myself getting upset with my mother for being tough on my cousin. "Murat is having a hard time these days. Don't you see? He's getting used to a new life; getting to know his new wife." She lets me be. "Is it because he's on Baba's side?" As I blurt this out, I wish I had not, but it is too late. I am well aware of the age-old friction between the two families.

"I'm sorry, Moeder," I add feeling badly. "Didn't mean to hurt you. I guess I'm so overwhelmed by everything in my life that fixing Murat's is more appealing."

"I can only imagine how difficult it must have been for northern-European cultured Christian city people to mix with near-Eastern Muslim farmer folk, and how you and Baba got stuck in the middle." I try to lighten up our conversation, "Can you see Oma in her fancy fur coat with matching leather shoes, handbag, and gloves to top it up, sitting down on a broken stool in Nene's rich-smelling little kitchen? One showing off her coiffured blond hair, the other hiding each string of her hair under a tightly wrapped black headscarf."

"Ha, that'd be a sight," she replies more relaxed. "It's a pity, your father's mother and mine never met." "Must have been tough raising a family in a country so foreign to you, even having to learn the language from scratch," I acknowledge her ordeal. She remains quiet, gazing away.

Noticing tears building up in her eyes, I hug her. "I'm glad you came." Her emotionality may not be just about the past, but about seeing me sick. "Ich hab' Dich sehr lieb," I whisper expressing how very much I love her. "Ich Dich auch, Adelheid," my mother responds in her usual controlled yet affectionate ways, omitting the word love, but calling me by the original source of my name – *our little secret*. "You rest now. I'll go for a walk," she leaves. Her calm demeanour, having allowed me to vent without retaliating, tells me how much she really wants to help me regain my health.

Macho

I keep pondering while my mother is on her walk; I cannot recognize nor reach my cousin – *my best friend. How true is our closeness that I've so cherished? Did he seek my company, even when we were kids, to some extent because I was part-European, his closest link to the West?* My cousin's young marriage has granted him a spouse with social status from his point of view and has opened the doors to citizenship in a western country. I don't want to believe it, but this is the simplest answer. *And the timing matches; him turning macho since his wedding, arguing with his brother-in-law and now scolding his aunt for no reason.*

Moeder returns, holding a tray with a hot cup of tea and a muffin. I decide to distance myself from my cousin's troubles for a while. *It's time to soak up her loving.* The days fly by and before we know it, she has to get back to her job in Turkey – *far too early for my taste.* "Promise, I'll be back as soon as I can," she hugs and kisses me good-bye.

"We better go," Ross points at his watch. *I'm relieved he took off work early to give her a ride – my absentee hubby.* "Sorry Moeder, I can't come along." "Of course," she replies. "You think I'd let you sit in the car for the half hour drive? Or let you breathe the airport air? I've worked too much pampering you to let it go to waste like that," she smiles. I wave as they leave, unsure whether I will live to see her again.

Zero

"Bummer, it's happening." I am alarmed sensing a fast rising fever. By the time I take my temperature it reads 40°C – *on my good old mercury thermometer from Turkey. At the clinic they warned me to come in right away if it hits 101; yup, it's sure past that in Fahrenheit.* I call the clinic to confirm. "Yes come in now," the nurse confirms. *Moeder left a few days ago, Ross is at work, and the other two, who knows.* I call a cab and go straight to the hospital.

While registering at the front desk, the nurse is nice enough to reply to my inquiry: "It's a typical reaction to repeat chemo sessions. Your white blood cell count has dropped to basically nil, turning your body unfortunately into a growing-ground for bacteria that normally roam harmlessly inside you and in the air around. Your body attempts to fight resulting infections by raising its temperature, but at this rate we have to get you on IV antibiotics right away."

For once, medicine I receive doesn't make me sicker than I already am. When my condition stabilizes, I celebrate the occasion by leaving the bed and curl up in the chair to look out the window. While gazing at the last of the leaves falling on this cold autumn day, a doctor whom I have not met before enters the room. "Congratulations on your shrunken tumors." Apparently, pictures taken at the time of my hospitalization, depicting my bulged up neck, were circulated at the weekly oncology meeting. *Wow, if for nothing else, I'm famous for my tumors.*

"The oncologists' panel discussed your unique case at length and collectively decided that an autologous transplant is the next step to take. Dr. Olsen conveyed this to you, right?" *Did she?* "We booked you in for December 5th," he adds nonchalantly.

So soon? I want to ask, but he keeps talking. "The nurse will supply you with the details of preparations that will start ten days before the transplant date." He continues, "A meeting prior to treatment will be arranged to elaborate on questions you may have in order to be well informed so that you can sign the consent forms." Before I can gather my thoughts, he leaves.

I am discharged from hospital once more, only to rest up for yet another treatment – the "ultimate one", according to my sister. We have been in touch only loosely since Aylin had moved to the Netherlands while both of us were still in our teens. She was not much of a talker so phone calls were kept brief and she was even less of a writer.

Last time we met was when I visited Maastricht to explore doctoral studies. But nowadays, she calls me regularly and keeps me informed on the medical front. Before the terms "bone marrow" and "stem cell transplant" were introduced to me at the hospital, she had mentioned them to me on the phone. "I'll fly over and donate you my marrow if I'm a match. I'll get tested as soon as you want me to."

First, my parents were asked to get screened for bone marrow compatibility. Once results arrived from Istanbul, I was called in for an appointment with Dr. Olsen. In her customary bluntness, she explained: "Neither of your parents is a match. Their markers are so different from one another that even the amount of indicators is off. This drops the chance of a match for you existing anywhere in the world to practically zero. You said you have only one sibling, right? Tell him or her not to bother to get tested."

So, I'll be my own donor, I understand. *I sure hope the cancer cells haven't snuck in that far,* I dread. Then I smile at the irony of my parents' racial diversity, *incompatible down to the bone.* None of this lessens the preciousness of my sister's thoughtful offering. *I feel so close to her again.*

Hook

In contrast, my relationship with my cousin-turned-brother is far from deepening. I attempt to draw a line between us by calling him solely Mick to distinguish "this new man" from my beloved Murat.

Far more crucial than this is my confusion as to why I am booked to return to hospital so soon. *And that for the treatment referred to as "the last shot".* Earlier, I was told that after chemotherapy is completed, I would be left to rest up for several months before any other treatment option would be considered. My recent hospitalization due to a nullified immune system and subsequent infection is clear evidence that I need to rest in between treatments.

Distraught by this change in plans, I call my family doctor Dr. Jackson. She kindly returns my call. Hearing the anguish in my voice, she says, "I'll talk to your oncologist and find out what's going on. I'll call you back in the evening." *What a sweetheart.*

I wait on edge, barely breathing whilst imagining horrid scenarios. *Why is the hardest of all cancer treatments scheduled when my body is so depleted?* To distract myself I get a glass of water from the kitchen. When I run into Mick, I want to relay my stress.

"Waiting for the doctor's call is making me crazy." I don't register much of a response from him. *Is it because I'm too overwhelmed to do so or because there is no hope for any communication?* I cannot tell. Engrossed in worry, I return to bed.

The evening hours move on, but the phone does not ring. *Five, six, seven, eight o'clock. Was it too optimistic to think that she'd remember to call me in her private time after a long workday?* Then it occurs to me to test the line to ensure no handset is accidentally off the hook. *My heart sinks further from rock bottom:* Mick is on the line, chatting yet again with his European girlfriend. In disbelief, I go over to his room.

"I'm awaiting a call. Please hang up and leave this line open." "Can't do," he replies. "It's not a matter of choice. I expect an after-hour call from my doctor." I reason, "If you must use the phone, why don't you go over to the fax line in the office? It's a separate number." *Considering I pay for both phone lines, this could be considered a generous suggestion.* I turn around to go back to my room, assuming to hear, "Oh sure, I'll do that." Instead, he spits out, "Bloody hell! You tell your doctors to call you on the fax line." I have nothing left in me to say. Shattered, my feet drag me back to bed. Looking at the clock one more time, I try to come to terms with the reality that past nine o'clock the possibility of a call is gone. *The nerve-wracking wait for the doctor's call will have to wait until tomorrow.* I lie down beside Ross who is already asleep.

When the phone rings at ten o'clock at night, I jolt up in surprise. *It's Dr. Jackson.* Hardly able to breathe, I listen attentively. "The change in schedule is good news," she assures me. "Recent medical evidence indicates that survival rates improve when the transplant is delivered sooner rather than later."

"My oncologist said this treatment is saved for the very end, if all else fails," I reiterate. She patiently confirms, "Yes, this has been the convention so far, but Dr. Olsen thinks the more aggressive approach of doing it as soon as possible could improve your chances in the long run." Still confused, but relieved by her describing things as "good news", my worn-out nerves relax a little. I thank her profusely and go to sleep.

Jump

Mick calls me to his room on the following day. *He must have hung up at some point last night – out of consideration for me?* Feeling more mellow with my doctor's reassurance, I am inclined to make peace. *He may want to know the outcome of the call,* I think as I walk over. He is holding out the phone. "She wants to throw herself off the balcony. Talk to her!" *What?* Muffling the microphone with the palm of his hand, he explains that his girlfriend, *"former" supposedly*, is so upset about his marriage that she wants to kill herself.

"She's not listening to me. Please talk her out of it!" I am as surprised at the absurdity of the situation as I am at my own response: "If she must, let her jump. I've my own life to save." I turn around, and crawl back into bed.

Next day, I hear Mozart's Requiem vibrate through the house. As beautiful as this haunting piece of music is, *how odd,* I think to myself. If not the melancholy conveyed in its notes, its title alone seems inappropriate under the circumstances. *Oh, I get it.* He is angry at me for yesterday. *Classy choice of retaliation, Mick.*

Might he also be acting up lately because I got sick? I used to be the strong one in our relationship, pulling him up cliffs in spite of being smaller built, letting him hold onto me when we went swimming in summertime. Even though Murat grew up as a boy in a male-dominant culture, he made allowances for me being an active girl since I was a "half-breed". My unusual situation within the culture we were raised in canceled itself out like a double negative somehow.

However now, I recognize that witnessing the frailty of my body may terrify him. *Distancing himself could be simpler than coping with intense emotions.* While the hair-raising melody resonates in the air, I ponder; *is my best friend pushing me away to avoid facing his fears? Going as far as counting me out altogether?*

6 ⚑

Shot

I have to return to hospital for a fourth time in four months. This time I am told to check in at the Tom Baker Cancer Centre. "I'm sending your father," my mother tells me on the phone. "I couldn't get away from work so soon again, but he was able to take off a fortnight." *There is no hiding anymore how sick I am and, in all truth, I appreciate my parents' support.*

My father flies over from Istanbul in time to accompany me through the ten days of preparation. "Ziyaretin için sağol, Baba," I greet him, thankful that he sacrificed his vacation time.

I had often thought about how best I could hasten travel arrangements for the lengthy oversees trip if anything happened to my parents, but this version had never crossed my mind.

I welcome Baba's presence, though I find his typically reserved mannerism amplified. *It's his limited knowledge of English*, I assume.

It doesn't occur to me how strongly his behavior may be affected by his fright of losing his daughter as he sees me hairless and with hollow cheeks matched by droopy eyes that mirror my weary spirit.

To make himself useful, he takes over the chore of grocery shopping, which is a great help at home while Ross keeps himself busy at the office. Mick decides for the first time to join Lennie on one of her out-of-town assignments. *My cousin's timing smells of avoidance of his authoritarian uncle.* Whatever his motivation may be, it is good to have peace and quiet at home.

My father's outings take a long time, but in the end he finds every single item on my shopping list. I can see him walking through each aisle in the store, meticulously searching the shelves, while a mixture of independence and embarrassment keeps him from asking for assistance. He also drives me to the hospital daily, waiting for hours while I undergo the tests and procedures necessary for my upcoming stem cell transplant.

Iron

Placement of a central venous catheter is the final step in the preparations. At the end of this minor surgery, I am left with a tube hanging out of my chest, the other end of it having been placed inside my heart. I am told that the veins in my extremities would not have been strong enough to withstand the toxicity I am about to receive. *The solution is to dump it straight into my heart.* It occurs to me that at times medical rationale requires focusing one's attention solely within the immediate margins of a problem.

On our way to the cancer clinic I ask my father to stop at a nearby park. The evergreen trees remind me of the reality reaching beyond the artificial hospital life. A squirrel running up a branch amuses Baba. He follows it with his eyes as it proceeds to feed on a seed. "Nazım" he names it affectionately. He is referring to his favorite poet Nazım Hikmet Ran. "Life is not to be taken lightly," I recall a verse he taught me years ago. "Live with utmost severity. Like a squirrel for example, anticipating nothing, preoccupied with nothing but living." I never knew what it meant – *until now*. With a refreshed alertness, I return to the car.

As we enter through the winding doors of TBCC, I am overtaken by an urge to vomit. *What's that smell in the air that speaks of disinfection and death?* My father looks at me worriedly and hands me his handkerchief while I fight back the gag reflex. When I breathe in the freshly ironed cotton scent, I have to chuckle. The realization that he managed to get his ironing done while visiting me is peculiarly humorous, especially in contrast to the otherwise bleak circumstances.

While growing up, the topic of ironing was laden with family drama. *Baba wanted everything ironed, Moeder ironed nothing – for sure not his handkerchiefs!* Neither of them missed an opportunity to repeat their opposing stances.

As a child, only just tall enough to reach the ironing board, I used to attempt taking on this chore, in the hope to create peace between my parents. *I don't know that I ever succeeded, but this moment of time travel has remedied my impulse to throw up.*

Admit

Admission turns out to be an elaborate process that involves reporting at various desks that are long corridors apart from each other. *Why does it have to be such an effort? It's not as if we're signing up for an exercise program here. Well, maybe that young blond with the sporty hairstyle over there could,* I pout to myself. Oddly enough, I continue seeing her again and again at the desks where I am registering. She has someone with her who could be her mother. *I don't know why anyone would drag along another person to such a tedious chore unless they absolutely had to,* I righteously think to myself.

Halfway down the list of stops to make, I feel too faint to walk or stand upright anymore and reluctantly ask for a wheelchair. By the time my father wheels me into the cancer ward, I am actually looking forward to the bed. When the head nurse welcomes us cheerfully, I understand that I have to endure an introductory talk about the ward before I can rest.

Hearing Baba respond to her with his broken English makes me proud. I am aware how difficult it is for him to do something he is not competent in, such as scrambling for words in a foreign language to make small-talk. Stimulated by this pleasant emotion, and also out of a customary courtesy for elders, I try to go along with the two of them. Having noticed my state, however, the nurse suggests, "Let's continue with the tour after you've had a chance to lie down."

My father drops me off at my new hospital room. This double room seems to have an occupant already, so I settle on the bed that is unused. An hour later, a little refreshed, I join the tour through the ward. There is a sense of generosity, both in space and in the quality of care. Most walls are decorated with inspiring paintings and each of the spacious rooms has its own television. I also notice an abundance of nurses compared to what I have been used to during prior hospital stays.

While the head nurse enlists details of visiting hours and shows us the guest and telephone rooms, I am absorbed in thought; *why am I admitted to this fancy ward?* "The Intensive Care Unit is in the next wing over," she explains. *Makes sense,* I note, based on the dire state most patients are in – *they look like zombies.* I feel terrible for these ailing people who in my opinion deserve the special attention.

The nurse goes on, "You'll be transferred to a private room soon." *Without requesting one? It must be a lucky mistake*, I conclude, *that I get to stay here.* Even though part of me registers how ill I am, my mind overrides this awareness by holding onto the image of a healthy self-sufficient version of me, for which it has ample data stored in memory. Denial serves as a powerful survival tool at this moment.

The next day, a nurse announces: "Collection time." My father volunteers to wheel me alongside her to an office with a machine that takes up half the room. "I'll hook you up to the cell separator. This machine will become part of your blood circulation for the next few hours." "I see; these cells are heavier than the rest and will be separated by the centrifuge." "That's it," she replies. "Did you read up on it?" "No," Baba grins while pointing at me, "engineer," utilizing his limited language skills effectively.

Noticing my interest, the aphaeresis nurse continues. "Blood stem cells are extracted from the patient – owing their name to the fact that they're the source cells capable of developing into any kind of blood cell; similar to the various branches of a tree originating from its own stem. The extracted cells are stored in a refrigerator while the patient receives a combination of high dose chemotherapy and/or radiation aimed at reaching even the smallest malignant growth. Left without further intervention, these drugs are strong enough not only to exterminate the cancer cells, but also the patient. Once sufficient time is allowed for the drugs to attack the cancer, the patient is rescued by injecting the strategically harvested cells into his or her body."

"Thanks, that makes it all too clear," I reply and proceed to translate for my father. He sits patiently beside me while my blood rotates out of me, through the cell collector and back into me. "This is it," the nurse turns off the machine after eight lengthy hours. "It's not optimal, but it'll have to do," showing us less than half-a-cup of thick white fluid. "I guess your cell production has slowed down from previous treatments."

Love

Once back at the hospital room, I try to sleep, but am too disturbed by the images of the day. *I'm surrounded by doctors making godly verdicts, sweet nurses caring for me and sick people about to die!*

Late in the evening, I hear someone walk in. *It's the blond from this morning.* "Hi, I'm Cecilia," she waves at me as she walks over to the bed beside mine. "Call me Celia." *What's such a healthy person doing here?* I am intrigued, but a brief smile is all I am capable of offering tonight.

In the morning, the nurses start preparing me for the upcoming chemo- and radiation therapies. The novelty of most medical treatments has faded over the past months, dissolving into the mundane reality of hospital life. What catches my attention at this instance is not this or that procedure, but my father who has entered the room.

When I get a chance to glance over at him through my action-filled surroundings, I see that he stands quietly at the other end of the room, by the entrance – *or exit? Is his physical distance indicative of more than staying out of everyone's way?* In spite of having traveled across the ocean to be by my side, a deeply etched boundary remains between us. Even so, I notice relieved that on occasion controlled interactions melted away under the intensity of the present circumstances. This has allowed for unspoken yet delightful sentiment to surface. *I'm finally convinced Baba truly cares for me.*

In the afternoon, when the rush settles down temporarily, my father and I have an opportunity to sit together for a little while before he has to catch his return flight to Turkey; work is calling. He gives me a restrained fatherly hug whilst I am absorbed by the real possibility that we may never meet again. Besides the recent treatments, I am also apprehensive about the new one to come – *it's hard to stay optimistic.*

This may be my last chance in life to tell my father how much I care for him. I whisper in his ear: "Seni seviyorum," verbalizing my love for him for the first time ever. Sentimental, yet frozen by the unanticipated emotional outpour, he stares at the floor and abruptly leaves the room.

The sadness I am left with after his hurried departure is lightened by the relief of having expressed my truth. *What Baba has never been able to say in words, he has expressed through his actions by flying over to support me.*

Roomie

My introspection is interrupted by the friendly greeting I receive from my roommate who has returned from another lengthy outing. I admire her vibrant appearance, but it leaves me feeling self-conscious about my bald head and lack of energy. Fortunately, my sense of intimidation lessens once we start chatting. "Was that your dad?" she breaks the ice, and before I can answer, goes on, "My mom helped me get settled, but she had to go back to High River. That's where we live. The commute sucks, but what can you do. Dave said he'll come as soon as he can. He's my boyfriend. Look at that, I can't shut up when I'm anxious. Anyway, do you have a boyfriend?"

We quickly warm up to each other. Finding out that we are both in our mid-twenties brings us closer, too. Our excitement is dampened however by the sudden awareness of what brings us together: We are both transplant patients. Celia explains, "I'll be getting the marrow of a donor. Leukemia is a blood disease, you see." "I'm set to use my own, presuming my blood is fine," I counter.

We compare notes in order to get a better picture of the treatments we are headed for. "Too much to digest and no time to cope," she criticizes the information sessions with doctors. From the bits and pieces we have gathered, both our treatments are usually kept as a last resort for patients with advanced disease.

I am reminded of one of the new oncologists' explanation at the information session: "While bone marrow transplant is a common procedure, stem cell transplant is a new option – and the only one possible in your case. Considering how varied your parents' markers are, waiting to find a donor for you would be pointless. An autologous transplant, where you are your own donor, is the only way to go."

With professional excitement, he added, "You're one of the first handful of recipients ever to receive this procedure in Alberta; it's quite new worldwide really." My face must have given away the scare of being a Guinea pig, since he continued, "This procedure has far fewer risks because it eradicates graft-vs.-host disease." From a scientific point of view, I find all this information interesting, though as a patient I feel queasy to say the least.

Odd

In spite of having tried to keep our discussion impersonal, both Celia and I are drained from talking about aggressive procedures that are about to overwhelm our bodies. On a cheerier note, she tells me, "I've been in remission for several months now. Chemo worked once more." This explains her beautiful short hair and her good looks. She goes onto telling me about the survival rates her doctors are predicting.

"This is my second bout with leukemia," she explains, "first I was diagnosed at nineteen." Following a dangerously close call, she had regained her health and, as if to forget it all, had gone back to her old life full speed, she conveys. "Once five years passed, my doctor quit follow ups. I figured I was cured." She sighs, "Before the end of that year, I kinda felt sick. I didn't think anything of it at first. But when I started coughing up blood I decided to visit my GP. After some tests, she told me the cancer was back. I never thought that I'd be scared of anything more than death, but I found out the hard way. Recurrence sucks!"

With a sunken heart I listen. "Years aren't enough to wipe out the memory of ugly treatments," she goes on. "This time things got under control after one set of chemo. But my doctor says if a cancer comes back, the risk of another hit is big. She warned me that this may happen much sooner than the first five years of remission I had. People like me supposedly don't make it beyond a year."

She reiterates, "It's such a tough choice. Right now I'm free of cancer. I feel well and wanna go on living. But ignoring my doc's warning is like playing Russian roulette. Then there's the bone marrow transplant. Risky business. It'll make me sick and who knows how long it'll take me to get over it. The thought of the grafted marrow affecting my organs scares me."

"I'm happy though," Celia cheers up. "They found me an exact match, an anonymous donor. Can you believe it? Some guy who doesn't know me happens to be on the donation list and is willing to get cut open to give me a chunk of his bone marrow. What a gem. Once all these troubles are done with, a healthy future awaits me. That's what my doc tells me. No more hospitals! They give me a survival rate of about sixty percent. That's great, right?"

"Sure," I reply, not sounding as enthusiastic as I would have liked to. "Honestly, I don't know what to make of these numbers," I add. "First they gave me a few days to live – no more. Then, my odds were raised to fifty-fifty. It came with an expiry date of a year though." "How's that?" Celia inquires.

"Beats me what the oncologist meant by that. Anyhow, then I heard them say I'd have a forty percent chance after that, but if there was a recurrence it would be the end. That'd be zero." She lets out a skittish laughter.

"The way you tell it, it sounds like calculating a payoff at a horse race." "I guess," I smile back, wondering, *had I told her how I used to feel like a racehorse on my high-strung educational track?* "Dave's brother works at the Edmonton Derby, and we go for a visit sometimes," she explains.

"They sold me on the transplant by raising my survival rate to nearly seventy percent," I go on. "Just as I thought that was a decent improvement, the other day I was told that my last CT-scan shows darkened areas which could be resistant cancer, and that'd drop the success rate to twenty percent. Enough already!"

"Yeah, forget all those numbers!" Celia jumps in. "Never liked statistics anyway," I reply. "You are one, I am one. I'm adding up 'fifty-fifty'; that's one hundred!" "Years?" she asks. "Sure, that too. We're going to make it, that's that." "I put my bet on you," she grins and raises her plastic cup. "There is a lot to live for!" "Cheers to that," I concur. "To our success."

Row

"Bye for now," Celia leaves the room when her partner arrives for a visit, whilst I remain in bed tired out from our conversation. I press the play button on my portable CD player – *another one of Moeder's thoughtful gifts to help lift my spirits. Comes in handy in this surprisingly noisy place.* I am enveloped by the sound of gentle classical music, the closest thing to a loving embrace I can find at the moment.

Didn't Ross say he'd come by after Baba left? I do my best to tune out any such thoughts along with the metallic announcements coming out of the loudspeaker beside my bed. Instead, I think back to my yoga teacher guiding us at the end of each class. "Lie down in Shava-asana," she instructed us, "in corpse pose."

By nighttime, the continuous roar at the cancer ward drops to a slightly less hectic version of the daily routine. Celia returns to the room after having been out since our chat. "I wanna run away. It's like Death Row here! Oopsie, were you asleep?" "No worries, I'm awake," I answer. "Only the dead could sleep around here." "I've been pacing along the corridors back and forth like an inmate, trapped and only sure of one thing; let me be anywhere else," she frightfully shares. "But you look so calm."

"Oh no," I reply. "If chemo hadn't knocked me down, I'd be screaming." Having found a listening ear, I go on telling my innermost worry. "Tomorrow morning is my big day. I keep visualizing that the dark spots on my last scan are just poop or something, but fear creeps in. What if they're tumors laughing at the treatments, ready to eat me up all over again?"

"The day of reckoning! And it's my turn in the afternoon," Celia responds. "When my boyfriend proposed this summer everything was so easy. We began looking for an apartment with a second bedroom. I started picking baby names already. And then this." "We're planning to get pregnant, too," I join her excitement. "I've been looking at replacing my two-door clunker for a four-door to fit the kids in."

"I feel better now," Celia replies. "We might as well get some shut-eye." "Does it bother you if I leave the music on a little longer?" I ask. "Hadn't noticed," she responds startled, "it's so loud in my head." She points her ear in my direction. "I like it. Will you turn it up so I can listen, too?" I increase the volume and we both stop talking in an attempt to rest.

Coffin

First thing in the morning, I awake to a nurse asking me to swallow some pills. *Good, I must have slept an hour or two.* "What're they?" I ask. "Something like a sleeping pill." "But I just woke up," I respond. "Besides, such things make me drowsy." "Believe me, you'll want these," she intensifies her tone to a plea. "You'll be spending the next hour in a box, so 'drowsy' is good."

Trusting her was the right move, I acknowledge when I overhear the technicians in the radiation department refer to the container they place me in as "the coffin". They position me sideways and, as though this narrow rectangular structure were not tight enough, they stuff cloth bags filled with a crunchy substance around me.

"Oh-oh," one of the technicians rearranges a bag he has placed too snug around my nose. "We want you still be able to breathe. It's just pasta inside by the way – to evenly absorb the irradiation across your whole body." I would normally reply, or nod at least, but there is no room for either. "Don't move." *As if I could.* "All in all, it'll take forty-five minutes and we'll turn you at halftime." *OK then. Where's Ross with his relentless offers of drinks when I need one?*

I feel sick, or rather, I would feel sick if I could sense anything in my body numbed by drugs that I suspect by now were not merely sleeping pills. I am in bed and don't know how I got back. *I've had enough of such freaky blackouts. One minute I'm somewhere and the next one I wake up somewhere else.* My internal pout is cut short by a nurse who has appeared by my bedside.

"May I ask why you're putting on another pair? You're already wearing gloves – and thick ones at that," I hear myself comment, not fully comprehending in this dozy state that indeed it is me talking. "It's protocol," she replies. "This chemo is so strong that a single drop of it would immediately tear a hole through my skin." *And what about mine?* I do not inquire aloud, realizing the irrelevance.

Sometime later, Celia is wheeled back into our shared room from her individual set of treatments. My heart goes out to her. *On top of all this, a surgical marrow transplant awaits her.* We are both too drugged to talk and take turns sleeping and staring into the blank for the rest of the day.

Burn

"This room is so big," Ross looks around in the private room I am newly transferred to. "I wish you could stay with me," I reply aching for affection. Seeing my husband for brief intervals has left me feeling undesirable. *Who'd want a bald 'n' bony creature like me anyway?*

Several colleagues visited me during the initial treatments, but since then no one dropped by. *My parents are overseas, my sister hasn't been able to fly over to visit, and Lennie and Murat are more and more estranged.* Then, Celia and I were separated because both our immune systems are attacked by the treatments we received. *Without the rescue of our respective transplants, we would wither and die in no time.*

"Let's put that big TV to good use," Ross suggests. "How about we pick up a movie?" *Am guessing that was a rhetoric question.* "Right," he looks at me as if registering the state I am in only now. "Let me zip over to the store and get one." While awaiting his return, I examine this sizable room. It is beige and feels dreary with two sterile beds and one lonely chair by the window.

A nurse comes by to check on me. "There were no single rooms left, so you got this one to yourself." When he returns, she alerts him, "Please leave your jacket outside and come in with clean shoes. Wash your hands thoroughly each time before entering this room. If you've the slightest sign of a cold, we ask that you postpone your visit. Your wife requires near-sterile conditions from here on."

"Understood," he sends the nurse off, places the movie in its slot and with the remote control in hand, stretches out on the spare bed. Shortly into watching this comedy, I cannot hold back, "what a dismal storyline." "It's just slapstick," he replies, obviously hurt. I regain perspective; *enjoying his company is all that matters.*

"Ha ha," I laugh out loud at a mediocre scene to make up for my sharp critique. "Ow," my grin comes to a halt. I have been medicated so much that I had not realized how badly my skin is burnt from radiation, especially in the tender areas around my lips, nose and eyes. Subdued by pain, yet determined to enjoy this break from the hospital routine, I refocus on the screen.

7

Stem

"You'll be fine," were Ross's last words when he left for home at the end of his visit. And today, being Monday, he is at work instead of holding my hand on this momentous occasion. "We'll transfuse your stem cells now," Dr. Weis announces.

I remember him from the panel of oncologists who had each explained what they were assigned to do to me, none of which I could really grasp at the time. Afterward, I signed countless forms giving my permission to proceed with the transplant.

Two things struck me on that chaotic day; how nice this doctor was and how illogical it seemed to have to consent to receiving drugs known to cause cancer to cure my cancer. "It'll take ten to fourteen days for these cells to graft to your bone marrow and start producing new blood cells," Dr. Weis educates me with a compassionate voice.

"Until engraftment is complete, that is your white and red blood count and platelets are up again, you'll be susceptible to infections, fatigue and bleeding. We'll remedy this as best we can with blood transfusions, antibiotics and other medications. We'll also monitor pain medication to make you as comfortable as possible." He then proceeds to inject my previously harvested stem cells back into my blood stream. Sudden coolness hits my veins.

"Straight from the fridge?" I begin shaking ferociously. I make out Dr. Weis comment, "She's gone into shock." I sense his strong grip on me while he orders his assisting nurse to hold me down on the other side of the bed. My last sensation is numbing warmth entering my body.

Morphine becomes a steady companion from then on, a button push away. Though, unlike hyped up descriptions of this drug, I find it does no more than mask the underlying pain. I come to know that the degree of relief depends on the level of affliction to be suppressed.

Lone

How can I be so lonely amidst a crowd? I catch myself thinking while watching hospital staff come and go. Besides the team of oncologists and the friendly nurses, there are lab technicians, a physio- and a psycho-therapist, a dietician, a pharmacist, and other people I don't fully register, all frequenting my room.

"No problem." The cleaner's smiling eyes break the monotony of the customary activity. He is wiping the floor clean. My vomit is no more than watery bile by now, but I feel sorry for having missed the garbage bin. A day later I manage to master the art of the projectile aim, having had ample opportunity to practice with each pill I am given to swallow. From here on, all medication, along with nutrition, is strictly administered via the central line in my chest.

The nurses begin a countdown to Christmas to bring cheer to the patients. This prompts me to do some counting of my own. *Blood transfusions are easy; one donor per bag. But platelets count for four.* It takes on average three to five donors to prepare a bag for each such transfusion, I am told. At the thought of thirty generous strangers' blood flowing through my arteries I quit keeping track.

Could I get Celia something nice for Christmas? I wonder, aware that going shopping or asking Ross for the favor is out of the question. My eyes scan the few items in the room. My ocean poster on the wall lifts my spirits – *ripped at its edges from traveling from one hospital room to another.* Get-well cards are lined up on the window sill. The few flower arrangements sent to me are apparently decorating tables in the common room because they pose a health risk. *In what sort of perverted reality can pretty flowers be deemed dangerous?*

My CD player is the only other personal item – and two disks. *That's it; I'll give Celia one of them. She enjoyed listening to them with me. Since it's going to be a used one, might as well gift her the one I like best.* No, a voice in me resists, *that would leave me with death!*

However nonsensical this inner dialogue may be, I acknowledge that after repeatedly listening to these two compilation disks, one calms my spirits while the other tends to stir up darker emotions. *It's volume I and II of a set called Meditation Classics, how different can they be,* my mind rules over my heart and a nurse agrees to deliver my second-favorite disk to Celia.

A few days later, the same nurse hands me a shopping bag, "Celia's mom asked me to bring it over." I peek in right away. *It's a beautiful warm shawl, so thoughtful.* A handwritten note is attached: "Thanks so much for your gift and we wish you a Merry Christmas." "How's she?" I ask the nurse, disappointed at not being able to chat with my friend. "As well as can be," she answers diplomatically. "Neither of us had a clue what we signed up for," I add, frustrated at how the short hallway between the two of us has turned into an insurmountable distance.

Tongue

"Ouuuch!" I pull off the last piece of the thick dead layer of skin on my tongue. "Chemotherapy is meant to kill cancer cells, but it also destroys other fast-growing cells such as hair follicles and the gastrointestinal tract." Someone had forewarned me about this. *But reality differs from knowledge – this pain got me weeping.*
Dr. Weis shows up. *Didn't I see him during his usual rounds?* "The nurse called me back. What happened?" "E' hur'..." I try telling him how much it hurts while the tip of my tongue is bleeding. "Why did you do it?" *Because half of it was hanging off already,* I want to say, or, *I'm bored out of my mind and on drugs, what do you expect?* occurs to me as another possibility.

Before my morphine-filled brain can collect itself, however, I hear him say, "Never mind." He turns to the nurse, "We need to avoid risk of infection and control her pain level." She administers a booster shot of antibiotics into my central line and presses buttons on the morphine delivery machine. *Guess she max'ed it ou...* I fade away.

I awake to a group of volunteers singing Christmas Carols at my door. *Losing track of time has lost its scare effect,* I note. *Or have the drugs numbed my senses altogether?* Relieved, I assess that my tongue has healed in this period. I ask to be weaned off the morphine – *I want my mind back. I want my body back, too,* I determine, and begin exercising my muscles in bed in order to soon be able to get up and move around again.

The first time I am able to leave my room, I walk over to Celia's with the help of a nurse; with one arm she supports me, and with the other she rolls along my IV stand. "She has pneumonia," we are informed by another nurse over persistent coughs in the background. "Let's visit once the added antibiotics kick in," my nurse encourages me protectively. I wave at my friend through the barrier of these two ladies. It warms my heart to see her smile back.

Next day I feel stronger, and stubborn enough to walk by myself. "Would you please put this shawl on my shoulders?" I ask the nurse – *haven't gotten that agile yet.* "It dresses up your gown nicely," the nurse remarks, "and it'll go well with the matching blue mask," she winks. "Better be safe."

She's so different, I notice once at Celia's room. In a matter of a few weeks, her appearance has changed from a sturdy athlete to a delicate porcelain figurine. When I thank her for the lovely gift, she whispers in a depleted voice, "Looks good on you." With a strained turn of her head, she points at the CD I had sent over, "And thank you, too." I lightly squeeze her toes sticking out from under the blankets, "Until next time," and return to my room.

Akin

"Dear God, please help Cecilia," I hear myself pray. "She's a good person, ease her pain." I cannot believe the words coming out of my mouth. *What am I talking about? I'm a hard-core scientist.* I am disturbed by the topic of religion surfacing suddenly, which was a taboo subject in my family while growing up. Differing cultural values put so much pressure on my parents' relationship that the matter of belief would have broken it altogether.

Avoidance was the unspoken agreement my Muslim father and Christian mother had come to. The resulting void grew further in my life when an elementary school teacher decided to be considerate about my parents' individual heritages. While her gesture contributed to less tension at home, having to step out of the classroom during religious studies had the contrary effect on my already tentative relationship with my new classmates.

One morning, shortly before this arrangement, I had walked to school as usual. A teacher, whom I had met only briefly, took me to another classroom. Unbeknownst to my parents, and my young self, I had been moved up a grade. This abrupt dislocation halfway through my first ever school term was disorienting. In addition to this change, being regularly separated from my new class felt less like a privilege and more like a punishment. While having to sit by myself in the empty hallway for the duration of a class, I had my first inkling of the power of religion. The pain of exclusion taught me undeniably the potency of such a common ground for people to unite and strengthen their relationships – *and inevitably create a barrier to outsiders.*

At public events such as commemorating the beginning and completion of a school week – *all of us pupils lined up like little soldiers in the school yard, dressed in matching uniforms, singing the national anthem* – a deep compassion grew in me for the communal spirit. At six years of age, I had begun feeling as akin to my community as an alien, but at least this time I was included.

For years to come, mixed emotions stirred in me whenever I heard the Turkish national anthem. When it was regularly broadcasted on our living room television, I would get weepy and stand up from whatever comfortable position I had been in and walk over to our hallway or my room. I would assume the position of attention and remain still until the last note of the melody played through the walls, standing tall in honor of the camaraderie I so yearned for – *all alone.*

Cheat

In contrast to the anthem, the muezzins' ezan, calling to prayer five times a day from Istanbul's innumerable minarets, had no such gripping effect on my young being; possibly because it was in Arabic which I was not familiar with. Perhaps it was also due to a lingering sense of exclusion from early childhood, emphasized by the men in my extended family going to the mosque in response to the ezan while the women stayed home.

Following a transition from public to private schooling, I found myself in a more heterogeneous environment, interacting with students of Islamic as well as Christian and Judaic heritages, along with some outspoken atheists. In contrast to my fluency in languages, I remained voiceless in matters of faith. It was as if my friends had access to a magic wand of sorts to feel empowered by, each calling it differently, but each believing in the same kind of power to guide them and help them succeed in their wishes through prayer. And the ones who were nonbelievers found strength in believing in the nonexistence of any powers beyond. Even though joining one or the other side appeared to be the safer choice, once more I could not commit to any particular group.

The emptiness left by a lack of alliance was filled with a passion for science. Books on mathematics, biology, chemistry and physics became my so-to-speak faithful friends and, over time, I became a scientist. The logical approach became my trusted instrument not only for conducting research, but for life in general.

It was most satisfying to formulate a solution to the age-old dilemma this way: If there was no spiritual existence, it was fine with me since by default I aimed to live virtuously. If, however, an omnipotent entity existed, then I was open to witnessing proof of such an all-mighty presence. This essential matter neatly taken care of, I focused my efforts on the tangible aspects of life – *that is, until my simplistic mentality and my supposed integrity were demolished by real life.*

And now, here in the hospital, I hear a prayer slip through my lips. *It's not a change of heart or an illumination. It's pure desperation.* Feeling like a cheater, unaware of any connection with an entity beyond my five senses, I nevertheless go on to asking favors of ambiguous "powers that be" to assist my ill friend.

Pass

"Merry Christmas," a cheery nurse greets me on Christmas Day. "Good news, your spouse called. The bad news is that your diarrhea hasn't stopped. We can't give you a day pass." "But you promised, just a few hours, please." "Let's wait to see what the doctor says," she leaves.

A young oncologist comes in. "I'm replacing Dr. Weis today." "He'd said I might be discharged by now." "It was a date we aimed for. It's even possible that a patient could leave within a week of a transplant, but that's rare. Besides, you started out compromised. Considering all, you're recovering well, but a whole day is too much without monitoring you. Let's give you a half-day pass. That's four hours. You can leave during the afternoon rest period. Make sure you return by 7 p.m. for the nurses to check on you."

"I bet it feels good to get unhooked," the nurse remarks while tucking the loose end of my central line under my shirt. When Ross arrives at 3 p.m. I am well-equipped to leave, wearing warm winter clothes along with a mask and adult diapers. "No thanks, I'll walk." I leave the wheelchair behind and lean onto my husband's shoulder. "I left the car running. It's in the drop-off zone," he assures me. "Oh good."

Relieved to have arrived, I slide into the passenger seat. *Am ready for bed.* "Let's get a movie," he suggests. "Sweetie, that's too much effort..." "But I didn't know what to get," he cuts in. Noticing his defensiveness, I admit to myself; *I'll try to be nicer from now on when critiquing his choice of movies.* Then I shift into holiday-cheer mode and decide to go along. *I'll ask for help at the store instead of looking through the shelves.*

"Something sweet and funny?" the clerk recaps. *Am not in the mood for my usual meaty topics tonight.* He throws a look at how tensely I am leaning onto the countertop to stand upright. While I self-consciously adjust my mask, he hurriedly searches through the pile of recent returns. "Not sure about funny, not brand new either, but this one is still popular. My girlfriend said she liked it and she's into romantic stuff." "Sounds good." I pay and return to the car where my husband has been waiting for me while I ran this errand – *some things never change.*

Once home, Ross assists me getting up the stairs to our bedroom. Passing by the living room, items lying around indicate that the other two occupants of our home are in town. Instead of inquiring about them, I decide to join my husband in disregarding any evidence of their existence.

After getting the TV set ready, he lies down with me on our bed. "I miss this," I smile. "Come under the covers." "Me, too," he replies, "but I can't stay. Harry asked me to meet him." As the previews roll on in the background, he continues, "He sounded down. You know, he has no one here. His family is back in

Aberdeen. And it's Christmas. I'd take you along, but you better rest. I'll be home in good time." He ends his obviously rehearsed speech and leaves before I can respond.

Disillusioned, my eyes concentrate on the screen. *Looks like a good one,* I sink into the story-line. *This young woman and the older guy remind me of us,* I console myself. Just as I get into their building romance, it becomes evident that the character I had identified with is about to die of cancer. Unable to press the stop button, I watch in horror as my biggest fear unfolds. I come to experience a new term I learned from Celia a little while ago: "bawling my eyes out".

By the time Ross returns, the movie has long since finished. His booze-breath, our delayed return to hospital and the nurse's rush to reconnect me to the various medications only marginally register, *unlike the sharp sting of rejection.*

Ring

A few days later, I attempt doing some of the stretching exercises the physiotherapist suggested. "At this rate, you may be home for New Year's Eve," Dr. Weis announces on his rounds; this is the first time he sees me out of bed in the morning. I also begin walking the halls daily, each time stopping at Celia's room. She is in bed once more. "I don't want any more pain meds," she protests, "I want out!" "I know," the nurse replies while proceeding with an injection in addition to the IV morphine. Once my friend dozes off, the nurse remarks, "It was a great match on paper, but unfortunately the graft and host are not agreeing."

Celia is in better form next time I walk by. She calls me in and picks up a ring from the side table, placing it on her finger with full attention as though it were the very first time. "Isn't it gorgeous?" she points her hand out at me with a dreamy voice. "Yes, lovely." "Dave got it for me. He's saving up for a real engagement ring, but wanted me to have this 'til then." Instead of the piece of fake jewellery, my attention is drawn to her skin around the ring. *It's scaling and pink – inflamed?* "The doc said not to keep it on much," she pulls it off hastily, returning to the harshness of reality. Dreams for a healthy future trickle away in her tears. Before starting to cry myself, I quickly leave.

Ice

Indeed, I am released on December 31st – *I'm free at last*. I say my good-byes to the caring nurses. "I don't know how you find the strength day in and day out to do what you do, but am most thankful that you do!"

I pass by Celia's room before leaving the hospital. She is holding a bottle of lotion and is slowly rubbing her hands. *Something about her is different.* With each passing day, the light in her eyes is a touch dimmer. "Is that for your skin?" "Yes," she replies with a quiet voice, palpably in pain. "May I put some on your feet? They may be hard for you to reach." "That'd be nice." I go on to dig through the layers of blankets to locate one of her feet. I am caught by surprise when I finally reach it – *icy!*

While carefully massaging Celia's cold feet, I notice her brittle skin. Her body feels hollow. *Partly vacated already?*

Sorrow overcomes me. *Alea jacta est,* a Latin term I must have picked up somewhere pops up; the die has been cast.

Goosebumps run down my arms. *Has my friend reached the point of no return?* Vague memories of slipping out of my body pass before my mind's eye. *Is there an inevitable fate or do we have a say?* My gloomy thoughts dissipate when I notice her feet warm up. Enthused, I rub them a little while longer before having to go. "I'll drop in when I come for my weekly checkups. And remember – we have a big celebration waiting for us this summer." "Yeah," she smiles back at me with her beautiful blue eyes.

New

What a surprise; Ross is extra-attentive when he picks me up with a bunch of shiny New Year's balloons. *Wanting to make up for his faux pas at Christmas?* Lennie and Mick are preparing supper when we enter the house. Lennie greets me in the kitchen. She holds up a spoonful of potato puree, "Thought it might be easy on your tummy." Mick is setting the table. "Welcome home, Sis." *His pronunciation has improved even more since we last talked,* I observe pleased.

I nibble on bits and pieces of the caringly prepared meal, wanting to be part of the dinner party. Friendly conversations remind me of the bliss I felt half a year ago on the tour-boat. *Maybe we can glue it all back together?* "Everybody smile!" Mick commands while he runs back to his seat after pressing the self-timer button, framing a jolly image of the four of us inside his camera.

Lennie tells me over dessert, "Back in Glasgow a whole school of kids have been praying for you, Ada. My niece is an elementary school teacher and she took it upon herself to get her principal to permit prayer circles in your name for the past month." "That's so thoughtful, please give her my thanks," I reply in appreciation of the gesture in spite of still being in limbo over this topic.

"Would you like me to make you a cup of tea?" Mick turns to me, his voice dripping with sweetness. *Is it the thyroid medication that makes me irritable?* I was forewarned about hyperthyroidism when my current dosage was increased to counteract the post-treatment fatigue. *Or is it about time I spoke up?* "Are you serious? A cup of tea? How dare you put on such an act? Where were you when I needed it brought to my bedside? When I needed a wash thrown in so I could lie on clean sheets?" My voice rises beyond my control with each statement. "When I needed you to hang up the phone so my doctor could..." "Don't talk to my husband like that!" It is not my cousin but Lennie who intervenes in his defense. *A reflex to avoid any reference to Mick's lover in Europe?*

Yes, it's not nice. Yes, I should've kept my mouth shut. But I couldn't help it... I am about to settle down, more from strain than self-control. "And you can't talk to my wife like that!" Ross bursts out at this moment. Months-long built up tension turns a spark into a raging fire. The two siblings go on to cursing each other with hostility I have never seen them in before. *Even our well-tempered Lennie?*

"Get out of my house!" Ross shouts. "You get out!" She retaliates, both of them feeling righteous, since, while we are the rightful tenants, she is officially our landlady.

No words are left to say. In an eerie quiet, each of us couples retreat to our respective bedrooms. I am devastated. *Have I destroyed everything?* Feeling responsible for breaking the peace, I sleep fitfully. By the time I get up, Lennie and Mick have left. "How could they've packed up so fast?" I ask my husband who is at home on New Year's Day. "Len starts her new position in Squamish on the third. They left a day early for Vancouver." Oh. "She wants to sell this place sometime soon." *Everyone but me was already clued in.*

Empty

"Which one shall I pick?" Ross consults me in the used furniture store. He concludes before I can walk over, "I'll get the solid oak desk for myself, and the two smaller ones for my crew." *Your crew?* I am not only too slow to walk but apparently also to grasp. "I'll have people working for me soon," he explains on this second day of opening up his own office. *Why, I would ask if I were able to think straight, couldn't this have waited another month?* I feel like an aimlessly floating leaf, dragged along by the current.

"For us," he emphasizes. *How nice, the raging river counts me in.* I appreciate my husband's ability to hold a vision, though all I can envision is resting in bed on this fourth day of having been discharged. "That one looks comfy," he points over to the swivel chair I am sitting in, "I'll take it, too." At the cashier it becomes evident that it is not only me but my bank account that is included in this deal.

With Lennie and Mick's departure, the house has an empty-nest feel. *It's just the two of us now.* We don't last another day before our habitual pattern resurfaces with an added twist. My cousin, giving us enough reason to be upset with him, had become a scapegoat for us to vent all our pent up frustrations.

And now, not only do our pre-existing issues continue, but our relationship is further burdened by new worries. The shock, the anger, the despair... all such overpowering emotions brought on by my sickness are silently ignored – *or so we think.*

Arguments erupt out of the blue, to the extent that neither of us can hardly complete a sentence without the other one cutting in. Matters escalate when Ross transfers the pressure of the new business onto my shoulders, "It's your fault if it fails!" *Isn't that oxymoronic? Another funky term you taught me. Who helped you out in the first place?* I might challenge him if I had the strength.

In this defenselessness, it briefly occurs to me that he may be wanting to voice a deeper fear of abandonment: *It's your fault if you die and leave me.* However, lost in my own woes, I counter his intimidation with a more subtle, nevertheless equally wounding, method. I point out his mistakes at every opportunity.

If I can't be happy, I might as well be right. "You broke it, don't deny it. I saw how your arm brushed against my Oma's vase." Irritated, he calls me "Madame Fastidious". What I really want to say is: *It's neither your fault nor mine that I got sick, but please be by my side.*

Pep

"The dark spots on your CT-scan are still there," Dr. Olsen reports in her customary dissociated tone on my first outpatient checkup. Her consistency is strangely comforting. *Who'd have thought I'd miss this one?* It has been barely a week since I left the cancer center, yet the familiar surroundings, along with memories of the good care I received in the past month, override the reason for being here – *for a fleeting moment.*

"They could be scar tissue," Dr. Olsen reiterates, "or resistant tumors." I stare at her in disbelief. "The suspicious areas noted on your scan before the transplant haven't changed." I feel cheated; *after all this, you have nothing else to say?* It finally occurs to me why an oncologist of all people would be prone to disengage from bonding with her patient in view of the lopsided risk vs. reward ratio. *Am thankful anyone ever chooses this profession.*

"How can we find out?" I ask as if discussing a third-party matter. "There is nothing we can do if it is cancer. You've received the maximum dose of any treatment possible. Time will tell. If in six months you're fine, they're probably leftover scars." She shows the courtesy of not spelling out the other option.

Wait and see... I've heard that before! "There must be something that can be done, right?" Shortly into my pleas, Dr. Olsen cuts me off. "You're wasting my time. Quit asking so many questions. Don't you see, I have other patients too!" She leaves the examination room. Next, her nurse escorts me out. "We're here to extend patients' lives and sometimes it's no more than months or weeks." *That's the worst pep-talk ever.*

I sit down in the waiting room, not knowing what to do. *I'm beside myself.* The uncertainty is so immense that an essential part of me dislodges. I had experienced such numbness before as a result of drugs during my recent hospital stays, but evidently my own biochemistry is as powerful. I truly feel detached, literally out of my mind – and body. Too much has happened in too short a time.

My life, my future, if I have any, is at the mercy of a few unidentified spots in my gut. *Will I die or will I live? It's that simple.* I like English idioms Ross has taught me. He laughs when I recite them incorrectly, but I appreciate their direct graphic impact, like so many visual sayings in Turkish. *Of course, "I'm beside myself". Who'd want to remain in a body that's nothing but a ticking time bomb?*

I walk over to the washroom to splash water on my face and afterward find myself at Dr. Weis's door. His nurse advises me to leave. "He rarely comes to this office. He's usually in the clinic or on rounds." *Yup, I know that.* "And he doesn't take outpatient appointments. You best be going home." "It's OK," I say, while my inside yells: *Nothing is OK!*

My determination soon pacifies this nurse into letting me stay. "What can I do for you?" Dr. Weis startles me while I am half asleep on a chair. "May I see you in your office please?" I ask, surprised by my own calmness. "I'm about to go home," he replies, "but alright." Upon briefly hearing me out, he shakes his head, "I would like to help you out, but I don't follow up with patients once they're discharged from my program." My spirit crashes on the spot. "Don't give up," he adds encouragingly. "Let me think about it."

Wait

The next morning, I wake up with sore glands and achy bones. *I felt run down ever since furniture shopping and then yesterday's stress did me in.* Following a weekend huddled under the comforter, I receive great news from the outpatient clinic, "You're booked with Dr. Weis for this week's checkup."

"Watch this cough," he warns me at the appointment. *Yes, anything you say,* I look up to him. "We can't give you any more chemo or radiation currently. Soon you'd glow in the dark." *Anything he says, I smile at.* "We could wait as Dr. Olsen suggests." *No, please no.* "Or, we can try to diagnose the remaining spots via needle biopsy. If that's inconclusive there is surgery." *Yes, please.* "But first, we need to get you stronger. General anesthetics would be too much on your body right now, and then there is the risk of surgical incision."

"Let's book you in for surgery in three months and I'll monitor you at regular checkups," Dr. Weis goes on. "Rest up in the meantime." "Absolutely," I nod enthused. *Ninety days of a nerve-wracking wait, but at least I'm in caring hands.* I postpone my usual visit to Celia on my way out of the cancer center. *With this cough it's best I stay away from her. And I also have a promise to keep to this angel of a doctor.*

In spite of the extra caution, the adrenalin rush that enabled me to get through the day fades by night. For the following weeks, microorganisms feast on my depleted body like hungry larvae on a cadaver.

8

Grab

I blink. Each time my eyes open I close them again, pausing at length with shut lids. *Let it be a bad dream, please let it all be a nightmare!* Blink. *Alright, if this all really had to happen, then let that be it.* Blink. *Stop the pain, now!* Nothing changes; my eyes hurt the same. The codeine pill that Ross helped me to swallow with a sip of soup has lost its effect. The ache of being alive has returned full blast.

It's not that I don't want to, I do want to live... I think. Imprisoned by depletion, I reconsider; *but how am I supposed to in this wasted junk of a body? How the heck did I make it this far? Then again, was this life really worth saving? Or would it have been more merciful to let me go?*

I am utmost discouraged that my sense of accomplishment for surviving the transplant was so short-lived as my body collapsed right after arriving home and has been that way ever since.

"Tiniest microbes in the air can be a health hazard," a nurse had warned me. "Your immunity is very low." *I now know what she meant. Weeks later, I am still bedridden.*

I'm even robbed of the choice to sign off! Suicide has been a hush word in my world, and euthanasia at most a conversation piece during intellectual debates; *a sort of friendly fencing, for nothing but the sport of it, clear of any consequence.* However, the pristine white symbolism of fencing is stained with life's sticky reality now – *no escape.*

Should a person have permission to end her own life? How about the life of a child? Is it murder or mercy when a father kills his baby daughter who is tortured by an incurable disease, squealing with each labored breath? In what world is it the norm to euthanize an ailing beloved pet, yet unacceptable to do the same for a loved one? I am appalled at myself, and at society at large, for so easily dismissing essential matters merely because they don't affect us directly... *until they do.*

No escape, indeed. In the vulnerability of my frail physical state I have nowhere to run, no job to be preoccupied with, no errands to take care of, *not even run to the washroom.* Everything is in slow motion – *except for my thoughts.* My conscience has caught up with me and grabs my attention without warning. And when it does, I have no other option but to show up authentically.

Pick

I call the outpatient clinic at Tom Baker Cancer Centre. "I'm still sick. I have to cancel this week's checkup." "Come when you can.

You've missed three appointments already. We've to keep monitoring you. And come in asap if you get a high fever." "Yes, thanks," I remember from the time before.

"And if you have no one to drive you and are too weak to come by yourself, we can arrange for a volunteer to pick you up." "Thank you very much," I reply, having no intention whatsoever to make use of such a service. *There is no way I'd take up someone else's spot who really requires such assistance.*

"Could you please transfer my call to the cancer ward, room 509?" I ask to reach my friend. *I wonder how she's doing. It's been a month since we were in touch.* Her mother answers. "Celia is resting. I'll tell her you called."

A week later, after finishing one more set of antibiotics, I decide to go to my checkup in spite of my body's need to continue resting in bed. Upon standing, my knees give way. Following several unsuccessful attempts to get upright, I remain on the floor and prop my back against the edge of the bedframe instead.

What now? A flash of sensibility leads me to reach for the phone on the night table and call the outpatient clinic. In spite of a brief temptation to yet again cancel my appointment, I say, "Could you please arrange a volunteer pick-up?" While waiting for the driver, I am distraught. *What if some other patient ends up in a bad emergency right at this moment and can't get the necessary help because of me?*

Guilt-ridden, my heart begins racing as if witnessing this fictitious person die in front of me. In this state of panic, a heat wave rushes through me. The doorbell rings. "That was quick," I wipe the sweat off my forehead. "I was in the neighborhood when they paged me. Are you alright?" the volunteer driver asks. "Feeling a bit weak. That's all." When we arrive at the hospital he places me in a wheelchair. Having no resistance left to appear independent, I slide into it.

"Do you have a caregiver?" Dr. Weis inquires at the appointment while examining me. I look at him blankly, not grasping his question. *Why would I need anyone to take care of me? I'm out of the hospital.* "Do you have any family?" "Oh, yes. My parents are in Europe, but they came over for visits. And my husband, well, he's busy." "Tell him to come with you next time." *What part of busy didn't he understand?* I protest. He persists while concluding my checkup, "I'd like to meet him."

"One more stop please," I ask the volunteer to wheel me to Celia's room. She is sleeping. I place a mask on my face for her sake and remain at the door of her room. The nurse updates me, "It's not looking good." *Come on Celia,* I cheer on silently. *We have to make it to summer.* As if she heard me, she opens her eyes and slowly turns her head my way.

There is something angelic about her, I notice, observing her quietly lie in bed. She has retreated further. Her presence is shifting away with each visit. *Are life and death polarities that have their own gravitational fields?* my scientific mind wanders. *When pulled close enough by either one, resistance becomes as futile as it would be for a piece of scrap metal near a potent magnet.*

While watching my friend being drawn away from life, I am left wondering why and how it was possible for this natural pull to reverse in my case. *What else is out there... or in here?* These glimpses into unspoken realms appear impossible. All I know is that I do not want to admit that my friend is dying. *She looks in less pain*, I console myself, *but also not fully conscious of the transition she's approaching – can anyone be?*

"You look pale. Is this a close friend?" the nurse ends my train of thought. I cannot utter a single word, *if I did, I'd break down*. "Would you like to speak to someone? How about we get you to the psycho-social services around the corner? They've nice lounge chairs in their offices. You can rest, and if you're up for it, you can chat, too. I'll check if someone is available."

"Don't worry about me," the volunteer says. *What's his name? Am I still having chemo-brain? Why can't I remember names anymore?* "I can run an errand while you rest and pick you up to take you home in an hour."

Bus

"Hi, I'm Ian," the social worker smiles at me. "Would you like to tell me what brings you here?" *Not really*, I want to reply. "It's too much..." I cover my mouth immediately to stop an avalanche of other such uninvited words. A tear drips. I wipe my nose with the back of my hand trying to look tough, "I don't cry." *For sure not in public.* "It's alright," he comforts me. "What's too much?" "I feel so guilty," I respond without thinking.

"Guilty?" *This wasn't what he expected,* I assess, hearing the surprise in his voice. I find myself filling the void left by his well-placed pause. "I let down my husband, my parents, my supervisor... Celia." Under the therapist's watchful eyes, I add, "That's my friend on the ward. We shared a room. I feel responsible; she's getting sicker while I'm getting better."

"How are you doing now?" "Well, better than before. I'm not out of the woods yet, but somehow I got to walk away from my death-bed." Saying this out loud for the first time makes me grasp the reality of it for a moment.

"I feel terrible that I let people down by getting sick – not doing my job, not being by my husband's side, not making my parents proud. And now, on top of all that, I take away someone else's spot." "How's that?" "By getting help such as this and all the medical care. I didn't die when I was supposed to."

The image of a city bus full of people at morning rush hour in Istanbul pops up in my mind. It often was so full that when more people got on at the next stop, some less fortunate ones near the exit doors were regularly squeezed out while the driver pressed the automatic doors to forcefully close up on them. At the risk of running late for school, I jumped out to help an elderly lady or a young kid back on whenever I could. *But now I can't! Can't help anyone and can't even hold on myself.*

"What are you thinking?" I hear the therapist. "I'm too sick to be of any use." "That's a big statement," he neutrally qualifies. Determined not to share images of the bus, which are too intimate, I hold back. Only to blast out: "Aylin was so unlucky, I couldn't help her either." *Where did that come from?*

Too late to retreat, I go on. "My sister, she was about to start university at the height of terrorist activities. In the late seventies, academic grounds in Istanbul turned into shooting ranges. We were confused whether these fights were instigated by devoted freedom fighters or mean-spirited militants. Baba reluctantly gave in to Moeder's pleadings – my parents," I explain, surprised at blurting out so much, but unable to stop. "I recall her trembling voice. 'Let's get her out while we can.' My uncle was to keep an eye on Aylin in Maastricht."

"That sounds intense," Ian listens on. "By the time it was my turn, peace was restored in the country; at least to the extent that a military coup ended daily killings on the streets, leaving us in the dark as to what may have continued behind closed doors." I pause only because I have no strength left to speak another word. "Why am I telling you this?" I whisper out of breath. "You've gone through a lot lately. Emotional tones of similar nature cluster in our minds, regardless of time and content," he explains.

"Just like what you're telling me of your childhood, a cancer diagnosis and following treatments can be equally disturbing and unsettling," he brings us back to the topic of the day. He adds, "Have you ever heard of PTSD? It stands for 'post-traumatic stress disorder'. It's a mouthful, but simply it means that when exposed to traumatic stressors there can be a major emotional impact. Seeing your friend unwell may be triggering some of these unprocessed feelings." I listen more to the calming tone of his voice than his words.

"I'd like to suggest we meet weekly from here on, and continue our conversation. I'd also suggest you join a support group when you can. You've had a long day. Shall we finish up with relaxation?" I nod pacified. "Clear your mind and visualize a pleasant scene while listening." Overtired, I welcome softly spoken words accompanied by gentle music.

Reminiscent of the times that my mother used to read Grimm folk tales to me in childhood, my body relaxes into a little snooze, until I am awoken to be taken back home.

Egg

"My husband, Ross," I introduce him. "Good that you came," Dr. Weis replies while they shake hands. "I'd like to talk to you about your wife's needs. This month is critical for her to regain some of her weight and stamina. It's essential she gets all the support possible for her upcoming surgery. I'd recommend that you see a counsellor together to find the best way to move forward. Here is her card."

"With all due respect, doctor," Ross cuts in. "We've been doing this for a while now. What I'd like to talk to you about," he mimics Dr. Weis, "is this brochure. I picked it up while waiting." I peek over and catch the title: "Cancer and Fertility – Your Options". "What are our options?" he inquires. "I'm afraid it's too late for that," Dr. Weis responds. Silence sinks into the room. "We were planning our first baby..." I begin to explain. "I'm very sorry," he grasps the matter. "The treatments you received before the transplant would've resulted in infertility, so it wasn't brought up again at the pre-transplant panel. I didn't know this wasn't mentioned." *Before my hubby makes a scene, I best jump in,* "And the birth control pill I'm on?"

"That was only to hinder bleeding while your platelets were down. We could change it over to HRT, that's short for 'hormone replacement therapy'." "Isn't that an old woman's remedy?" "It replaces something you'd normally produce. Actually, the standard dose is a fraction of natural levels at your age." "I'd rather not." "We can start low and adjust by increasing incrementally." *Nope.* "Alright," Dr. Weis gives in when I do not respond. "Let's take you off the pill and see what happens."

"Arrogant bastard!" Ross vents while driving home. *I like him,* I am about to say, but choose to abstain. Regardless of this being how I really feel about my doctor, I fear that it could lead to yet another discord. The air is thick with unexpressed emotions as we avoid discussing the underlying matter of mourning the loss of the family we were about to build. *Even if he were able to,* I admit, *I'm in no shape right now to process this bit of news.*

During the following days, I come to understand that my hormones have been destroyed at the source – *my eggs are cooked.* Imminent sensations prevent me from dwelling on this depressing thought. One moment I lie under a blanket with a heating pad to fend off chills, the next moment a hot flash bursts out of nowhere. I kick away the covers as fast as I can and pull off layers of clothing. *I'd tear off my skin if I could.* Shortly afterward, dripping wet, shivers start taking over again and I layer up, only to repeat this cycle a few minutes later.

Bar

I obligingly begin HRT a week later. Dr. Weis adds during the same appointment, "Your recent CT-scan didn't tell us anything new. It's not exact enough to determine whether there is any change in size. And the needle biopsy we tried was inconclusive and left you in too much pain to consider doing it again. We've no other choice but wait out the surgery. You keep getting stronger, alright?"

I stop by at Celia's room on my way out of the clinic, *as always – well, as often as can be between fatigue spells and cold bugs.* She is awake this time and I am relieved to see some life in her eyes. We chat a little before she gets back to resting.

Once home, I am alone as usual. I cozy up on the living room sofa. *Great pick, Moeder. Pretty and comfy.* I cuddle up in a blanket and unwrap a candy bar for lunch. *It has a few peanut chunks in it. That's a legume, right? And that's veggies in French, so it's alright then,* I justify in my worn out mind. Didn't someone say chocolate is a vegetable? Kidding aside, I don't feel like eating anything even if there were healthy food at home. *My gut is a mess.*

First it was the heavy treatments that damaged my GI tract, then I lost my sense of taste and smell, and now it is the trying wait for the surgery. *Do I or don't I have cancer? That is the question...* I imagine a man's voice with a British accent – *wait, shouldn't that be a Danish one? Hamlet was after all...*

Alright silly mind, straighten up, I tell it. My brain feels like an overstretched elastic band, wobbly and unable to pull it together. I pick up a book to read, *that'll help me focus,* only to be reminded that my vision is still blurred from chemo-therapy. Before I know it, I begin dozing off again, and place the book back on the side table, right beside the intact candy bar.

Spill

Upon coming home from the office, Ross sees me resting on the sofa. "Why are you so moody?" he asks. "Sulking at me like that," he talks to himself while turning away. *He couldn't be confusing my tiredness with moodiness? Or is he transferring onto me his own state of mind?* He returns to the living room sipping a glass of dark ale, the head foaming over. *He was too hasty,* I observe, being well-trained by "the master himself" on the art of pouring a pint. "Do you want a divorce? Is that what you want?" I hear him yell at me suddenly. I freeze. My eyes remain fixated on the brown stains growing with each of his agitated spills on my antique kilim.

My mind departs... *What a nice trip that was,* I reflect on my last visit to Turkey as a single woman. I had traveled inward into Anatolia and bought this hand-woven wool carpet in Cappadocia, the Turkish name for this utopian landscape being Göreme. The literal translation "cannot see" was descriptive of early Christians in the area taking refuge from Roman attacks by building elaborate underground cities; depths of structures reaching ten or more stories into the earth. *Wishing I, too, could hide right now – any old cave will do.*

"Who cares what you want, I'm calling a lawyer!" Ross stomps out of the living room and walks toward the front door. But then, he settles to drink up and, after picking up a six-pack from the fridge, heads upstairs. *His rants are increasing in frequency,* I find myself noting with the objectivity of a research scientist, while the emotional blast continues burning my gut like a hot cannon ball.

It is me who stays on the sofa this time, unlike the too many other nights when he comes home late, "wasted" in his terms, and falls asleep in the living room. *Initially I used to feel lonely for him, yet, in time I'm appreciating sleeping free of baritone snores and a stale breath.*

Balance

"What do you do for balance these days?" the counsellor at the cancer clinic asks. On this second visit, I feel more myself. *This is alright*, I think to myself, *combining this with my regular checkups. I'd have expected a woman, but this guy is fine.* My first involuntary visit recently helped me overcome my stigma about seeking emotional support. *We go to school to learn math, and take courses to learn driving. Why not go to a therapist to learn about coping with life?* I come to terms with it.

I admit to myself that I also plainly yearn for someone to talk with. *I've Ross, but he either sleeps or watches TV to "chill after a long day's work," as he calls it. Contact with Lennie and Mick is cut for good. Weekly calls with my parents are mainly to touch base. For the rest of my friends, I now know what "fair-weather friendship" means. And then there is the lady I met the other day in the park, but I'm not going to pour my heart out to just anyone.*

"Balance? As in blah-lance?" I reply. "Sorry, couldn't help it." "No worries," Ian responds softly. "We need all the comic relief we can get around here. "What makes you think it's 'blah'?" he inquires. "Isn't balance boring," I answer, "middle of the road, predictable. Why would I want that?" "What if balance isn't just a wash-out in between good and bad experiences and is something else altogether?" "What do you mean?"

Ian takes a piece of paper and draws a horizontal line on it, placing the letters "g" and "b" at either end. "If that's the scale reaching from good to bad, where would you place balance?" He hands me his pen. I scribble a capital "B" on the center of the line. "I see," he replies while drawing a tiny triangle below the line, right underneath where I placed the "B". "Does that look like a seesaw?" he adds. "Yes, it's not called a balancing act for nothing, right?" I respond. "Right," he says, with a tone that I am learning does not necessarily mean he agrees with me, but rather avoids confrontation.

Ian then proceeds to draw a new line, starting at the end of the horizontal line that has "g" marked beside it, slanted upward to the center tip of the sheet of paper, and repeats the same for another line tilted upward from "b", uniting the latter two lines at the top, completing a large triangle. "How about this?" He writes "BALANCE" across the page. "Oh, I see. I was thinking linearly, but you went from a line to creating a surface area by drawing a big triangle."

"That sounds like a mathematician talking," Ian responds politely. "What could this be symbolizing in our lives?" "You introduced a new dimension," I smile with the gratification of having solved a puzzle without understanding its meaning. "Yes, balance is a whole new dimension, an integrated state. When we're able to manage the good and the bad and whatever else in life, we reach a sustained level of wellbeing. Our bodies know it by maintaining equilibrium – it's called homeostasis. And our minds know it by feeling at peace."

"Hah, never thought of it that way," I am surprised. "Is that what my yoga teacher used to refer to? 'Hatha Yoga –balanced union of mind and body,' she kept telling us." "Perhaps," Ian smiles.

9 ♫

Run

"Are you sick or are you well?" Ross shouts through the handset. *I don't know what to say.* He is upset at me, and I am upset at myself, for not functioning right. "Yesterday you were fine when you dragged me to the park, but today you say you can't come down to the office to give me a hand for half a day? I ask you to sit at the desk. How is that tougher than walking?" He hangs up before I can reply, not that I have an answer.

Each time I think I am making progress, depletion claws me back down. Distraught, I wish it away. Unable to hold a perspective on what my body has endured, I focus on how well it ought to function, *like it's always done.* I am further disheartened that these frequent episodes of fatigue may seem fake to my husband. *No wonder he's pulling away.* However, the truth is, the physical drain aside, awaiting the exploratory surgery by itself is too much to cope with.

What if the cancer is not gone? Might as well be walking up to the guillotine. I cannot imagine going through that arduous experience again. Rather, the opposite is more the case: I cannot get the harrowing images out of my mind for a minute. It terrifies me that the instant I relax in the slightest, cancer could overtake my body immediately. *It did the first time around!* I still feel punished for trusting the doctors at the onset of symptoms. Both of them continue their daily routines as if nothing happened. *It was me who was wronged, but their lives are intact. They're the ones who made a mistake. Why am I the one who suffers for it?*

"Stop being such a worrywart," Ross dismisses my concerns anytime I want to talk to him. "Shit happens," he encourages me in his way. "Get on with it!" *Or is he as delirious as me, hopelessly wishing to put this behind us? Move on, don't look back. Run – run far away from this craziness. Oh how I wish, if only I could...* I begin feeling more and more alienated from my familiar circle of family and friends. It is as if they take it personally that I cannot function like I normally would. *Is my hubby punishing me for getting sick?*

And then there is Myrna. *She doesn't know me really, but treats me nicely for no apparent reason.* I fondly recall the day this retired teacher entered my life. I was resting on a park bench two weeks ago, when our eyes met at the very moment that an unseasonably early robin sang on a low-hanging branch between us. "Spring is in the air," she smiled from behind the snow-covered tree and walked around it to sit beside me. "Soon enough we'll see flowers." *Hah,* I snickered inside, too aware of how much longer the landscape would remain white. But her cheeriness felt good. "Have you ever considered uncertainty is to freedom what soil is to a flower? It isn't undesirable; it's actually necessary." "Right. Like the 'degree of freedom' in science," I added spontaneously. "And freedom is essential for life. Ergo, uncertainty gives life." I enjoyed her playfulness.

Since then, we meet for strolls whenever I am able and other times talk on the phone. *It's so unlike me, to open up to a stranger like that.* This subtle shift feels as if I entered another Lebensabschnitt, a new phase in life – *or may be another universe? Parallel universes,* I iterate, *what if they exist? Isn't it inevitable in infinite possibilities? Or, time travel,* I extrapolate. *If space can stretch in inexplicable ways, why not time, too?* It is not logic talking, but a mind that searches for an out. *Go back, reverse to before the cancer; rewind more, to before the wedding; and take a side step, enter another universe, another reality... free of deceptions and misdiagnoses; go one step further: without any disease. No lies, no illness... Could I bear such joy?*

Cry

"What do you mean, you cashed it in? It was a cash wire to begin with!" I am livid. *My parents said they sent it to me. How did he access it?* As I ask myself, I recognize the redundancy of my question. *Just like with my credit card, he undoubtedly used my bank card.* "I bought a few computers and an IT system and was scanning through our accounts to find a way to pay for them. Et voilà, I found the money – the exact amount to cover the bill." *Did he move funds from my personal account to our* joint one and wrote the cheque from there? "What will you do with so many computers?" I ask, wavering from the crucial matter at hand. *Why do I do that; undermine my own position?* "I have a new graduate working for me now," Ross proudly announces. *I wish I could cheer him on.* "Soon I'll hire more guys. And then there's the intranet system to connect everyone within the office," he adds excitedly.

I stare at him in disbelief. "We needed it, Babe," he replies, his tone now somber. "We? My parents made the wire-transfer to send me to the States. You know how badly misdiagnosed I was. They made a huge gesture so that I can get a second opinion on my treatments. I told you all about it. How Moeder got this idea from one of her students' parents to get me a checkup at Mayo Clinic. Do you know how long it takes to save up that many thousands of dollars in Turkish Lira?"

"I am your safety cushion. Don't be a mama's girl!" *Oh no, that's a foul hit below the belt.* Having been in more than enough fights with my husband, I get a sense on how things are going to unravel from here on. It takes all my discipline to bring the roaring steam engine inside me to a halt. *I'd still go for it if it weren't for this damn exhaustion,* I confess. I am painfully aware that I don't have any spare energy to spend on such games, *yes games they are indeed.*

I feel torn inside. It hurts as if it were an open wound. *Like a Turkish saying; içim kan ağlıyor, I'm crying blood inside.* I do not know what to mourn for first: *admitting to my parents that their help is gone, seeing through my husband's tactics, or having lost my independence when my used-up savings would've sustained me just fine?*

At this moment however, what bothers me most is that I am not able to hold up my end in a fight. Even though this is a shallow response to what has taken place, it is the only issue I can face without completely falling apart. Ross uses the pause that resulted from the lack of my counter-attack to leave. I stay behind in our bedroom, pondering the dynamics of our arguments.

Play

Hearing the house door close with a bang, I suspect that he has headed to the pub. Frazzled, I call Myrna who is becoming a consoling friend. "Can I run something by you please?" I hesitantly inquire. "Of course," she replies softly. "If I am to judge by the tone of your voice, this may be another one of your 'reality checks', right?" "Yes," I nod into the phone.

"My dear, I will listen to you, but first, I want you to hear my words: Trust thy self." "Thanks, but lately I find myself distrusting my senses. Nothing is what it was. I want to believe whatever people tell me. When the doctors kept saying not to worry, I hung onto their promise that I was stressed but otherwise healthy. And now, I want to believe that all is well in my marriage, but..." I cannot hold back tears, "I don't know." "Tell me," she encourages me to go on. "Things between us haven't been smooth from the start, but we worked it out somehow. Now though, he feels so far away. Today for example I couldn't feel any warmth between us. Instead I saw cold-blooded calculation when I looked in his eyes. Am I becoming cunning?" "I doubt it," she reassures me. "Whenever I ask him to explain himself on a matter that bothers me, I end up defending myself on an irrelevant topic."

I continue sharing, "Now I see that he cleverly poked me in a sore spot and diverted the attention from what really matters to a topic he knows I react defensively to." "Oh dear." "Today, when I didn't bite on his bait, he walked out." "Sounds like it's not confusion but clarity you're gaining. It seems to me your eyes are opening up, and he didn't appreciate you seeing through his thinking. There is nothing wrong with you." *What a relief.*

"Take a moment to calm down. And know that everything that irritates us about others leads us to a better understanding of ourselves. Jung knew what he was talking about. You're familiar with him?" "Sure," I reply, not wanting to let on my Literaturlücke, an embarrassing gap in my knowledge. *That's the Swiss psychoanalyst who talks about dreams,* is all I know of him.

I hesitate, *shall I tell her about the missing funds?* But then decide that this is a private matter and leave it at that. "Thanks so much Myrna." "Call anytime. Bye." Although reassured to some degree by our conversation, I continue reflecting.

"You're like an open book," Ross had told me during one of our many chats in bed – *a well-loved past-time in our early days, cozied up under the comforter on Sunday mornings.* I yearned for someone to share intimate aspects of myself with and he seemed to enjoy listening to my stories; *they flowed easily when cuddled in his arms.*

Tales of my tomboy days were among his favorites. "Your seaside adventures and climbs in the concrete jungle are fun, but the best is how you returned your weekly allowance and earned your own money." He understood this was unheard of in the society I grew up in.

In Turkey, it was a matter of status that the daughter of a good family did not work – *none of the other girls, or boys, did, nor did they want to; even Aylin bobbed along carefree.* I had my mother to thank for talking my father into permitting me to tutor kids in school. That way, year after year, I saved up enough to purchase things to my own liking – *like the speed-bike Baba didn't approve of,* I grin with satisfaction. It was empowering to make such decisions. The many hours I spent tutoring allowed me in return a sense of self-reliance.

Today, when Ross had nowhere to run, he poked me in my tender spot, calling me "mamma's girl". He knows how I hate accepting help from my parents, or anyone else for that matter. *I should be self-sufficient at all times. I should be the one helping them.* Aside from these disturbing thoughts, an undeniable truth about his priorities becomes clear. *Betting that he'd get a charge out of me, he chose to play me instead of owning up to taking the funds.*

With the newly gained insight, looking back, I realize that this pattern has been the norm rather than the exception in our relationship. "Attack is the best means of defense," he used to tell me reminiscing on his boxing days. *I never doubted he was anything but a true sportsman.*

I am left wondering how Jungian analysis claims I am to understand myself better through this aggravation. *Does it reflect on how I, too, treat myself with disregard?*

Widow

The phone rings. My heart skips a beat; *is it my sweetie wanting to make up?* "Hi Ada," Myrna's voice comes through. "Oh, hi." "Were you expecting another call?" "No, no, it's OK." "Well, Dear, I wanted to ask you to visit me tomorrow afternoon. The weatherman predicts a warm day. A Chinook wind is on its way I heard him say. How about meeting at our usual bench at two o'clock?" this spry retiree invites me. "A little stroll followed by a cup of tea?" "That sounds nice. Thanks." "See how you are in the morning and let me know, alright?" "Sure, bye."

"I'm sorry we had to cut our outing short," I apologize. "I woke up thinking I was up for it." "Not to worry," she comforts me. "I'm glad you told me. You have to listen to your bod' and my wish for you is that you speak up for yourself more." *I've an inkling she isn't merely referring to coming in from the cold.*

Her home feels enchanted, filled with ornaments and paintings, each one emitting a spirit of its own. While my eyes soak up the graceful displays, she explains: "I couldn't leave them behind. They're laden with special memories. After Will died, Toronto wasn't the same anymore. Right after my retirement, I moved here. This house is a third in size, plenty big for me, but a little crowded for my decorations. They give me company. I grew up on a farm near Cochrane and have been missing the Foothills and the Rockies for quite some time." She stops recollecting.

"Enough about me. Let's get you cozied up. Wrap this throw around your legs and I'll get a pot of tea going. There, I hear the kettle boiling." She comes back with a tray of homemade cookies. "I don't mean to impose..." "Not at all. I have all day. You just tell me when you'd like to go home."

What does she want from me? I wonder. *Can't she tell I've nothing left to give?* Myrna's friendliness is unfamiliar compared to my interactions with other people; *I'm the one who tends to others' needs.* "Relax," she says as if she heard my inner chatter. "It's time that you look after yourself. Have a cookie with your tea." "Thanks."

I wake up smelling a whiff of cinnamon in the air. *My nose is working again!* I am pleased that this side-effect of chemotherapy has finally reversed. "Fresh from the oven," she brings a big bun over. "I must have fallen asleep, I don't usually..." "That's good. Get all the rest you can. I had prepared the dough this morning so it was perfect timing for baking the buns while you rested."

"It's absolutely delicious," I mutter, enjoying the warmth in my mouth with each bite. I hide the disappointment of my taste buds lagging behind my sense of smell in their recovery. "I'm sorry, I best be going. My husband may be home soon." "No apologies necessary around here," she reassures me. "You take good care now."

Flush

At the slim chance of my sweetie coming home early, I want to be there to greet him. I desperately wish that we can make up and put yesterday's tension behind us. *Oh, my tummy, I think I'll throw...* I run to the washroom before I can finish my thought. *Bummer, should've known better.* I watch the remains of the cinnamon bun flush away in the toilet bowl. In the euphoria of starting to smell again, I hoped to put everything behind me and forget that I was on IV nutrition only a short while ago. I make a mental note to stick with broths, continue taking daily digestive medication and not get carried away like that again. *Easier said than done.*

While gargling to get the bitter taste of bile out of my mouth, an involuntary glimpse in the mirror startles me. *Who's this person?* An aged face looks back at me with darkened wrinkly skin around the eyes and mouth, a leftover from radiation. Little bristles are growing on a few spots where hair used to be, accompanied by a few follicles of eyebrows and an odd eyelash here and there starting to come back.

Compared to this, the lump sticking out of my throat last summer wasn't that bad a sight. Ross must be sick and tired of seeing me like this. I do my best to pretty up by covering my head with a favorite scarf and putting on a nice cardigan, and wait up for him. Several hours of anticipation later, I have to accept that I have to go to sleep.

Two days later, Myrna calls midmorning. "Come over for lunch tomorrow." "Sorry, I can't." "Why is that, are you unwell?" she inquires. "My digestion is poor lately." "Am sorry to hear that," she responds. "How did you manage with the treats you had here last time?" "It was a bit rough," I reply, too self-conscious to tell her how bad it really was. "How about I make you a mild chicken broth from scratch? With a free-range chicken and organic vegetables?" She insists, "We need to strengthen that bod' of yours. I also have some remedies you can try to see if they help your digestion. I'll show you when you get here. Shall we say one o'clock?" "OK. Thanks." *Why is she so nice to me?*

Kid

Next day, I arrive at 1 p.m. sharp at Myrna's door, *the habit of punctuality learned from Opa.* My maternal grandfather used to begin eating at the very hour he had invited his guests – *whether they showed up or not.* "Smells good in here." "It's almost ready. Can you have fruit? I cut up some in case you're early." "On an empty stomach, I'm not sure. I usually have it for desert."

"Yes, that's how we used to eat it, too, until we discovered food combining. It's about eating foods in the order of digestibility." "Makes sense," I concur. "Fruits are easiest to digest, easier than any meat for example. Give it a try with one or two pieces today and see how it sits with you." Cautiously I nibble on a slice of apple.

To my pleasant surprise I get a sense of taste, but my mind does not register "apple". *Have my taste buds been rewired wrongly?* "I drizzled a few drops of lemon on the fruit to keep it fresh," she interjects as if reading my mind once more. "I don't read minds, just expressions," she smiles at my startled face. "Food is ready. Let's eat." "This tastes so good," I exclaim cherishing each sip. "It's the first time since chemo," I reveal more relaxed.

"Glad to hear that," she replies. I gave you a little cup for starters. Let's see how you do with it. Here is a thermos I filled for you to have more for supper if you find it agrees with your tummy. And this is that digestive tea I mentioned. Start with a quarter of a cup a day. If it works, great, but if not, let it be. There are lots of other things we can try to help you with."

"You're so nice," I reply. "I learned these things while helping Will with his cancer. Might as well use it to help you, too." "What happened?" I tentatively ask. "It was pancreatic cancer. We did everything we could, but it was his time." "And you?" "End-stage lymphoma." "Incredible." "I have a surgery next month to find out if the treatments worked." "It's not your time yet kid; I can feel it in my bones."

Soon after, visiting Myrna for lunch becomes a ritual I look forward to every few days. Each time, she sends me off with "leftovers", which I soon realize are well-planned meals for me to consume when home alone. *I don't know how she managed to crack through my self-dependence,* I ponder, half-aware that there is not much of any resistance left in me.

I adopt her habit of blessing the food before consuming it. At dinner, I notice Ross's eyes on me while holding my hands over my plate. "What's that for?" When I proceed to tell him about it, "Watch out," he warns me. "I bet Maria, Myra, whatever her name is, turns out to be a missionary wanting to hook you in."

It

Into the second week of our new lunchtime routine, I begin feeling awkward once more because of Myrna's generosity, and also wonder if it I should create some distance after Ross's comment. "I'm most thankful for your loving care, but may I at least reimburse you for the cost of the food?" "No." There is a hint of being offended in her voice. She pulls herself together quickly. "How about this: I cook for you, but you only, to build you up for your upcoming surgery – no sharing with your husband. He can eat anything, but you need special care. It's my get-well gift to you." Against all my effort, a tear trickles down my cheek. Noticing this, she hugs me. In the safety of her embrace, tears build up to a flood, quietly rolling off my face.

"It's alright," Myrna assures me. "You don't have to carry the world on your shoulders, none of us does. I can tell you're a responsible person who takes on far more than her share. But, for once, now that it's your turn to receive, you don't know what to do." *How did she figure me out?* Speechless, I listen. "It seems to me that you were a gifted child, right?" I nod shyly. "I taught such kids for many years and you'd have fit right in. "We all have our gifts of course," she adds. "No point in getting a big head over God's creation. Indeed, since my retirement I volunteer at a special needs school and find these children as precious as the bunch I taught before – if not more."

I reminisce on the price this supposed giftedness came with. Having been two years younger than my classmates for most of my schooling left a mark of insecurity. At eleven, my body fit in more with the flat-chested boys than the girls who began developing at thirteen. *I felt excluded from the female club.* Even when my body eventually developed, I lagged behind my classmates' teenage cliques, and found solace in my imagination and in science books instead. Only in my final high-school year,

I begun opening up. *Am I ever glad I did, for that was the seed for my friendship with Fulya and Berna.*

"There's something refreshing about you..." I hear Myrna, "humility." "Actually," I hesitantly open up, "when I was a kid, I wanted to please my parents and make others around me happy. At the start of each school year I worried that I was going to let everybody down when I didn't have it anymore. I wasn't sure that, after the summertime fun I had, I'd still be granted it."

"It?" "Yes, the gift. I knew that it wasn't me who solved the problems and understood textbooks. It felt more like something was entrusted to me." "And that's why you didn't attach your ego to it," she finishes my thought. "That ambivalence must have been hard on you in the past, but now it works in your favor. You clued in early on that nothing is for certain. All of our lives, our bodies, our abilities, are only temporary."

Sniff

Three days left to the surgery date, my nerves are at the verge of collapse. My countdown turns from daily to hourly. Ross is home for supper tonight. While we are both in the kitchen, he sneezes. "You don't have a cold, right?" "No, just a sniffle." "What do you mean?" Anxiety rises in me. "Don't worry. It's nothing serious. I'll sleep it off overnight." *But what about me?*

Ever since my intestines are healing, my husband has moved back in our bedroom. We are no more than roommates at this point, with no physical contact – not as much as a good-night kiss on the cheek. *Has he returned for me or our orthopedic mattress?* Tonight, I move out to the guest room, unwilling to risk getting sick so close to my surgery. By morning, however, I find out that it is too late. The droplets of sneeze that shot through the air the night before transferred ample viruses to initiate an infection.

Shortly after leaving a message for Dr. Weis, his office calls me back. "Come in this afternoon." Shivering regardless of all the layers I can wear at once, I drive myself to the clinic. "Let's get you on antibiotics right away," Dr. Weis says after looking in my throat. "Don't cold symptoms appear a few days after initial exposure?" I ask surprised at the speed of it. "Normally yes, but your immune system is in its infancy. That's also why it most certainly will turn into a bacterial infection. I'll let the surgeon know that we have to postpone by ten days." "But that's well into April." "You behave now, rest and get better, so it doesn't become May, alright?" Dr. Weis leaves. *Yikes, more of this tense wait?*

It's doctor's orders, I tell myself, *camp out in the guest room from now on.* Myrna continues her loving support by bringing food to my door. "You're too kind," I thank her. "You'd do the same," she sounds casual, as if her help were merely a cup of sugar I get to borrow from a friendly neighbor. She indeed knows me well, I would do the same. *Except, until I met her, I'd have limited myself to helping a friend, not an anonymous person like she does.* "We're all one big family," she adds synchronistically, completing our conversations as if listening to my thoughts.

Key

I feel more comfortable in Myrna's company every time we meet. She sounds genuinely interested in my personal story and I enjoy hearing more of hers; how she takes her volunteer work seriously for the duration of the school term and then takes the summer off to travel the globe, always starting and ending by stopping over in Seattle to visit her son. *Did she say his name was Stephen?* She was a stranger a little while ago, but now she feels close, indeed like a family member; *the wise auntie I never had.* "You're in a rough patch right now, and you deserve all the care in the world," she replies once more with her impeccable timing.

"Be, where ever you are," Myrna tells me while staying for a visit after bringing over a thick bowl of borscht. "It's no use to wish being anywhere else. A little fantasy once in a while is fine, but you know what I mean, right?" *I don't.* "See, if my tour-bus drops me off in London during a downpour, I can go through the rest of the day preoccupied wishing I were in Rome for a better chance of sunshine, but I'd miss out altogether on that day." *OK?*

"I'm saying that undoubtedly you're in pain, and wishing you were healthy. That's most understandable and I pray that you get well very soon. In the meantime, I'd like you to consider experiencing things more attentively." *I appreciated her wry humor to begin with, but now she's lost me.*

"Sit with your current state," she responds to my probing eyes. "Be here, be still. Being present for life is the greatest present you can give yourself for the rest of your life." *Sounds like a riddle, but I think I'm starting to get it.*

"More to the point," she continues somberly, "the key is to grow with our suffering, not to run from it or grow from it, but with it. The path to sanity is <u>through</u> – that simple."

I listen on, trying to absorb what she means. "Your recent circumstances aside, let's consider your upbringing for example," she makes an approach from another angle I gather. "You were a bright girl in a man's world and had a split life even at home. Your parents demanded you speak their individual languages. Add to that their own cultures and religions. Isn't Constantinople..."

"Istanbul," I interject in defense of more than five hundred years of history. "Yes, of course," she tolerates my interruption. "Isn't Istanbul built on two separate continents? How symbolic." She continues, "Anyway, the point I want to make is that you had to cope with diversity and with strong opposites early on. You were immersed in it, unable to escape, and eventually you learned to integrate this. What was a vulnerability became a skill; and now, you're stronger for it. You're not falling apart in the midst of adversity, you face it. You've looked death in the eye my dear. That's no small feat at any age."

"Similarly, maturity comes from owning our pain, and once we heal our wounds, we become better servants. Your time will come," she adds, "to help others." *Servant? I haven't signed up for anything like that!* I panic. Ross's words of caution alert me. *What if she has a hidden agenda?*

Next time Myrna suggests, "With your permission, I'd like to offer you Reiki. Maybe it could speed up your recovery from the cold." "What's that?" I ask skeptically, my trust in my new friend shaken by doubt. "A form of healing art. I simply channel universal love energy through my hands onto your body." She adds, "You remain totally clothed and there needn't be any physical contact if you prefer." "I'm alright with that," I reply, not out of conviction, but because my insides ache for human contact.

I reconsider Ross's earlier warning. *He doesn't know her at all. I don't know her well either, but I know how nice it is to have her companionship.* Indeed, unlike my usual relationships, I feel supported by my new friend's presence. *Short of dragging me to some faraway village on a religious mission, I don't mind if she has another agenda.*

All I know is that she has a good heart. And she can't be too fanatic if she practices some Eastern sounding healing. From then on, each of our lunch meetings ends with a session of this intangible therapy called Reiki followed by a short stroll in the park when possible.

10

Flow

Through allegedly closed eyes, I peek at Myrna waiving her hands over my body. *This can't be bad for me, right?* I wonder, unsure if I am subjecting myself to witchcraft. I enjoy the part when she proceeds to holding some of my body parts with her tender yet strong hands; my abdomen, a thigh, a foot... and especially when she cups my head. *For the sake of plain old touch, I endure the rest of this so-called therapy.*

A few times later, I ease more into the experience and notice recurring sensations. My otherwise shallow breath opens up and my constant worries have less of an edge. "I have this feeling of something falling off me," I tell her at one of the Reiki sessions, "some weight being washed away kind of, leaving me lighter."

"Nice."

Then, at yet another session, I have the notion of expanding as if I were a deflated balloon that is being pumped up. I open my eyes to ensure I don't float off.

"Is anything the matter?" she inquires. "My fingers and toes tingle. I feel, hmm, full... It's so lovely and warm." "Oh good," Myrna replies. "You've entered your body." She further responds to my questioning eyes, "Universal love invites your being to trust and inhabit your body wholly again, as it's meant to."

Over tea afterward, she explains: "All sickness originates in energy blockages. When things get plugged up, a part of us retreats." "Where to?" I ask. "That may be difficult to describe to a scientist," she laughs. "In my world, we're beings of energy with souls that reside in physical bodies. When a soul's free flow through our earthly existence is inhibited, illness shows up. Every time we clear the way and enhance harmony between body and spirit, healing takes place."

While I try to follow her line of thought, she continues, "Simply, health is living a genuine life. To thine own self be true. Start right here and now with yourself." In contrast to feeling cocooned in a loving way when held by her, listening to her ideas stretches me far beyond my comfort zone.

What's she implying? I am intimidated. *I'm an honest person. And does she mean I blocked something in my life and made myself sick?* My mind is overloaded. I excuse myself to leave early, attempting to hide my injured feelings.

"Live your life fully. Embrace it truly," she emphasizes. "The rest unfolds and flows. Rather straight forward, isn't it?" She adds, "It's been a powerful session," and concludes her comments while I put on my boots. "Don't think too much about what I said. Go home, rest and drink some warm lemon water to flush your system."

I decide to do exactly that. *I've to look after me for my surgery in two days.* On my way home, a verse I read at schooltime revisits me from memory. *"Wisdom is truly knowing; true wisdom is knowing one's self."* Yunus Emre's words I recall from an old literature text book come alive. *What are the chances of a Canadian churchgoer and a Turkish mystic saying the same thing?*

Cramp

"Promise. We'll do our best," I hear a familiar voice. Through reflections dancing in the oxygen mask placed over my mouth and nose, I make out the shape of someone approaching me – it's Dr. Knowlton, the nice gyne-oncologist. Her compassionate squeezing of my hand is the last thing I register.

"I'm Feng, Dr. Knowlton's assistant," a young man introduces himself. I look around while he continues talking and realize that I have been brought back from the operating table onto a hospital bed. *So cramped in here,* I note, trying to see through the cracks in the curtains surrounding me. *I bet there are three more patients in this room. Ooh, talk about "cramp" – my belly aches!*

"Preliminary biopsy results are negative," Feng catches my attention again. In the relief of the news he brings, I am taken by his oriental face, *angular features wrapped in such a smooth complexion.* "We examined everything as closely as possible. Dr. Knowlton decided to proceed with a hysterectomy since there was extensive scarring in the pelvis. We also pulled out your intestines and looked around for any other organ damage, but everything else looked alright, so we put them back in."

"In a few days we should have a complete report," he continues. "In the meantime, make sure to keep the pump going for several more days to avoid clotting," pointing to the medical device that looks like blown-up stockings squeezing my legs in regular intervals. *I've waited a few months, I can handle another few days.* I crawl out of bed. "Watch it," he warns me while giving me a hand. Hunched over, I walk toward the sun rays gleaming through the window. For a moment, there are no stitches or worries – *nothing but the joy of being alive.*

"Just sip the broth part," Myrna encourages me when she visits later that evening. "Yummy," I appreciate the nutritious chicken soup in spite of being groggy. She leaves shortly afterward to let me rest, leaving a card by my bedside. Inside she has written: "*Happy recovery to you, my dear Ada. You are a radiant being of light and love. Remember the power of this affirmation and let it help you heal.*" These words are as nice as... oh no... The food comes back out – having lost its goodness on its way up. *I hope the same doesn't happen to how I feel about her fine words,* I am concerned. *Lately, I find it difficult to relate to her.*

Free

On the third day, Feng shows up again at my hospital bed. "Great news," he grins. "It was all scar tissue, according to the biopsy report. Some of it was rock-hard, but Dr. Knowlton cleaned it out well." He adds on his way out, "She'll come by in the next day or two."

I'm free! The funny sensations in my gut aren't anything to worry about; it's simply my organs dancing around in there to find their new places after having been aired during surgery.

I would wait for Dr. Knowlton normally, to thank her in person. But I have a life to live – *starting now!* Ignoring the pulling pain radiating from the metal staples lined up on top of my pelvic bone – my scar nicknamed "the smile" by one of the nurses, *"the scream" through clenched teeth would've been more appropriate,* I correct in my mind – I get dressed, pack my small bag and make a b-line for the exit.

Wait! Must share the super news with Celia. While making my way over to the cancer ward with each painful step, I recognize that the additional two days of bed rest may have been sensible. *Nonsense,* my adrenalin-filled spirit shakes this thought off with the sort of vigor that a wild horse rejects reins.

Why is my friend's room so... desolate? Her personal decorations are gone. "Where's she?" I ask the first nurse I can catch. "You mean the girl with leukemia?" she looks at me apologetically. "She's gone." *Dead?* I cannot grasp the magnitude of the news. As if I were punched in the gut, I crumple onto the chair in my friend's room.

Everything around me is blank, generic... lifeless. I see this place through a shroud of disillusionment; *a machinery – the heat of one body barely gone, space is made for the next one to die.* I am flustered. *Scream or cry?* Neither. Instead, a horrendous guilt overcomes me. *Was I so preoccupied with my own stuff that I didn't care enough for her? I didn't even gift her my favorite CD.*

"You don't look so well," Ian observes. My feet have brought me to his office. "Lucky that my client cancelled, so that I could take you in," he adds. *Lucky?...* "What's up? What are you feeling?" *Feeling?...* Incapable of anything but staring straight ahead with dead eyes, I remain seated for what seems a long while. Then, I get up and leave. "I'll expect you at our regular appointment," I hear him say from behind me.

Tour

"A cancer cell starts out as a normal part of our body," Ian lectures me next time. "A mutation alters it from being like the rest of the healthy ones. Have you ever considered; in their ability to destroy, they teach us the hidden capacity in our bodies." *This guy is starting to sound as nutty as Myrna. My friend died, what does anything else matter?*

I let Ian continue merely because it saves me the trouble of having to talk. Unaware that he may be trying to access my frozen heart by a detour through my mind, I endure his words as I would elevator music.

"Strategic... resourceful... intelligence..." *What's he getting at?* My curiosity wins out over my ignorance and I start listening again. "Consider tapping into this power to navigate the rest of your cells, organs, toward regaining your full health?" I hear Ian's excited voice. "Can't hurt to try, can it?"

He's starting to sound like a used car salesman, I decide, to avoid getting involved in whatever he is explaining. "Here, I'd like you to try this." He hands me a recording, "It's subliminal messaging. Listen to it when you rest. Use stereo earphones. It's meant to release fear and strengthen the core of your unconscious mind." He adds, "You're a research scientist, doesn't this intrigue you?" *And you're a professional counsellor, doesn't this embarrass you?* I keep my comment to myself.

As I get ready to leave, while unable to thank him, I do get a sense that this is a kind gesture on his part to reach through to me in the numb place I have fallen into.

Rock

At home, on my way to bed I look at the recording with suspicion. *Isn't hypnosis dangerous? It turns people into puppets!* I am terrified of losing any more control over my life by experimenting with this. At the same time, Ian has managed to pique my interest. *I'll play it for a few minutes to check what it's about. I'll keep my eyes open to stay awake.* My index finger tensely placed right above the stop button, I proceed to play the hypnotic program.

Health-affirming messages are tactically sprinkled inside a pleasant story. They are read out loud in such a rhythm that the sound alters between my right and left earpiece, creating the sensation of being gently rocked like a baby. *This indeed is calming. Maybe Ian and Myrna's ideas aren't as crazy as they sound.* For the following seven nights, until my next counselling appointment, I commit to listening to this recording for half an hour each time before bed.

In the mornings, I notice awaking less tense. My worries are not as suffocating. Even the shock of having lost Celia begins to soften. I am still lamenting her death and continue being burdened by a sense of responsibility. But the suppressive intensity is infused with some space, permitting me to breathe a touch more freely and letting me believe that things will work out fine after all. I would call this hope if I were not terrified of this term. *Last time I hoped for the best, my life fell apart!*

Try

"That's a dirty word in my books," I rebel. This startles Ian who is attempting to cheer me up by quoting Alexander Pope, "Hope springs eternal." He inquires, "What's so bad about it?" "It's a dressed up version of denial," I defend my stance. "It's a drug. It blinds you to believe everything is alright, and then, bam! You hit the wall head on. And it's even taking the edge off missing my friend. Is that it, she dies and I forget?"

"Of course not," Ian consoles me. "The importance of an event doesn't lose its value just because you suffer a little less for it. In order to cope with traumatic experiences, we have to find healthy ways of toning down the emotional pain. If we don't, we keep turning our wheels in the suffering itself. Then it's not only the loved one's life that is gone, but also our life that is lost. Especially in the depleted state you're in, we need you to produce less stress hormones. Imagine the good you can spread once you're well; do a good deed in memory of your friend, help others who suffer…" *He has done it again,* I notice. *This guy has a way of sweeping away my resistance.*

"Remember me mentioning PTSD at our first meeting?" Ian continues. I nod. *Post-traumatic stress disorder. Creepy word, though it's starting to make sense.* "Yup. I thought that's what soldiers suffer from. But I see now that this sickness stuff is not unlike being in a war zone."

"Cognitive therapy is a useful tool. However, from the sessions we've had so far I can tell that you've developed the ability to observe and analyze events quite well." *Years of scientific training haven't gone all to waste.* "I'd like to propose something different to you," he goes on. "It's called Energy Psychology. In a way, it combines modern psychology with ancient eastern philosophy."

I liked yoga, and acupuncture is helping me with the pain. The thought of getting pierced again had scared me at first, but Dr. Choi turned out to be very gentle, placing needles on my body with artistic elegance. In view of these positive experiences, I am open to exploring further.

Ian explains, "One method in particular that I use is EFT which stands for 'Emotional Freedom Technique'. It could seem far-out at first, but I find it effective with PTSD. It's understandable why you're so distressed and I'd like to see if we can remove some of the intensity with this." *The hypnotic stuff was good. I'll give this a try, too.*

When he proceeds to demonstrate how this technique is done, I have to bite my lip not to burst into laughter; *tapping like a monkey on his chest, head and hand.* "Go ahead, laugh," Ian remarks. "It works anyway. See these points as switches along an electrical circuit. By tapping, you turn them on, and thus complete the flow within the circuit. When electricity runs through all the channels, the whole house lights up." *Guessing the house is me?*

"Repeat after me," Ian leads me. *In for a penny in for a pound,* I quote Ross in my mind and go along. While tapping, Ian says things like, "Even if I lose my identity, I'll get over this." He later explains, "You're not alone. Lots of people fester with deep-seated fears and identify with a quality they think they can't live without, even if it causes them suffering.

"Look at an overburdened mother, for example. Even if she has the choice, she may remain in the martyr mode because of an old trigger. At least once, a terrible event may've happened when she indulged in caring for herself, which led her to believe that bad things <u>always</u> happen when she puts herself first. And over time, the familiarity of this misconception could make it appear normal and safe. Through EFT she may be able to clear such a blockage, which would allow her to step out of dysfunctional patterns. Don't you think that's freeing?"

He ends each session by inviting me to state: "I completely love and accept myself." *Will I ever?*

Mission

"Kenya?" I put my cup down. "Yes, I'll be leaving next week," Myrna tells me during a teatime visit. *Ross got it right, she's a missionary!* "With what you've been going through, I haven't had a chance to tell you about it." *Or, has she been cautious, not wanting to scare me off?* "My travels in the summer usually involve missionary work. We're currently building a school in a remote village in Kenya. I wouldn't be going until my volunteer work here is over at the end of the school year, but our priest who oversees the project broke his ankle and requires help."

Shortly after her departure, I become lonesome. *Ian is good, but he's a therapist, not a friend. And my hubby is only drifting further away.* At first, I was pleasantly surprised when he agreed for us to see the marital counsellor Dr. Weis had recommended. *But the plan is aborted – or maybe "his plan" was to go only once?* I do not know anymore, our communication is broken.

At the second appointment, while in the waiting room awaiting Ross's arrival, the couple's counsellor approached me. "We're fifteen minutes into it. You're paid up for the hour. Would you like to come in?" *She turned out to be right assuming he wouldn't show.* This session was different than what I experienced with Ian, or the first time with her; she did most of the talking.

"There are conditions that can adversely affect both partners in a marriage, such as tendencies to alcoholism that can lead to mood swings, anger outbursts..." She spoke in general terms and went on to emphasize the impact of stressful relationships on one's health. On my way out she added a phrase that went something like this: "Don't forget, the denial of some state of affairs is the implicit acknowledgement of it. Don't take my word for it, take Freud's." *What was she implying with any sort of denial?* Unable to take on any more or do anything about it, I left.

The feeling of concern this counsellor emitted was so distinct that it lingers on. *What can I do to improve my wellbeing? Didn't I read somewhere that longevity rates go up when cancer survivors join a group?* Further encouraged by recalling Ian's suggestion from a while back, I attend a cancer support group meeting.

My initial reservation about sitting in a circle with strangers subsides after personal introductions – *everyone here knows the life-altering impact of cancer firsthand*. Soon I start looking forward to these gatherings and develop a kinship with two individuals in particular: Pam and Nicky.

See

"The C-word is avoided like the plague at home", Pam confides in group. Her husband and nearly-adult children have shut down emotionally in response to her struggle with breast cancer. As her feelings are blocked from flowing to her family, her heart pours itself into our support group. This setting offers us a safe place to share our struggles and to vent our worries. Also, her motherly care eases my hurts while my recent remission gives her hope.

Pam's health is not improving after her treatments. Each week she looks frailer – even her strong will starts fading. *The thought of witnessing her being consumed by cancer is unbearable.* The memory of Celia is too fresh in my mind. Cowardly, I pull away. I quit coming to the group meetings altogether. I try staying loosely in touch with Pam, yet soon I even stop calling her. For a while I remain in hiding.

One morning, however, I awake with a strong sense to contact my new-found friend and right away dial her number. "I don't have much time left," she utters laboriously. Terrified, I register her message. Knowing that I could not forgive myself otherwise, I quickly pick up a bouquet of pink peonies from my garden and head off to visit her.

Different hospital, different room, but the same struggle. Upon entering her room, I hold the flowers in front of me as if to shield myself from her pain. Her husband takes them with a forced smile and goes on to telling me superficial details about the oxygen machine that pumps air into her failing lungs. Fluid build-up is drowning my friend inside her own body.

Helplessly, I throw myself into the farthest corner of the room and stare at Pam in disbelief. Her body has turned into a bag of bones draped over with prune-like skin. Her hair resembles the scarce spikes of a porcupine after a fierce fight. She is sitting in a chair wrapped in a blanket. Supposedly, she is eating lunch, *more like gazing at the unappealing food.* Whenever she glances over at me, my frightful eyes search for other places to look at.

Gift

Pam is so weakened that she is leaning on her elbow to prop up her head. When her arm tires her head slips and takes a tumble. While she slowly gathers herself, I remain stuck in that moment. In my mind's eye, I am seated in that chair – or one just like that at one of the hospital rooms I stayed at a short while ago.

The biggest excitement of the day is to finally get out of bed for a short while in order to eat lunch sitting upright in the chair – the only other piece of furniture in the barren room. Food is the last thing on my mind; I've absolutely no appetite –

from the drugs or from despair? Who knows... I am barely hanging in, floating somewhere between here and thereafter. Oh, my head is so heavy... As I lean on my hand, it gives way and my head slides down my forearm...

I am startled back into the current reality. An insight hits me: Of course it is heartbreaking to helplessly watch how the illness is taking over my beloved friend's body, and I am utmost concerned for her. *However, what terrifies me most – even more than feeling for her – is my own fear of dying.*

Owning my share of emotions allows me to pull myself together and focus on my friend. My eyes don't frantically roam to avoid Pam anymore. Now that I look at her attentively, I notice an ethereal radiance about her. "I'm not scared of passing over," she says reassured by her strong faith. "It's the journey that worries me. I'm afraid of enduring even more suffering before I'm released. I don't know that I can take it anymore." Selflessly she adds, "At least I've had a full life, but you're so young. You've become a darling daughter to me. I pray that you enjoy life and are spared such anguish."

After pausing to catch her gurgling breath, Pam continues: "Doesn't anybody see?" she cuts through the discussion between her husband and the doctor who has stepped in the room busily assessing the ever-expanding fluid levels in her lungs. *She's protesting not being witnessed in her transition.* I nod at her, acknowledging her truth. I admire how she embodies facing death and loving life at once. I walk over and begin rubbing her back gently – this could be the last time I get to touch her in this life. "I love you" whispers itself out of us in the same moment. Teary eyed, we embrace.

The following day, her husband phones to save me a trip to the hospital. Our next meeting will be at Pam's funeral. In spite of having had many months to prepare, he sounds stunned, repeatedly mumbling, "But the doctors said she'd live a little longer..."

There is nothing to cry about, I assure myself. *She's unchained from her pain.* Life will go on without her. Nonetheless, I am bewildered. I drive around for quite some time until coming to a halt on the edge of a cliff overlooking the river valley and the Rockies. Gazing at familiar peaks in the distance calms me.

But then, unexpectedly, I begin screaming. I stop, ensure that all windows are tightly closed, and then lose myself in violently flooding tears. Emotions buried deep within me free up as they are given permission to surface by mourning for my friend's parting. I weep for Pam, for Celia – and for me, too. Eventually, I settle down with puffy eyes and a hoarse throat. This release feels like a good-bye gift from my dear friend. *Thanks Pam,* I smile internally.

One

Light-headed from this tremendous experience, I step out of the car to get fresh air and walk over to the field nearby to rest. While lying down on the ground, my hands brush against the grass. *Have these little leaves always been this supple?* Reminded of Pam's labored breathing during our last visit, I become aware of my lungs contracting and expanding perfectly well without any effort. I thankfully inhale the spring air.

Oxygen, I ponder, *one second my friend was breathing it, however difficult it was, and the next, she was no more.* Assessing this element's place on the periodic table, I acknowledge that it is one of many, but potently different; the threshold between life and death. *Even its symbol is neat: O – full circle.* It protrudes in my mind's eye out of the periodic table pinned to the wall of a long-forgotten chemistry lab. *"The GOD element,"* I sensationalize playfully.

Has soil always smelled this rich? I am drawn back to the present. As I exhale, my full weight from head to toes sinks into the ground. It is reassuring to know that I cannot fall down from here. *I'm held by the earth underneath me.* When I look up at the vast blue sky, I cannot help but wonder when its colors have ever been so brilliant. Sun rays dance on my cheeks. I breathe in deeply once more. *Has air ever tasted this delicious?*

I am surprised at how vivid everything is. It is as if I have awoken from a long dream. *Is this how good life can really be?* It is so inviting... but also overwhelming. *I dare not be happy or else all falls apart. Merely nine months ago, the same sun rays cheered me up on my wedding anniversary and look what happened next!*

Anchored in my breath, fear's grip is not as tight at this moment. I am able to discern that, aside from similarities in these two experiences, I have a new sense of being grounded. *Has "bubbly happy" morphed into something more substantial?* I am briefly reminded of images in a dream from a while back, reliving the sensation of falling through concrete into an ocean of new realizations.

In spite of intermittent notions of an expanding awareness, I am also unavoidably aware that a short while ago I was unsure whether I could, or even wanted to, live anymore. In fact, past experiences are so fresh in my mind that I shake my head as if to erase everything. My many chats with Myrna and sessions with Ian have undoubtedly been useful in better coping with life's mysteries, but the rawness of physical pain and emotional loss have a way of oppressing all else.

And the risk of a relapse? I can't go there. I do not have the capacity to contemplate it. I am alive now and I am in remission. That is all I can cope with. *Pam died, but I'm still here.* "Be at peace wherever you may be, my dear friend." I get up and straightening my jacket. This is the time to think of nothing but taking in one more breath and inching forward one more step.

Brand

The disconnect between Ross and me has grown further since my surgery. *How can two people coexist without interacting at all?* Evidently it is possible to do so under the same roof. Most of the time I sleep in the guest room or he sleeps on the sofa. On the few occasions that we share the same bed, possibly out of an urge to prove the validity of our marriage, one of us is asleep – *or at least pretends to be.*

We have settled into a time-share arrangement; he putters around in the house in the early mornings and evenings, while I take my turn late mornings, afternoons and late evenings. In contrast to the overly engaging fights, nowadays we do not speak to each other for days on end. While thankful for the quiet, I am distraught by the underlying tension. I want to get better for the sake of us both.

"It's almost half a year since your transplant. You should be fine by now," the resident oncologist determines at my monthly checkup, shortly after explaining, "Dr. Weis is on vacation." Void of any emotion, or rather, overwhelmed by emotions of her own while void of any empathy, she goes on with her eyes focused on my file instead of me: "Your blood work is slowly improving. All is proceeding according to protocol." *Have we got a heartless Olsen-protégé here?*

Her words hit me hard. *I'm a failure.* "Whatever it says on those papers," I reply, "I'm disappointed with my recovery." *She doesn't know how ambitious I am. If the standard is half a year, my norm is half of that. And here we are, six months nearly over, and I'm so depleted as if no more than six days passed.*

As much as I want an answer for myself, I want one for my husband's sake. With an engineer's mindset, I wish to define a problem and solve it. "I'm trying my best, but..." my voice cracks while my pride crumbles. *I despise failing more than she can imagine.*

I want to fix me and get on with life. These white-coated experts ought to know what to do next, right? Dr. Weis, whom I usually see at my checkups, exudes confidence with his mature and well-experienced mannerism, however, he has not been specific on my progress. "Be patient. You're improving each month." *It doesn't feel that way to me!*

A sensible side of me recognizes that this young doctor may not be the best one to consult. *She looks under thirty. If I'd* studied medicine over engineering, she'd be my senior by no more than a couple of years. How well would I've been equipped to give advice? But who else to turn to right now?

"Don't be so fearful," her face reddens when I dare to tell her, "I can't leave the house for a whole week sometimes." "You should. Don't be afraid to go out." "I want to, but I can't find the strength to get out of bed most days." "You managed today." "It was hard work." "Well, do it every day." "I would if I could."

The verbal duel ends with her handing me a piece of paper. "Take this requisition form to the front desk; it's a referral for psychiatric assessment," she states impatiently. "You're depressed. He'll prescribe you something for it."

Am I? I self-examine. It is true that at times I have felt low, outright despair, during the past months while I was acutely ill. *But now that the worst is over?* Attempting to follow her logic, I try to remember at what other time I have felt stuck in bed like this without being physically sick. *When I found out about Ozan's cheating!* Indeed, back in Istanbul I was so devastated that I didn't want to open my eyes to a new morning. Everything felt dull and gray. And I had to drag myself out of bed each day for months.

This is different though. "Yes," I acknowledge, "on and off, I've felt depressed lately, if that's what you're referring to. But what I'm telling you now is physical. My mind wants to get going, but it's as if gravity is tenfold and I can't fight it most days," I describe the incapacitating fatigue. I want to get out, pick up my life from where it was abruptly halted, move on with my dreams... *pragmatic plans rather.*

My words fall on deaf ears. Seemingly too afraid to own her own humanity, she cannot step beyond the rigid compartments created for her in the name of medicine. *It's not a helper in front of me, but a judge who has rendered a verdict.* I feel branded and tossed aside.

Psycho

"You're showing a normal response to abnormal circumstances," the psychiatrist summarizes his observation after questioning me on what is going on in my life. *That's a relief.* "Let me run a test. It's a standardized questionnaire."

Trying to make out upside-down letters on the top of the stack of papers in front of him, I gather it says "Diagnostic and Statistical Manual of Mental Disorders" – *sounds heavy.*

The questions turn out to be far less troubling than what I expected from the title. While things proceed smoothly, I let out a chuckle – *not the best thing to do while being assessed.* "Do you do some things excessively, again and again?" this older gentleman has just asked while at the very instance repeatedly tracing his pen over the same letters in his notes. *Is this about obsessive-compulsive patterns?* Unable to hold back, I gesture at his hand, "Do you mean like that?"

The tone of the appointment changes markedly after this moment. I discover the cost of my quirky sense of humor at my next regular checkup at TBCC. Dr. Weis, who has returned from vacation, reports: "In my absence you managed to get yourself diagnosed with mild anxiety."

"Really? I was sent in for depression." "You can't stay out of trouble for long, can you?" he winks at me, which lets me know he sees the complete human being that I am. He adds, "I wouldn't worry about it. I, for one, would be anxious, depressed, and all else, if I were faced with a life-threatening illness."

Clock

Whatever I may have, or not, been diagnosed with, it becomes painfully clear that rebuilding my stamina is far from straightforward. Nonetheless, determined to return to my studies in the fall, I attempt to reestablish a daily routine.

Optimistically, I draw a flowchart for my many plans as I would for an engineering problem. However well-intended, each day that I try to run prescheduled errands for the house or our business sets me up for disappointment. When I do succeed in following through with an activity, I collapse afterward. I have no other choice but to simplify my chart – until the end product is this:

9 am wake up, 10 am breakfast, 11 am catch up on news in my research area, noon prepare lunch, 1 pm eat, 2 pm stroll or medical appointments, 3 pm rest, 4 pm snack, 5 pm tidy up home, 6 pm cook supper, 7 pm eat – with or without Ross, 8 pm watch TV, 9 pm shower, 10 pm small snack, 11 pm bedtime. How difficult could it be to keep up with such a boring list?

These items, most of which my body fails to follow, at the very least serve the purpose of reminding me to eat throughout the day, which I would otherwise forget. Most days, it is noon by the time I am able to get out of bed. The dizziness I feel when upright does not dissipate until well into the afternoon – *it's as if my heart can't pump enough blood to fill my head.*

Whatever energy I muster up is spent while repeatedly putting on, and taking off, several layers of clothing. In spite of being on hormone replacement, hot flashes remain a part of my reality. For the rest of the time I feel cold, even on increased thyroid medication. Often I am too depleted to leave the house or be upright for any length of time and revert to resting.

In the end, not a schedule but heat waves dictate the rhythm of my day. The burst of a hot flash propels me out from under the blanket. *This is the moment to seize, put on the kettle, grab a handful of nuts and dried fruits, or when possible prepare food for later, before diving back into bed.*

Flirt

Irises, poppies and daises are blooming in my little garden, their bright colors always a welcome sign of the short-lived Calgary summers. Today, however, this sight makes my heart heavy – *Celia and I were to celebrate.* In honor of my departed friend, I pull myself together. *Enough of this tiredness!* With determination, I deliberate what to do and decide to include Ross in my plans. *Enough of distancing, too!*

I splurge on a weekend package at Château Lake Louise. *It's time we rekindle our romance.* I know Celia would cheer me on for this. Recalling Dr. Weis's suggestion to increase my HRT dosage, I take this as a trial run, and also consume a number of herbal remedies claiming to counteract menopausal symptoms.

I don't care about side effects at this point as long as I can be a bit more functional for our outing.

"I'm fine, mon amour," I attempt to assure my husband, *and myself.* I gesture him to stretch out beside me on the hotel bed overlooking my favorite mountain peaks. "But," he is hesitant, his eyes pointing to the still pink line above my pelvis. "The doctor said my scars are healing well, inside and out." *Not the greatest line to spruce up an intimate relationship.* He excuses himself, "Meet me at the Saloon," referring to the in-house restaurant-pub.

After he leaves, I study myself in the full-size bathroom mirror while changing into something dressier than the tracksuit I was wearing on our drive out. *Beside the big scar on my belly, I have a cut on my left breast – from the diagnostic biopsy; another one more to the center of my chest – from the central line; a few more spots on my body – from some other tubes stuck in me during procedures I forget; and a saggy neck, leftover from my bulged out thyroid.*

On my way to meet him, I roam through the hotel gift stores for a piece of lingerie to cover up reminders of the past. *This teddy will do – its style is simple, but it's silky smooth to the touch.* I don't let the price tag deter me. *I want my hubby to see me as his wife again, and not some sick patient.*

Upon entering the restaurant, I hear someone nearby cough. I am frightened by the many people and the blowing air ventilation. *Surely, sex is no more risky than entering this whirlpool of germs.* I walk over to sit beside Ross at the bar. He's in a good mood. He is wearing the shirt I gifted him. "Suits you well Sweets," I compliment flirtatiously. "What would you like?" he replies contently. "Hot toddy, please." *Chilly in here.* For the first time in months, we both enjoy sitting and eating together. I enviously watch him dip his fish and chips in the tartar sauce whilst I chew on a plain salad topped with pieces of cooked chicken breast. *Can't risk an upset tummy tonight.*

Once we retire into our hotel room, he goes straight to bed. I pretty up in the bathroom. He is half asleep by the time I come out. "What took you so long?" he inquires, finding the answer to his question when I disrobe and reveal my newly acquired outfit. "Nice," he responds with less enthusiasm than I anticipated.

Should I've picked the black one instead of this plumb-colored one? Do my scars still show? Apprehensive, yet set on making this night special, I lie down beside him. I slip a mint from my lips to his which I had freshly unwrapped and hid inside my mouth. "What are you doing?" he turns his face away. *Seemed like a sexy idea to freshen up booze and garlic breaths – guess not.* "Go to sleep." He rolls to the other side of the bed, putting an end to my wishful thinking.

For the following hours, self-doubt roams through my head. *Did the scarf I wrapped around my neck not match? Did it cover too much of my chest and turned him off?* Eventually, I allow myself to consider that his rejecting may not be all about me. *Is alcohol affecting his manhood? What else could it be doing to my hubby?*

In the morning, Ross is gone – *to breakfast without me.* To make the best of the remaining time, I decide to take a dip in the heated pool. *I managed to have no sore glands this morning in spite of the two-and-a-half hour drive yesterday and even after eating at the crowded bar. Maybe I can get away with this bit of fun, too.*

With each stroke, the warm water glides along my skin, *kind of being caressed.* Afterward I step in the whirlpool. The pulsing jets feel good on my tight shoulders. *Haah, kind of a climax,* I kid myself as I ease into this release.

After the brief exercise, I am exhausted and to my relief find a seated shower. Soaping up arouses rare yet fond memories of Ross and I bathing each other. *What happened to that innocent care and gentle curiosity of exploring each other's bodies? Can't blame it all on cancer; a good ninety percent of my skin looks and feels the same as before. Did life get too real too soon?* With no answers, I let these thoughts wash away down the drain.

This swim becomes my highlight of our weekend outing. At check-out time, we find each other at the reception and drive back home without exchanging a single word.

11 ▣

Click

*H*ow's Nicky? I wonder about my number-one guy in the cancer support group. He often comes to my mind while I am confined to bed-rest after returning from the mountains. At first, I think it is purely incidental that I am reminded of him.

Having failed to revive my romance with Ross is bothersome. *Why can't he open up to me?* I wish that we could share our concerns, and especially mourn together the loss of the vision to create a child together – *four max, we agreed on, one on each arm*. My hysterectomy alone is reason to talk, and his personal issues probably stir similar emotions that could bring us closer, but the unexpressed mutual pain ends up pushing us further apart.

Nicky and I have not been in contact much outside regular group meetings. Alongside his health troubles, a toddler and a newborn keep him and his spouse busy.

Even so, *we clicked right from the start,* with affection I think of this thirty-some, *and handsome,* professional basketball player. *We'd both been deemed too fit to be sick.* Strangely, what almost killed us was also the reason that brought us closer.

Nicky's misdiagnosis resulted in his hip pain not being taken seriously until the bone cancer spread into his pelvis. Aggressive surgery left him bound to a wheelchair, but this did not curb his joie de vivre.

In his adorably crude style, he made sure all of us group members knew beyond any doubt that he continued satisfying his wife in alternate ways. It is this blunt courage, I realize, in contrast to my struggles with sexuality that intensifies my admiration for him these days.

At our last group gathering, he had mentioned considering to have his body severed from his torso down in order to eradicate the inoperable metastases. *That's a man who wants to live at all cost!*

Wondering whether he followed through with this controversial procedure, I decide to call him. A recording in his husky voice comes on: "You can reach me at Agape." *Is this one of his twisted jokes?*

Recalling that I had not seen him at Pam's funeral, I inquire at the hospice by that name. To my dismay, I find out that he is indeed registered. *But he looked so robust last time I saw him?* I tell myself as though I forgot how cancer too often corrodes from the inside out.

Bad

"You're paying for the sins of others, my son," I hear someone preach to Nicky as I approach the room. *He didn't strike me as the religious type.* "Thank you Father," he replies in his ever-so-manly voice. *Is it true faith?* I ponder while waiting outside the door.

Not for me to decide, I conclude while the priest exits. "Hey Nicky!" I try to cover up my confusion with cheer. "Ada! How're you doing girl?" "You tell first," I divert the attention back to him.

"Couldn't persuade the surgeon to cut me in half," he reports. "What's the point in holding onto limp legs and a few rotten organs? Short of that, we ran out of choices. I don't want my kids to remember me any sicker than this, and it's not fair to my wife to clean up my mess. She gets enough of that with the little ones. So I moved in here." "Bummer." I am otherwise speechless.

"There must be a reason for this shit," he goes on in his down-to-earth tone. "Chrissie asked me to chat with her priest – she's the devout one in the family. He's convinced that we suffer for the souls stuck in purgatory. I hope he's right.

"This is so damn painful, not just the sickness, but my girl; my boy is too young, but in her eyes I see how scared she's. She knows something bad is going on." He looks at me with mournful eyes, "This better be helping someone out there to be set free."

Pierce

Unable to wrap my head around his thinking, but well aware of his desire to find meaning, I nod in agreement. I decide to see Nicky as much as I can. When I find that I am able to visit him every second day twice in a row, I become hopeful about holding to a schedule and consider volunteering at this hospice. However, when my fourth visit is delayed by a week due to a cold, I have to admit the prematurity of my ambition.

Nothing has prepared me for what I am about to witness upon entering the building. Nicky's distressed voice is audible from his room. I run over to find two heavily built caretakers holding him down in his bed. Even after all he has gone through, Nicky has enough upper body strength left to fight them off.

"I don't wanna die!" he yells. "It's all bullshit!" I can only guess that he is referring to the concept of suffering for someone else's redemption. *His eyes are about to pop out of his skull!* It is devastating to witness this otherwise laid-back man in such misery. A few minutes into this heart-tearing drama, he goes quiet. From behind the two big men, I make out a petite nurse holding an emptied syringe, *presumably tranquilizers.*

Feeling drugged myself, I stumble backwards toward the exit. *This isn't right!* The image of Nicky's delirious eyes pierces through my being for days to come.

Me

"I want to die happy," I pout during my counselling session. "Tell me more," Ian inquires. "Death... no, dying scares me.

We'll all go someday, but no one teaches us how. Most of us live as if we were immortal – so carelessly; treating our health as if it comes in infinite supply. We're all spoiled, so demanding of our bodies, just like a brat mistreating its parents."

"So, you're distinguishing between your body and yourself?" "Yes, of course," I respond short-tempered, assuming Ian has missed my point. *Right,* I notice the significance of his observation afterward. Ever since parting from my body that ominous night in hospital, my awareness has shifted. *It's been so subtle and natural that I hadn't noticed it before.*

"You're right," I reply apologetically. "I never thought about it. Before, I used to identify with my body ignorantly. Asking it to always function, pointing out the bad stuff all the time. I saw ugliness when I looked in the mirror. Chubby thighs. And when I looked at my hands, I saw bulgy knuckles."

"What do you see now?" Ian invites me to look at my hand. I nearly break down in tears as I truly see my hands for the first time; limber fingers with knuckles that function perfectly. "What I despised of as imperfection is actually what makes me 'me'."

Ian smiles, "Anything else?" "I appreciate my body now. It's awful to say this, but I abused it for all these years. I had to experience dying to gain the right perspective. My body is not some lowlife extension of me. It's an incredible structure with its own intelligence that allows me to live. Look at how well it has healed from a complete crash?" "Glad to hear that," he responds.

"Once we're able to be appreciative of being alive, for living in our bodies, we may be better able to cultivate gratitude for fellow people, too. And, taking it one step further, we can see our planet as another sort of a body that allows us people as a whole to exist, and treat the Earth more gently." *Didn't see that coming.* I am surprised at how Ian arrived at this mushy sounding tangent from my first comments. *He's different. His lovey-dovey side is alright though; I get his point, I think.*

Die

Next time I go to visit Nicky, I am told, "Family members only," and am sent off. At the following cancer support-group meeting, our coordinator Gina informs us of his passing. "Let's commemorate Nicky's life by contemplating what keeps us alive and lively," she suggests after saying a few words of sympathy. "One word everybody," she looks around the circle of the ten of us sitting submissively in our chairs.

"My children," one starts, which reminds me of the photograph Nicky had shown me with melancholic pride, a two-year-old in a frilly dress holding a sleepy infant in her arms, aware that they will grow up void of any memory of their father. "Purpose," another one utters. "Prayer,"... "being loved." "Amen to that," someone budges in. "Hope," "will,"... words are spoken into the circle by various members.

"Medicine," I add in defense of science. Gina laughs, "Yes, that, too." "Miracle," comes from another participant. *Now, that I couldn't have said aloud.* "Isn't that the case," she emphasizes this powerful word and concludes the exercise, and with it, the meeting.

I am stirred by the mystery that this term suggests. I want to push it away, because I fear it to be discrediting of my hard-earned engineering persona. At the same time, I feel the pull of an indescribable curiosity toward it. This inner oscillation leaves me mesmerized as if I were staring at a swinging pendulum.

I try to refocus on the news of the day. *Nicky is dead.* I am by no means getting used to the death of people I care about, but am more accepting of the idea. *Sweet Celia went pretty much unconsciously. Pam taught me that it can be done with dignity and that we've at least some say in the matter. And then, Nicky, handsome Nicky... the terror he fell into makes me want to die well.*

I want to die happy, indeed. *Add it to the list of paradoxes I stumble upon lately.* I want to go as contently as I would leaving a dinner table after the most delicious meal; full and satisfied. *I best start practicing now – my track record is poor. Last time I was on my way out, I couldn't come up with more than few occasions I felt really alive. Dying well requires living well,* I realize, *so that when the time comes I can say I tasted it, took it in whole-heartedly, chewed on ideas, gulped down pleasures, spit out a few bones... lived fully!*

I remember Ian's words at the end of our last session: "A sage named Tagore once said, 'And because I love this life, I will love death also.'" *Oh, so mine isn't a novel idea.* My mind seems to store up information that I cannot absorb all at once, rehashing some parts later when I am more receptive.

Relieved not to be alone in this, I open up to embracing life more fully – *including its end phase.* I commit to exploring and practicing dying daily. While I am unsure how exactly to do this, the intention alone seems to have an effect. I notice that living more attentively brings to surface unconscious patterns. I find new choices in my day, sometimes as simple as stopping eating at the sensation of completeness instead of stuffing myself until a physical fullness, or rethinking eating up what is left on my plate out of habit. Even in such minor actions I begin sensing that my life takes a turn from heaviness to a lighter and freer self. *An old me dies, and a new me, "more me" me, surfaces.*

As part of my learning, I also focus on releasing my relationship with my cousin. I have been hanging on to our emotional tension out of an inability to let go. *Add to that the loss of my fertility, probably my career... my marriage?*

When it gets overpowering, I remind myself that this is a daily practice and not a race. I also loosen up by amusing myself. *Take for example the French term for orgasm: petite mort – not a bad idea to befriend death after all.*

Fair

I awake more sore than usual in the morning. *Ou, it hurts to swallow – wishing I had no throat.* At this terrifying image, I close my eyes to settle down. *OK, let's see what we've gotten her.* I examine myself imitating one of my many doctors. As I slowly palpate along my neck, I notice that it is lined with tender lymph nodes. They are so enlarged that it is bumpy right under my skin. These symptoms remind me of dreadful tumors.

It's not lymphoma, I calm myself, *it's just a cold. Tumors don't hurt, these do! What happened?* I attempt to grasp the sudden change in the state of my health. *Yesterday was a good* day. Even my sense of humor was starting to lighten up – *I felt that good*. But today is a whole different story. *This isn't fair*. I yearn for being like I was the day before. *What have I done wrong to deserve such punishment this morning?*

I want to create a cause and effect link, to make sense of life. However, this is not motivated by curiosity, but by blindness caused by stifling worries. Frivolous thoughts repeat in my head like a broken record. *If only I find the reason for why I fell sick,* this morning's sore glands being merely a symbol for last year's devastating cancer episode, *then I'll finally understand it all and avoid getting sick from here on...*

Bite

"Why me?" "Yes, why did so much have to happen to you?" Ian responds at another session. "You've had more than your share to deal with in your young life." "I'm over the self-pity," I update him. "That was the past little while, when I was sick." "What I want to know now is why I survived when others die? Good people. They deserved to live, too. Did I steal their spot by staying alive?" "Are you serious?" Ian responds startled. "Do you still have survivor's guilt?" "Yes," I reply, annoyed that he is not validating my emotions which he usually does so well. Disturbed by exposing this raw inner quandary, I cut my appointment short. *I wish Myrna was here. She'd know what to say. More so, she'd give me Reiki which always soothes me.*

Too many unanswered questions roam in my mind. I am so weary at this point, that the only way I know how to cope, or possibly evade coping, is to busy myself with never-ending thoughts. *Getting physical may help*, I consider. *It's time to cash in my rain-check!* I recall my yoga instructor's invitation from before my diagnosis and enroll in the summer course. Tamasi instructs me less demanding postures than the rest of the class as I shake from weakness even during warm up stretches. This gentle East Indian woman places her hand on my back for support and whispers, "Rumi says: The wound is the place where Light enters you." Tears pour down my cheeks.

"Let's try something new, or perhaps ageless," she takes me aside after a few more unsuccessful attempts at keeping up with class. "Tibetan Rites may be right for you. They're five simple yet powerful exercises. You can begin with using supportive blocks to help along. At first, do no more than three repeats a day whenever you can. They're meant to activate your energy centers and build core strength. In time you may be able to increase to twenty-one repetitions. But no hurry, it can take years." While whirling around like a dervish, she adds, "This is not about performance. The point is to do only so many that make you feel good." I am confused, yet willing. "I'll give it a try not to try too hard." "That's the spirit."

Tamasi also fills a need for a female voice in my life during after-class chats. "I ate a double fudge brownie yesterday," I admit as if I were in a confessional. She listens with big eyes. "It may be brown in color, but it's made of white sugar and white flour. You know, the stuff cancer feeds on... I stared at it for a while, knowing it's bad for me, but couldn't help my craving. When I didn't eat it, I felt deprived. And once I ate it, I felt rotten. I did the wrong thing – again." "Sounds like a lose-lose dilemma," she responds. "I prefer win-win myself." *I'm not impressed by being mocked.*

"One brownie won't deprive or kill you. You know that, right?" *She reassures herself that I haven't lost it altogether, I guess.* "Whenever I have a strong emotional response to something, I look inside. What lies beneath? Befriend your mind so that it permits you a peek into beliefs you hold subconsciously." She proceeds to pack up her belongings, now that class is long over, allowing me time to absorb her words. *Even then, I don't get it.*

"Please tell me more, how does it work?" "Well, Ada, it's best for you to find your own answers. But if you really want my opinion, could it be that your fear of mortality has reared its head, saying 'Look at me, pay attention to me'? This could be an opportunity to get to know yourself better." *Even more? Haven't I done enough of that lately?*

"Why else do you suggest your concern to do something wrong is disproportionately linked to eating that one brownie? It's an invitation to let you know where your energy leak is, how your self is not in sync within itself. We all deal with this. A blaming game is often easier than facing the underlying truth. But in the end the latter is far less costly – and life-giving. Use the symbolism of taking a bite, or not, as a way to accept the reality of your mortality – more precisely, the mortality of your body. And consider what, or who, may possibly be moving on when the time comes." *That rings a bell. What part of me was floating off back when, away from life? It was so pleasant transitioning from this life, yet now the thought of it scares me.*

"Also meditate on what this brownie stands for," Tamasi goes on, "that this little dot of a thing can have such a pull on you and your will? Sweetness, warmth, love? How else can you supply this to yourself in a way that it's a win-win in the end? Either way, make peace with your death, and your life will blossom in ways you never imagined." *Wow, that's richer than any brownie.*

Daughter

"What a nice surprise," my mother greets me at the airport. "You're well enough to pick me up!" She has kept her promise and is visiting me for a second time in a year, now that school in Turkey is out for the summer. Once home, she is pleased that I have prepared the guest room for her this time.

"Haven't heard from Mick and Lennie since their move," I report, which I know she would like to know even though she acts disinterested. "We have one month together," she changes the topic while giving me an uncharacteristically warm hug. *I guess she still considers me in the "ill" category.*

Ross politely attends the dinner I have prepared for the three of us. By next morning, the frailty of my physical condition becomes evident again and I remain too weak to leave the bed for the coming days. "Demands I put on my body keep backfiring," I share disappointedly, "leaving me more depleted than I start out with." Moeder comforts me, "Let me take care of things while I'm here."

It's easier to talk with her, I notice. *I feel freer to express myself.* I have shed some inhibitions and false beliefs on how I ought to behave, as Ian had claimed would happen as a result of therapy sessions. *Moeder is the litmus test* – having feared her disapproval for years. In return, she responds less critically and acts more accepting of my recent changes.

She also picks up caring for me from where she left during her first visit; she cooks, keeps the house sparkling clean and holds me often – a treat always, *as it was whenever it happened while I was a kid*. I rest my head in her lap while she sits at one end of the sofa and I stretch out across it. "It's growing out the same way it did when you were a baby," she pats my short hair. "New hair, new body. Let's call this your new birthday." "How about 're-birthday'?" I iterate. "Many happy re-birthdays, mein Liebling Adelheid," calling me her darling for the first time. She bends down and kisses my forehead.

My mother's loving is like a panacea, allowing some of the chronic tension to release that has built up from having to get through each day. Sometimes she finds me curled up in bed in pain and holds me tight while I remain in the fetal position and indulge in her care. Other times, we converse – *it's mostly me talking, wanting to be heard by her, and also to include her in my ever-changing life.*

"The more I try to comprehend the events of the past year, the more perplexed I get, Moeder. When ... what ... how? I rolled through the to-do list of 'take these pills, stay still while we poke you, press this button for more morphine...' Faithfully, I followed orders. First it was heavy chemo, full-body radiation, then the transplant, and later the surgery. I compliantly endured all these intrusive procedures. Miraculously, I made it, so far at least."

"If I died, I'd have been a mere statistic. Since I lived, medical technology claims to have scored against cancer. What about me, the human being who hosted this unwelcomed guest? Did I not partake in this venture? What about life? How did it find its way back into my beaten-up body? Could this be just a random lottery?"

"One must go through the deep experience of sickness and death to arrive at a higher sanity and health," my mother breaks her silence. *She's quoting Thomas Mann again; her habitual way of conversing without personally committing.*

"I don't know any of the answers," her voice sounds more real now. "Possibly some of it was luck and some of it destiny – kısmet, as they say in Turkish. All we can do is do our best and hope for the best. One thing I'm absolutely sure of is how thankful I am to have my daughter back." *Hearing her vulnerability warms my heart.*

Break

What I want to tell my mother, more than anything, is the experience I had shortly before her first visit, of passing over into another realm, away from this life – *and the absolute peacefulness I tasted for what felt like an eternity.* At the time I was so confused that I had no words for it, no comprehension of any sort. Months later, I still have no understanding of it, not in a worldly way, but a lingering impression – *and a yearning to be filled with that vast serenity once more.*

Isn't it ironic, I would like to say to her in the logical ways she taught me to speak, *that on one hand I very much want the release I felt when...* I hesitate merely thinking it, take a deep breath and continue my imaginary conversation – *when I died. And on the other hand, now, back in the land of the living, often enough I feel crippled by the fear of dying.*

I want to share with Moeder recent happenings that have led me to distinguish aspects of my being, not as an owner who takes them for granted, but as a witness who honors having them – *like the insight I had about my body the other day with Ian, and also about my mind with Tamasi.* She told me not to criticize my thoughts when they go astray, but to observe what a potent tool the mind is and find ways to train it to work better, *not simply for an engineering job, but for living better.*

Moreover, I sense a separate emotional body of sorts – *as I am not my mind, neither am I my feelings*. After plenty of therapy, I discern that my response to a situation is conditioned by past experiences. I am convinced that I have a say in releasing old drama which in turn allows me to shed emotions I had previously assumed to be essential parts of me. And then there is the "I" – *is this what Myrna called "soul"?*

I have since read about these topics in books, but nothing intrigues me as much as actual sensations of this inner core I have experienced – *as real, and as vague, as dreams...*

I cannot tell Moeder. This is not a topic to approach intellectually – *which I know to be her "modus operandi"*. I let all this be, concerned that it could stretch our relationship too far. *I want to enjoy our new-found closeness, and not to break what good we have.*

12

Chain

How can it be any harder than before? With teary eyes, I wave good-bye to my mother at the airport. The time for her to return to Istanbul has come too soon. Not being acutely ill this time, the separation pain stings even more. It does not help knowing what awaits me at home after her departure.

Things between Ross and me are beyond "adrift" – they're as severed as Nicky's gut was going to be! When our second wedding anniversary approaches, I reminisce. *Was I really as happy as I claimed to be on our first anniversary?*

Hey, that's when I got sick! How bizarre is that? The sharp onset of illness coinciding with this special occasion carries the kind of weight that forces me to be forthright. I shamefully recognize how much I gave in to wishful thinking. *The drinking and outbursts were there from the beginning.*

But... I was healthy then. I was successful, and invincible... or so I thought. He seemed like a man who could use help, *and I envisioned myself as superwoman flying to his rescue.* I believed I could manage. I was wrong. I recall Myrna's words of wisdom: *Could admitting this be part of "being true to myself"?*

What was my driving force? *Lacking direction and meaning in my own life? Were his troubles a distraction to bury my own sorrows?* Something else I was wrong about was that everybody, given a choice, would prefer to change an unhealthy situation for the better. *It sounds so logical,* I want to hold onto my naïveté, *but experience has worn it off.* I have to accept the power of addictive human nature.

Our individual lives, *having become invisible to each other,* collide at a most unexpected instance. Ross arrives later than usual. *The pub session lasted longer,* I assess from his squinty eyes as he enters our home. Next thing, a hefty key chain buzzes by me, an inch away from my face – *courtesy of a skilled boxer's aim.* I cannot help but stare at the indent it leaves on the wall before dropping to the ground. "Clunk!" The sound makes me jerk. Something in me dies.

"You failed me!" He breaks down in tears. "You weren't supposed to get sick!" *How does that justify you nearly smashing in my face?* I want to strike back, but cannot speak. *You sucked me dry!* I want to challenge him. *You deceived me.* Nothing comes out of my mouth. I don't have the strength for a confrontation. In my silence, I realize that this is a symptom of a deeper matter. *None of this is about me. He's not out to hurt me; he's the one hurting worse.* I underestimated alcohol as a destructive drug. *Is booze his cancer? Until he comes to terms* with it himself, he can't make a choice for the better – and I can't help him either. I am reminded of the marital counsellor's words. *This is what she was referring to!*

Eye

I wake up with a crystal clear notion in the morning: *Have to move on solo.* I may not be able to recall her name, but the counsellor's message has gotten through to me. *Can't afford to drag on things any longer.* Even so, I try talking myself out of it. *I'm not strong enough to leave the house most days. Am told not to even take a shower when alone for risk of fainting. I'm scared of him,* I pile up further justifications. *He kicked me out of the house before, shoved me out the door when mad at me.*

All aside, *I cannot break my vow! It's sacred,* I acknowledge the degree of commitment I feel toward my husband. I promised my life to this man with the solidity of a religious statement, *except in my case it's my belief in integrity holding me to my word.* At this tormenting moment, it dawns on me that my idealistic way of life has reached a breaking point. This allows me to finally see the blatant reality beyond habitual attitudes: *I also have a responsibility toward myself.*

I find a note on the kitchen counter at breakfast. "Meet me at Calgary Tower's swirling top at 7. You make my world spin round, Babe." It's the 29th! He hasn't forgotten our second anniversary. How romantic he can be. Heavyhearted, I rest up to be able to go out in the evening. *It's like I'm invited to a funeral, not a celebration.*

While walking over to him in the restaurant, I applaud him silently for facing me at the elegantly decorated dinner table. *Can't tell when last we sat across and looked each other in the eye.* One thing I can tell, however, is that he has had a few of what he calls "brewskies" already. *I can't take this anymore,* I hear a deep cry inside. An old voice cuts back in; *but how can I do the unthinkable – break my vow? I don't want to break up, but I don't have the luxury to break down any further, either.* I continue agonizing while he orders appetizers. *How can I do this on our anniversary?* Maybe this is the right time. I want to connect candidly with the man I love, even if it means going our separate ways. I build up the courage to speak up.

"Ross," I reach out and hold his hand apprehensively. "I agree with you." "Good girl," he teases me, then looks puzzled. "Agree on what?" *This is tough.* I sweat, *this is no hot flash, it's fear.* "You know how you brought up the topic of divorce a few times. I agree." *Yikes. This isn't how it was supposed to sound.* I beat myself up as if there were a nicer way to say this.

My husband of two whole years, *seems twenty at times,* retreats his hand. He curls back into his chair like a snail pulling back into its shell. I have never seen him like this – *not even when he was about to lose me in the hospital.* His usually domineering sharp eyes look aimless, insecure... *Is this the real man behind the facade?* I am guilt-ridden – *a bad mom who's leaving her baby boy. But what about him disappearing on me when I needed him in the hospital?* The truth of the matter is that I abandoned myself first, neglected my own needs, in wanting to be accepted as a woman, an engineer, a wife. "I'm very sorry," are my last words before taking a cab home.

At the house, I pack some of his clothes in a suitcase with the sentiment of sending "my boy" off on an outing. I put aside household items to get him started; collapsible chairs and our camping table, our air mattress, along with kitchen essentials.

He sleeps in the guest room for the next three nights. Under the hurt of feeling rejected, I sense that he may be relieved that I am setting him free of my health burden, sparing him initiating the divorce which clashes with his Evangelical upbringing. On the weekend, I drive him, my dear husband, to his new apartment. "Let me give you some space," he says while we hug after emptying the trunk, "then we'll talk this over." "Sure," I reply. *Who knows, maybe he's right, if we could deal with everything else as amicably as this separation...*

Faith

The house is so quiet. I look around in the living room. *No one else's clutter, no tension, no arguments.* I don't even have to fight over space in the fridge now that the boxes of beer cans are gone. I fill the shelves with veggies instead while exploring the raw food diet. With my green drink in hand, I settle on the side of the sofa where the sun is shining in. The warm rays feel good on my aching bones. I take a sip of the concoction of dark leafy veggies I just made in the blender. Sensing the thick yet smooth fluid run through me is invigorating – *Popeye got it right.*

Feeling a touch relaxed, heavy thoughts take over. *Is this a time to rest or is it the proverbial calm before the storm? What if another disaster is waiting around the corner?* As the momentary sensation of pleasure dissipates, I notice realistically: *Can't afford wasting the bit of strength I'm rebuilding on such morbid thoughts.*

"Stress is a killer!" the headline of a health care magazine laying on the coffee table catches my attention. As cliché as this sounds, I now know how true it is. *Worry is cancer of the mind, it occurs to me. But why then do many of us spend so much time worrying about things? Why do we live in a fear-based society?* I reconsider how fear is used as a tool for teaching from early childhood. We are warned not to touch the hot stove, "It'll burn you!" "Don't err away from the straight 'n' narrow, or else the big bad wolf will get you!" I also acknowledge that fear of the unknown is a basic survival instinct across the animal kingdom. *But, what if we can outgrow it?* I explore: *What if instead of fueling old habits we could drop them?*

Excitement overtakes me. *What if fear is a kind of training-wheels to keep us safe until we evolve beyond it and move forward freely?* I am reminded that this bold thought may stem from the church sermon that Myrna had invited me to a few months back. "For God has not given us a spirit of fear, but of power and of love and of a sound mind," was the theme of the sermon. *It had given me goose bumps.* Afterward, she had introduced me to her priest, briefly telling him about my recent medical and marital troubles. It felt good to be in the company of such welcoming people.

"Would you like to make peace with God by accepting Jesus Christ as your Lord and Savior?" he inquired toward the end of our conversation. Observing my hesitation, he added more casually, "You're welcome to join our congregation anytime."

"You see, it isn't that easy," I wanted to explain myself. "With a Muslim parent, and a Christian one, things get tricky. As a child I was haunted by which of my sweet grandmas would inevitably end up in hell if I dared to pick one or the other religion; Oma or Nene? And now, I respect all beliefs, but can't get myself to choose a particular one." "I understand," the priest replied kindly and retreated. While Myrna and I walked out of the church, his compelling Bible quote lingered in my mind.

I take another sip from my drink. *What if fear is absolutely unnecessary?* I am startled by a subtle shift in this moment from leading a mental argument to listening to an inner voice. *Just considering this feels so good*, I sigh, and resume iterating. *If I ran into a bear in the woods void of fear, I wouldn't give out fear vibes,* I recall a warden's comment that animals sense this. *I could use my wits to think more clearly and, most importantly, calmly. And if it came to having to use pepper-spray, a pair of steady hands would come in handy during such a critical incident.*

I find this to be a far more serene, *and sane*, way to live. *I'd still remain aware of risks and dangers, just without the added hype needed before to get my attention,* I affirm. I acknowledge that healthy fearlessness can only be attained through highly conscientious living. *That surely takes practice.* "I commit to practicing fear-free living," I declare to the empty room.

Belong

While such insights enhance my outlook on life, the immediacy of a practical matter grabs my attention. A formal letter from

Lennie's realtor states: "You are to vacate this townhouse by October 1. The owner prefers it empty for showings." It is peculiar that this notice reaches me within days of my husband's departure. *They weren't on talking terms last I heard! And Lennie didn't have the guts to tell me herself?*

What am I to do? The reality of my life is inescapable: *I can't go back to my studies, I've no way of earning a living, and now I don't even know where to stay.* Without anyone else at home, I feel safe to express myself on paper. I take out the teddy-bear journal that Berna had gifted me and start writing. Until today I had used it more for recording events, mainly listing medical matters. In the newly found privacy, I am freed up to pour my emotions into it. This, after all, is the closest thing I have to talking with a friend. *Nothing like a real friend, but at least this one won't leave or die on me.*

I am distraught about having fallen from building a high-powered career to below the poverty line. *"Forget the career!"* I cannot stop, *"Forget having kids! Forget marriage! Forget your best friend! FORGET NORMALCY!"* The tip of my pen rolls onto the page. *"Fuck it all!"* There I say it, rather, write it in bold letters across my journal. I cannot stop. *"I've had enough of my prudence and correctness! Is this where it was supposed to get me? I'm pissing mad at the world!"* Good, another power word I learned from Ross's rich vocabulary.

Initially, I used to get offended by such language. It felt unnecessarily vulgar when he went on "F'ing this," and "F'ing that." "Get over it, it's just a word," he would respond. I get it now, I see his point. I wish I could get over him as easily. *But how am I to wipe him out of my life? I promised my life to this* man... *for better or for worse*. I find myself oscillating between new perceptions and old patterns.

I continue recording weighty dilemmas. *"As abruptly as I was imprisoned, now I'm free, they say. Apparently complete remission is achieved – unless proven otherwise that is. The beehive of doctors and nurses runs around at the hospital while I'm flat out run down. I'm cancer-free, yet far from well. Where do I belong?"*

Guest

Shaken to the core, apathetically I go through the following days, not knowing how to solve my immediate housing problem. I cannot afford a place of my own, but shared accommodation is out of the question with my health needs.

What if I stay with my parents, I consider for a moment. *How would I endure the long trip?* I ask myself, unable to deny that I can barely make it to the grocery store and back once every ten days. *And the big-city pollution, the crowds?* If I were sturdy enough to travel, healthy enough to interact with people without having to ask first if they have a cold, I would be well on my way to getting back to normalcy, in which case I could return to university and complete my doctorate. *Only if...*

A padded envelope arrives in the mail. *Spain?* The sender address is unfamiliar. *Who do I know there? Nobody.* I proceed opening this well-taped up packet. *Myrna!* She has written me a long letter, telling me about her mission's ordeals and successes in building the school in Africa. *"One of our volunteers is going to Spain and I will hand this to her to mail."*

While opening up the next page, a little pouch falls out – it has a key in it. *"Praying that the key reaches you. It is for my house. Am sending it along in case you may like to have a change of scenery."*

Guessing she means getting away from my husband, presuming we were still living together. *"Feel free to stay in the guest room as long as you would like. It is available until three days before Christmas. Then I am back and my son comes for a visit."* Her spontaneous timing catches me by surprise once again. *Oh dear Myrna, you're the best.* Her gracious offering allows me more time to plan for my future housing.

Rush

I force myself to sort through my belongings and begin packing. The most sensible solution is to give away as much as possible and pack up essentials for storage. *A box a day keeps the chaos away*, I tell myself. *Got to pace myself to prepare for moving out. And the last week doesn't count because I must rest up for the day of the move*, I remind myself. *Can't be getting sick in the middle of it.*

We deserve a nice break now, I permit myself, while stretching a piece of tape across the filled box. I am so thankful to have my body back that I find myself referring to it as an entity of its own; *it's more than "me" now, it's "us"; "my buddy and I"*. When this slips out in public, people often ask if I refer to a partner. "Oh no, it's the royal we," I grin back. I don't bother telling anyone that I have begun a completely new relationship with my body, and each and every organ in it.

"Thank you my dear stomach," I say upon eating, as I know of a time not so long ago that it was an open wound not able to digest anything. Thank you, heart, I say, remembering the murmur resulting from the tube going straight into it. Brain, thank you, too, I add, grateful to have my mind back after it had gone numb from the toxic radiation and chemo. I shiver, recalling intrathecal treatments straight into my spinal fluid.

Stretching my feet out, I go through the pile of mail I brought in from the front door and pick through the rock climber's magazine. Members of my department bought me a one-year subscription as a get-well gift. Reading the interview on a recently deceased professional climber catches my attention. "It's the thrill that keeps me on the cliffs, demanding more of myself each time. I thought I'd stop with the birth of my twins. They're so adorable, I want to see them grow up," he was quoted before his last and fatal climb.

What is it about extreme sports? I think, relating to the intense urge that cost this man his life. I contemplate my share of pushing myself, be it rock-climbing without appropriate gear or paragliding in questionable weather. Next on my list was bungee jumping and skydiving, anything to stretch myself beyond my comfort zone. As timid as I felt socially, I had begun stretching my limits physically within a year of living in Canada.

An adrenalin-driven climbing adventure comes to mind. My eccentric friend Pete and I were once again attempting to scramble alongside climbers that were in full gear; their helmets, harnesses, footgear and ropes in place. When it started raining, the sensible ones left. By the time we came to our senses to descend, a hailstorm literally nailed us to the rock face.

Without the security of any anchoring, a daring adventure had turned sour in a hurry. The wetter the rock got, the more slippery its surface became. Both of us were searching for cracks that yielded enough grip to hold on – *for sheer life, it felt like* – though, it would have cost us no more than a broken limb to free fall from the height of a rooftop. Even so, I was catapulted out of dull existence into vibrantly living for a few exhilarating moments. I felt alive while having to be acutely aware of the strategic positions each of my fingertips and toes were in.

Fortunate for us, the storm that day passed in time to let us get down with only minor scratches and bruises. Once on the ground, I was so shaken that I could not stand upright; my legs turned to jelly and buckled under me. Pete and I remained sitting on the ground for a while, leaning against each other, drenched yet glad to have made it. *I'm cured,* I realize, not having any gnawing urge for such craziness anymore. With gratitude, I wiggle my toes on the coffee table. *Being alive, being granted a life in this body, is enough.*

To Be

When possible, I combine my medical check-ups with a therapy session. Ian expresses his concern for my financial situation. "Are you on disability?" "No. I'm not interested in such stuff. I plan to continue my studies in the winter term," I respond firmly. "And then I'll get some teaching on the side." He looks at me with apologetic eyes that say, *"I don't believe you, but I don't want to burst your bubble either."* "Admirable as that is, please keep it in mind. Processing can take weeks to months."

Afterward I drop by the cancer clinic for my appointment. *My numbers are better*, I rejoice, studying the printout of my blood test results as if it were a report card. On my way out, I stop over at the adjacent park. I pass by Drama students practicing on the lawn. I am finally well enough to notice my surroundings and realize that the Tom Baker Cancer Centre is part of the university grounds. I try making light of the past year; *I haven't quit school. I've just been attending the Faculty of Medicine at the opposite end of campus from Engineering.*

One of the students is rehearsing Shakespeare's famous line: "To be... or not to be... That is the question..." I cannot keep a straight face at his overly melodramatic tone. "To be and to love! That is the answer!" I yell over. Seeing his confused look, I feel bad for disturbing his concentration – *at first that is*. Right afterward, I congratulate myself. *Way to go Ada, you rebel.* Feeling a touch taller, be it from my new-found cheekiness or the good news at the clinic, I walk back to my car.

Speech

"Would you like to speak to oncology students on Wednesday?" Dr. Weis asks at my next check-up. "It's a weekly seminar in our department. We invite guest lecturers; we have a last minute cancellation." "I'd be delighted," I reply immediately. The idea of being back in a scientific setting, not as a study object but as a speaker, *on the right side of the equation,* is luring. And the possibility of reaching out to medical students surpasses any excitement I have had teaching engineering – *those were interesting, practical topics, but this, this is about life itself!*

"Does medicine help us evolve as humans, or merely extend our lives and wreak havoc with the natural flow of life?" I begin my talk, intending to provoke and catch my audience's attention with this rhetorical question. "If it weren't for incredible experts such as Dr. Weis, using extreme measures, I'd have lost my life. Instead, I made it, yet struggle with chronic illness." Inspired by Nicky, I describe this in biblical terms, "It's quite like being stuck in a sort of purgatory." I emphasize in a moment of passion, "neither dead nor alive."

Gripped by the memory of my friends, I go on, "I'm compelled to speak frankly to you about this side of the story, in honor of others who haven't made it." I find myself steering away from my notes. "Am I a mishap? An experiment gone wrong? What is the world to gain from this damd person remaining partially alive? And what am I to gain from an undefined disability that pins me down?"

I deliberate further: "Ever since my hospital days, a cloud of indescribable tiredness descends on me abruptly – and even when it eases off, it remains hovering over me, ready for attack anytime without notice. You may think I'm depressed, that it's in my head. It is not. Lacking a solution for my predicament, experts prefer to label me with whatever it takes, in order to sweep such inconvenient matters out of sight."

"This will happen to a set percentage of you, too, sitting in front of me in this room. Can't fight statistics." I want to engage the students, "The question is which one of you will it be?"

"Objectivity has its place in professions like ours," I continue. "But if I learned anything this past while, it is this: Take life personally. Last year I was one of you, studying to become the best in my field of practice. I was so absorbed in my research work that all else felt secondary. Now, I have no career to speak of – nothing but a case study to deal with. That is: me. How do I keep clear of cancer and regain my health? How will I pay my bills in the mean time?"

"I was trained scientifically just like you, to concentrate on a problem at hand. That's a useful tool, but please, don't just focus on the tumor. As much as your patient loses out, you do, too. You then limit yourself, cut yourself off from the big picture. Become the doctor you'd want to entrust your own life with."

I go on feverishly, "When you get short-tempered with a patient, and believe me you will, I hope you'll remember my words. Treat them the way you'd want to be treated having to decide on a life and death matter at the end of a long night of partying. Yes, the shock, the drugs... it makes us look dumb and distracted, but the reality is, we're under the influence of one too many shots of chemo."

"When some of us fall behind in our expected recovery, it's bad enough that we can't keep up. Labeling us doesn't help, it's just convenience..." I am signaled by the coordinator to wrap up. As I attempt to gather my thoughts, I feel naked, overexposed. I excuse myself, step off the podium and leave the lecture hall.

Heart

"I messed up! It was humiliating!" I depict the talk that ran amok to Tamasi after the yoga class on the following Friday. "I had prepared a nice speech. It was supposed to be professional and friendly, but then I got carried away!" "Now, now. Don't beat yourself up," she consoles me. "I ruined my opportunity, not only to make a meaningful contribution, but to present myself as the sensible scientist I used to be."

"Stop thinking and end your problems," she interrupts. "Listen to Lao Tzu." *Who?* I rumble on distraught; "Worse yet, I damaged my relationship with my doctor."

"Open your heart!" She startles me, clapping her hands sharply. *That's harsh. I could cry right now.* "See it as spiritual CPR," she explains herself, not that I understand what she means. "I've to go," she puts an end to our conversation – *her monologue rather.* "Have a nice weekend." *Nice?* I remain seated on the gym floor. *What's nice about anything? Why was she so cruel to me?* Subdued, I go home.

At night, I light a candle, cross my legs and meditate before bed. *That's what I call it at least, but probably I do it all wrong.* After having returned the hypnosis package to Ian, I decided to give this a try. He had suggested during earlier visualization exercises to imagine a pleasant scene. Lately, I have been practicing recreating the image of swimming in the bay of my childhood, at sunset – one last plunge in the Marmara Sea at the end of a hot summer day.

This being my imagination, I want to introduce a dolphin to join me in the shallow waters. Ever since I was little, I developed a deep affinity for these animals that symbolize playful companionship to me. But so far – *for the umpteenth time* – the moment I am about to add this benevolent being into the picture, a shark shows up instead. I have to abort my fantasy each time this sharp-toothed creature tears off my leg.

Tonight, the same scenario plays out. The shark appears – *what else's new?* When it is about to sink its teeth into my flesh, something unusual happens. Its bite does not get stuck in me, but goes through me. At first, I shake it off as inconsequential – *it's a fabrication of my mind after all*. The emotional shift, however, is potent. I find myself void of the predictable anxiety that arises at the instant of impact. Instead, I calmly observe the threat flow away. *It's so peaceful.* I sleep less tensely this night.

"And a few more practices later," I report to Tamasi after the next yoga class, "the shark still arrived uninvited, but it remained at the periphery, which then allowed the dolphin to finally manifest in my vision." "Good," she smiles. *I have a funny feeling this has something to do with last week's "spiritual slap".*

I note a surprising familiarity between this soothing serenity and the mind-boggling dream I had some time ago: When I fell onto concrete, instead of a fatal collision, gentle waters greeted me. *Could this be indicative of how I believed a lot of things were "hard facts"? Is that how I found myself in head-on collisions with authoritarian settings?* Everything in my life, be it at work, at home, and with the doctors initially, felt like a fight. *It's as though I was confined to a boxing ring, not knowing things could be any different outside it.*

Illness ripped apart what I knew to be solid ground. Unusual experiences began surfacing amidst this disarray. At first they seemed to be far-fetched. But now, I wonder if it is the other way; that I have fallen through illusions to witness a congruent reality of its own, *one that is best not analyzed, but lived with fluidity.*

Mad

"That was interesting," Dr. Weis remarks when I see him next. I flinch. "I'm so sorry. Didn't mean to rant." *What a good man. He's still talking to me after that speech disaster.* "On the contrary. It was an unusual style, but you struck a chord with the students. Too bad you missed the lively discussion afterwards. They asked if you could return for another seminar, and perhaps stay for a questions and answers session. Are you available in the winter term?" "Absolutely," I respond, relieved that it had not gone as badly as I imagined. I am also glad at a renewed chance to reach out. *Now I'm ready for it.*

Afterward, at counselling, Ian urges me once more to complete the medical disability application. "Have you done it yet?" Observing my resistant attitude, he reminds me, "You accepted sick-leave benefits, right? "But they were for a short while." "How different is this?" "Those were my basic rights. I had paid into it and my husband took care of the paperwork." "You also paid into long-term disability from each of your pay cheques." *Long-term – I don't want to think about that.* "Look, here are the forms. I'll help you apply. It's not guaranteed, but I can't see why you wouldn't get it."

Ten days later, I receive a reply. *That was fast.* "Your application was rejected." I call the number at the bottom of the letter to find out why. *Am sure Ian will ask.* "These benefits are exclusively for people unable to work due to a severe medical condition," I am told. "Yes, that's why I applied." "Ma'am, our files show you're earning a steady monthly income." *Wouldn't that be nice if it were the case?* Dumbstruck, I hang up.

Ian recommends I seek legal advice. "Income sharing is a tax strategy couples utilize under certain circumstances. Essentially, a portion of the combined income is reported by the lower-earning spouse to lessen taxation," the legal aid lawyer informs me. *Is this your parting gift, Ross?* "We're not together anymore," is all I can say. The unyielding determination I had admired in him when we first met now feels more like a bulldozer driving over me full speed.

"We could look into making a case for you," the lawyer goes on. *With what energy? At what cost of angering the dragon? And truly, I don't want to fight the man I grew to love.* I remain silent. *I don't expect any of this to make sense to an outsider.* "In the case of a divorce, the standard procedure is dividing everything in half, including a joint business." *That'd destroy our new business. It'd be the end of my hubby's lifelong dream, and with that, of him, too.*

I lose my last hope for reconciliation. To ensure the most peaceful separation, I sign over my rights to the business in return for whatever portion of my capital he can pay back.

"Shit! Shit! Shit!" My yelling echoes through the parkade while I walk back to my car. An inner voice replies: *When stuck with manure, make fertilizer.* I laugh out loud. *I've gone completely mad! So be it.*

13

Open

Tamasi approaches me after our last class. "You look pensive. Are you alright?" I sum up my disillusionment about feeling conned. "I'm sorry to hear that." She sits in silence with me for a while.

"It may be impossible to accept this, given the way you're feeling currently, but 'blessing in disguise' isn't a meaningless saying. Look at your illness. However gruesome it's been, this set you free from the vicious cycle of admiration, continuously having to achieve more and more to get to a place of feeling loved." *She noticed?*

"Now your eyes, and your heart, are opened. You're gaining the ability to see things for what they are – in people and inside yourself, to make healthier life decisions. It's painful right now, but in time you'll come to appreciate the rewards of true naked love."

While half listening to her, I notice: *There is a silver lining to my separation. In the worst of times, when I need support the most, I'm moving on by myself.* I do not limit myself anymore by the belief that a woman cannot manage without a man. *I've broken off an unspoken cultural law!*

"This is a book I'd like to lend you," I listen to Tamasi again. "You've a strong urge to analyze and unite, be it people or ideas. Have a read of these sutras – Sanskrit scriptures." Noticing my confused look, she explains, "Raja Yoga is yoga of the mind; a more abstract approach toward attaining balanced union. The quantum leap from instinctual existence to mental synthesis was significant." "Funny term," I interrupt. "'Leap' sounds so big, but 'quantum' is tiny." "That's how it works." She elaborates, "Day doesn't turn into night in a moment; it's an ongoing process. Yet, then comes a moment, we know it's nighttime. But that's beside the point I'd like you to focus on."

"The next shift is from being stuck in mental constructs to intuiting life," she continues, bringing me back from my diversion. *Resolved to getting me un-stuck?* "Einstein put it well: The intuitive mind is a sacred gift and the rational mind is a faithful servant." *Really? Did he say such a thing? Or is she messing with me? Then again, her words are attractive,* I am reminded of recent introspections.

"Here is the contact info for a shamanic healer," she adds. "He's good, if you ever feel like it." *Doesn't she realize what a stretch it is to consider leaving logical analysis? And then the thought of leaping into something as inexplicable as intuition? I am torn between curiosity and defensiveness. And shaman? Why is she doing this to me?*

A-wake

On my way home, I have to blink twice while driving by General Hospital – or rather, where it ought to be. Later, I watch on the news that it was demolished. *It's gone!* Overwhelming memories flush through me like a tsunami. *The very hospital room I was diagnosed in is no more.*

Fitting, really, I ponder disheartened; *people I loved are gone also.* The optimism I work so hard to rebuild disappears instantly. *My career is down the drain – I was so close to completing my doctorate. My self-confidence that I'd always figure out a way to earn a living is lost.* I recognize how simplistically I had relied on my abilities all along, never considering a complete crash of my health and strength. *My life savings are no more. "Our baby" is dead* – the mutual business endeavor as well as the hope of bearing a real one.

It would've been simpler if I died, too, I consider, admitting to myself that it may have been more convenient for everyone to mourn for me and move on. *I'm here now, but the old me is gone.* The energetic, productive, helpful me has been replaced by a listless understudy, inept in her new role of existing without doing or achieving much at all. *What's the point of it anyway – so much pain and struggle, for what?*

Quit searching for a reason, a voice inside orders me, *begin creating one instead.* I pull myself together as my mind quietens and frantic quandaries dissolve. Before moving forward, however, I have to bring closure to the many losses I suffered recently. Affected by the finality of the hospital demolition, I say out loud: "It's time for a funeral!"

It'll be a cremation, I determine. I locate a small wooden box and stuff it with symbolic photos and belongings. *For once, I'll disobey condo regulations.* I prepare a little fire pit in the backyard. *I'm ready to release my past and the "past-me" with it,* I cheer myself on. *Can't do it without a eulogy!* I proceed to scribbling one down.

In the evening light, dressed warmly in my coat, I ignite old newspapers inside the make-shift pit. Placing the wooden box, *my coffin*, on top of the building fire, I begin reading: "So few arrived – that's me, myself and I. Then again, no one else knew really. She, the dead, Ada-of-the-past, she was a good person; she had her quirks like all of us, but meant well and gave it her best. She was serious and fun, fragile and resilient. Some thought she was too complicated, others saw her depth."

I ad lib from there on, "Pity she died so young, so many unfulfilled promises, so much potential wasted. When she shined, she glowed brightly, yet she was afraid of her own light – as if it were a wildfire. We gather here to honor her life and to cherish the signature she left behind: she lived and died for love. She's at peace at last, freed of worldly worries. Let us lighten our hearts and go on living in love and peace, also."

Shaman

Hearing my words stops me in my tracks. *Under the appearance of being a driven person, in truth, whatever I did, I did for love.* Excelling in school was not for recognition by officials, but to be accepted and appreciated – *in short: loved* – by my family and society at large. I never took credit for my achievements or built a sense of accomplishment on them. *That explains why my diplomas and award plaques remain packed away in boxes to this day.* I was too busy trying to prove my worth, my love-ability to the world.

This revelation stirs me so much that instinctively I decide to follow up on Tamasi's suggestion and call the shaman. *So, that's a "medicine man".* I base this on my shallow knowledge from Western movies. *Let's see what this one has in store that an MD doesn't.* "I'm Eagle-fea*z*er." *This guy isn't First Nations!* From his inability to pronounce the "th" sound, I gather that he is of Germanic descent. For the sake of trusting my yoga teacher, I don't say anything. *I'll chalk it up to a pleasant drive out to Banff if he turns out to be a scammer.*

"I take you on a shamanic journey," Eagle-feather instructs me. "You lie down and I drum." His rhythmic beat calms my breath and slows my heart-rate. *This'd be, hmm, like lying on the examining table,* I play with thoughts, while stretched out on the floor unsure of what is expected of me. A little while into this, I doze off. *I guess it's the ongoing drumming,* I deduce to justify why I am able to follow the intense imagery during my subsequent dream. *Standing beside a river, I'm drawn to watch eddies swirling at the edge of the water. When I step closer for a better look, I tumble into the gushing current. My eyelids twitch as I brush by boulder-size rocks and prickly branches. The river eventually opens up to a delta, and a little further I find myself afloat in the ocean. I sense a tug on my arm – a dolphin is nudging at me with its snout.*

"Open your eyes." I wake up. *It's just the shaman touching my arm*, I register disappointedly. He places a candle on the ground beside me and proceeds to wave his hands from over my belly onto the candle, cupping away air as if he were clearing off a pile of sand. The candle blows out, but he keeps at it, reigniting the flame. After repeating this innumerous times, he finally stops. "Never seen any-zing like it," he dryly remarks. "Dark Energie extinguished ze light too much, but I cleared it." *Is this advertisement for his services? I don't feel different. Is he a sha-man or a show-man?* "Your pover animal: Bear." "They scare me." "A big Grizzly." *Sigh. The image alone makes me want to run the other way, even after fearless living affirmations.* "I saw a dolphin in my journey," I want to trade. "Yes, Delfin is a goot friend. But, Bear is it, to protect you. Get so close it can devour you. Nuzzle in its unter-belly. Bear helps you best like zis."

"Same viz suffering," Eagle-feather orders me further. *Did we change topics?* "Hug your grief, your pover is stuck hier. Let it engulf you and spit you out ze ozer end." *Come again?* "Magic lives in ze impasse - ze Alchemie of dying into life." For a moment his words reach me, not logically but like a vivid dream.

"All is one," he continues. "You lose nozing. Ven you cry for a loss, look for vat you gained. Cancer didn't take from you zat life von't take back one day, so wie so. You have an in into zings most people don't have any Idee about. Look at it as an initiation." "And you lose no one, eizer." *That's it!* My mind is back in action. *This has gone too far.* I am about to protest, "Bu..." He cuts me off, "Ze pain you feel, ze grief, feeling guilty for zem being gone and you staying behind," – *how did he know about this?* – "zat's not about anyone else.It's about Du; a cover up for you feeling shortchanged, for zey're not here anymore to fill a need in you. Get over your guilt. Ve're done. Vatch for aftereffects in ze next days," he walks me to the door.

That was something else, I shake my head in disbelief in my car. The hour-long drive back to Calgary passes in a snap. *Am so perplexed, don't know how I manage to get myself home.* Aside from the agitating comments, I feel nothing out of the ordinary, except for added exhaustion, and go to bed early. At night, I am startled awake shaking. *Earthquake?* is my first response, having grown up with such seismic activity in Istanbul.

It's solid rock in the Prairies as far as the eye can see, I come to my senses. *It's internal,* I notice. *Is this what the shaman warned me about?* I am unsure whether it is his doing or my tired mind playing tricks. Nevertheless, once I get a sense that this is of no imminent danger, I release into it. The jaggedness I felt at first settles into a slight rocking motion inside; *like swinging in a hammock,* I envision while falling back to sleep.

Warm

Am so glad Moeder bought this sofa-bed. I admire it in Myrna's garage. I like it more than anything because it is not only comfortable, but it reminds me of my mother. *It'll fit in the studio suite perfectly,* I assess – *offering seating at daytime, and double as my bed at night.* I have delivered a security deposit for a rental unit and feel more settled knowing where I will reside as of the New Year. Ross's promise to repay me in monthly installments when we completed divorce papers has given me the confidence to sign the lease.

Moving out of our home was tough, I acknowledge, having had to work extra hard to clean out the house while struggling emotionally to leave behind a big chapter of my life. I contemplate the recent months, noting that the uncertainty has felt worse than dealing with illness because this time the responsibility of making life decisions is not on doctors anymore; *it's all on me.*

This one will be a piece of cake, I am content with the minimal amount of furniture for my upcoming move: a small kitchen table with two interlocked chairs, neatly piled up on my sofa, right beside two well-traveled suitcases – *what a journey the three of us have been on.* I glance at fifteen boxes stacked along the wall – *will have to figure out where to put these. Coats, boots, bedding, pots, they take up a lot of space,* I justify. I did not have the heart to throw away bulky photo albums, or give away my plentiful books and some of my hefty engineering textbooks.

Myrna's splendid offer came in such good time, I note relieved. Staying in her home for the past eight weeks has been a delightful breather. *It's like a healing temple here. No rush, no fuss.* Each day, I look out at the Rockies from her living room, listen to classical music, and read the sutras in Tamasi's book. *A few months into it, the verses don't sound like complete gibberish to me anymore. I cannot grasp them – yet?* Regardless, I continue the practice, hypothesizing that such old text would not otherwise still be revered in this day and age. *If I keep reading, perhaps its veil will lift someday?*

I reflect on the shamanic journey quite often. *Not "if", but "how" did it cleanse me and align me toward better coping* with ever-changing circumstances? I surprise myself with having a lighter outlook on life and a new-found resourcefulness – *makes dealing with adversity so much easier.*

However unfathomable they are to my logical mind, the multitude of extraordinary encounters make absolute experiential sense. As with cutting-edge medicine that saved my life, intangible interventions have come my way to enable a deeper sense of wellness. *Just like carrying separate ancestries in my blood, I now carry the health-giving magic of modern and ancient healing in me!* At this peaceful conclusion, a long sigh of relief pours out of me.

While witnessing the resulting harmony in my life, I recall the day on which I was pressed to either put a deposit down for the studio apartment I liked, or keep searching for another rental place to move into before Myrna's return. The timing pressure aside, this particular suite was within my tight budget and felt homey. I simply took it, without dragging my energy down with superfluous worry, regardless of not knowing how to bridge over the time from when I am to leave her home on the twenty-second to the first of January, the day I get possession.

As I reexamine dates on the calendar, I see it is the 5th of December. *A whole year has passed and I feel more alive than ever.* I reflect on my initial diagnosis. *Isn't anything in life fifty-fifty, really? In the end something either happens or it doesn't.* I am learning that life has a way of flowing in its own rhythm.

Now that I have located a rental place for after Christmas, I also ponder how not to let Myrna return from Kenya to a garage full of my belongings. *I appreciate her kindness and won't infringe on her generosity.* While searching for a cost-effective way to store my items, I wish I could reach her. *Maybe she'd be fine with it after all and give me permission for the ten days?* I take a step beyond my introversion. "*Steven 206-859-6591*", is written on a sticky note on the fridge – *so it's with a "v", and is that a seven?* My second guess turns out to be right. "This is Ada, Myrna's friend. Is this her son Steven by any chance?" "It is he," a friendly voice responds.

After I explain the matter to him, he reassures me, "Don't fret it. From the sounds of it, you left plenty of space in the double garage for her car to get in and out. I might not even rent one this time, and if I do, scraping off snow from the windshield won't kill me, will it now," he chuckles politely. "That's such a relief," I thank him. "Did you say you're moving on the first? I'm not leaving 'til the second. I can give you a hand." "You sweetheart... I mean, that'd be great." I feel warm with anticipation.

First

Receiving a call from my school friend Fulya on the same evening is the icing on the cake on this special day for me. We have not seen each other in six years, since our graduation in Istanbul, but have remained in contact – *no more than every half year, really, but each time it's as if we never parted.* Her move to California with her husband had sounded very promising for both of their careers. And shortly afterward, I had received their announcement of a baby-boy.

In spite of being the farthest away on the East Coast, Berna kept Fulya and me abreast on each other's news. *That's how I* heard about Fulya's separation around the same time as mine. It surely was no one but Berna who also informed Fulya that this is my stem cell transplant anniversary.

"Happy first 're-birthday'!" Fulya phones me. *She had no other way of knowing this term.* "Teşekkürler," I thank her. Yes, I've survived one full year." "Let's celebrate! Come to San Francisco for Christmas, well, to Palo Alto. But, söz," she promises, "I'll show you around SFO, too. We've plenty of space for you. It's just my boy Kaya and me in the house. I got enough points to fly you over." "Fulya, what a..." "Don't mention it. Hadi naz yapma, özledim seni." She tells me she misses me, motivating me to accept her invitation.

"Tamam, geldim," I take her up on it. Releasing self-limiting inhibition frees me up to enjoy life. *Ian, it worked!* Besides the energy psychology sessions, I am reminded of my yoga teacher's words: *This is a "win-win", Tamasi! I get to visit my dear friend <u>and</u> tie over the week-and-a-half before moving into my new place.*

The three-hour-long flight tires me as much as intercontinental trips used to, *but I make it.* However awkward it may be, I am glad to have followed Dr. Weis's advice to ask for wheelchair assistance. Fulya is unable to hide her upset when she sees me being wheeled out of the gate whilst wearing a mask. "Where's Kaya?" I want to meet her son. "With his dad," she explains. "He has a cold and I thought you might want a few days of rest. You'll get to see him soon enough."

Sevgili dostum, I am touched by my dear friend's thoughtfulness. The memory of her ailing father throughout our studies comes back to me. *That's how she learned to care about these things.* I am remorseful about my ignorance at the time, self-absorbed like all of us eager students, minds narrowly focused on books and hearts closed tight. *Oh, except when I was goo-goo eyed over some worthless lover. All the while, not giving my friend the empathy and support she deserved.* "Üzgünüm, for back then," I apologize. "Don't worry, you didn't know any better," she responds nobly.

I regain enough strength for sight-seeing on the third day. Nature draws me more than the city. Fulya pulls the passenger seat down like a recliner. "Let's get you comfy for the forty-minute drive to Half Moon Bay." Once there, my eyes soak up the endless view. On this hazy day, it looks like the ocean knows no limits and rises beyond the horizon onto the heavens.

Beloved blue waters, here we meet again. Fulya tucks her arm around me while wrapping a quilt over our shoulders. We walk into the gusting wind, to the edge of the beach where the waves crush into the silken sand.

Inhaling the oxygen-rich air is dizzying. *Salty, yum!* I ease into a soothing sense of connectedness with all. *The ocean breathes through me... I'm drunk with loving life.*

Overview

Invitation (Prologue)... diving into the adventure.................. 11

1. Thirst..... the immediacy of a life-threatening shock............ 13
2. Happy.... flashback to 1st wedding anniversary.................... 38
3. Date....... desperation and denial... 50
4. Granny... end-stage cancer, dying into life......................... 71
5. Light...... an unwilling return to flesh and bones,
                                    a motherly embrace........... 92
6. Shot....... final chance at life and a fatherly farewell....... 115
7. Stem....... holding on amidst the reality of death,
                                    the ultimate treatment....... 131
8. Grab...... flashback comes full-circle, a new start,
                                    vulnerable yet authentic..... 150
9. Run........ inescapable realities of illness and life................. 163
10. Flow..... an engineer's mind and energy healing,
                                    facing existential fears........ 181
11. Click...... hypnosis and discernment...................................... 206
12. Chain.... breaking free from habit... 221
13. Open..... yogic shamanic healing, 1st re-birthday................ 240

Well (Epilogue)............ putting it all in perspective................. 254

Acknowledgements.. 257
About the Author... 258

Well

Eighteen years later, I am here still – in awe of having made it this far. Admittedly involuntary every time, my visits to the realm in between living and dying have been most enriching. Resulting frailties have prompted me to examine with brutal honesty my reasons for holding on and also discern at what point to let go. Along the way, presence and stillness have become my guiding posts in keeping myself aligned amidst ever changing circumstances.

Scary as it can be, learning to yield to life's cycles gives me a sense of lightness and clarity. I had ample opportunity to prioritize what is essential and let go of what is not, by urgency at first and later by choice. I can now live the gratitude of being alive with certainty. This led to a mantra I live by each day anew: Life is worth it; live it well while you have it.

I have learned to not fight time's irreversibility, instead to accept its reassuring nature. Once we know, we cannot go back to not knowing, such as the fact that death is one breath away. This helps me center in this precious life. It encourages me to further live my truth, which is based on aspects of ancient – and hopefully one day common – wisdom I am most attracted to.

What were initially mental concepts over time turned into heartfelt knowledge and eventually infused me wholly. Authenticity, true integrity, loving compassion, service to humanity... are not merely amicable traits to aim for, but personal values I am committed to embody. I believe such detached passion not only transforms ourselves, but may contribute to enlivening wisdom – might it leave a ripple effect on its evolution?

Integrating my multi-nationality taught me to also appreciate the multi-dimensionality of life. I focus within without distancing myself from others. In this state, I find myself tapping into an essence that unites us all, with a sense of inter-connectedness both mundane and divine at once.

My heart, my life really, was torn to pieces. Through it I have been blessed with a soft gaze to see the world for what it is; a myriad of souls dancing in an ongoing flirting and mating of spirit and matter – some with grace, others not so. However painful, outright insane, it can be amongst us humans at times, I practice shifting from reacting defensively to enabling a nurturing space for life to unfold in its fullest. I witness events we call miracles spring out of this place.

I came to taste infinite love I have heard Rumi speak of. In this expansiveness, I know that love is as universal as gravity – and the most potent energy of all. In such awareness, the joy of being alive flows through me with the ease of a simple breath.

May you be well and may your journey be as fulfilling.

                                             Ada Y. Akanay, 2014

Acknowledgements

This book has been in the making for quite some time. I give thanks to dear ones who nurtured me whenever I hit rock bottom so I could find the energy to move forward: my parents Rosemarie and Hakkı Bolkan, along with my Canadian parents Marg and Don Mantle.

I would like to give thanks to friends who have continuously encouraged me to write and have held a loving space for me over the years: Esen Türay, Margaret Ardan, Lynne Ronneseth, Grant McFetridge, Ömer Çetiner, Ann and Ray Frost, Saskia Evers, Iryna Spica, Paulo da Costa, Fran Aitkens, Yeşim Kaman, Zeynep Onen...

My special gratitude goes to Prof. "Corky" Brittan, whom my kind friend Nil Brittan introduced me to. It is wonderful to be understood and to be guided gracefully. I give further thanks to Michael Boyle who embodies balanced living so well. Randall Recinos I thank for brightening my world with visual harmony. And Monique de StCroix I thank for capturing the beauty of life.

I would like to thank caring and competent doctors and scientists dedicated to improving medical therapy. My thanks also go to gifted healers who facilitate holistic healing. And I bow to all who bless my words with their pure presence and embrace life in its wholeness.

About the Author

Dr. Yaz Bolkan is an award-winning multi-lingual, multi-genre writer.

While methodically studying energy healing techniques and timeless wisdom, she also has a doctorate in engineering, university teaching certificate, philosophy of science schooling and professional psychotherapy training.

Extreme encounters along with subsequent disabilities enhance her holistic vision of life, whereby she passionately empowers audiences to explore and arrive at their own life-transforming truths.

For inquiries regarding her writing and speaking engagements, she can be reached via: virtuswiz@gmail.com

Photo: Virtus Ventures

Made in the USA
Charleston, SC
05 August 2014